About the Author

AMY BRYANT grew up in Virginia and now lives in New York City. This is her first novel.

POLLY

PLLY

a novel

Amy Bryant

HARPER **PERENNIAL**

NEW YORK ● LONDON ● TORONTO ● SYDNEY

HARPER ● PERENNIAL

P.S.™ is a trademark of HarperCollins Publishers.

HarperCollins books may be purchased for educational, business, or sales promotional use. For information please write: Special Markets Department, Harper-Collins Publishers, 10 East 53rd Street, New York, NY 10022.

FIRST EDITION

Designed by Sarah Maya Gubkin

Library of Congress Cataloging-in-Publication Data

Bryant, Amy.
 Polly / Amy Bryant—1st Harper Perennial ed.
  p. cm.
 ISBN: 978-0-06-089804-5
 ISBN-10: 0-06-089804-6
 1. Teenage girls—Fiction. I. Title

PS3602.R947B69 2006
813'.6—dc22

                                          2005046704

07 08 09 10 11 ❖/RRD 10 9 8 7 6 5 4 3 2 1

For Bruno

acknowledgments

Special thanks to Claudette Sutherland, Bruno Blumenfeld, Sascha Alper, Larry Weissman, Jeanette Perez, Annie Keating, Kim Hawkins, Rick Vartorella, Amy Zavatto, Jennifer Morse, Elizabeth Goodman Artis, Helen Rahrer, Susan Whelihan, Alicia Krueger, Liz Kelly, Emily Webster, Gary Karshmer, Chris Artis, Dan Marotta, Carrie Kania, Kevin MacDonald, Muriel Jorgensen, Jennifer Jankowski, Yona Deshommes, and my family.

PLLY

one TOMMY

"MelissaSimpsonHeatherStoneTammyHardenStacyMetford . . ."

The front office secretary hadn't bothered to drum up any enthusiasm for the announcement of the drill team winners. The junior high school didn't have tryouts; instead all the girls who were interested put their names in a box by the gym. Only twenty names (plus ten alternates) were drawn. I didn't know any girls who hadn't put their name in the box. My classroom was quieter than it had ever been. Even the boys were interested.

". . . AngelaDavenportChristySwansonPollyClark."

I thought maybe I had imagined the secretary had said Polly Clark, but then Mrs. Heath beamed at me. Mine was the last name called before the alternates, and the only name called in my classroom. I slipped out of my seat, suppressed a smile. I bent down and loaded my books into my backpack, conscious of my classmates' stares. I had hoped Katie's name would be

called, too. Katie and I played soccer together. We went to the
roller rink together. We hung around the mall together. But
Katie didn't even make the alternates list.

The kitchen at the rear of the cafeteria was dark, and the lunch
tables had been moved off to the side, the orange plastic chairs
stacked on top of them. I perched on the edge of one of the
tables, wondering if this was how the cafeteria always looked
at the end of the day, or if it had been set up like this for the
drill team meeting. All around me there were girls in bunches
of three or four, but I didn't see anyone I knew well enough
to go up to.

Mrs. Evans, who taught public speaking, was in charge of the
drill team. She clapped her hands, and everyone quieted down.
Mrs. Evans had big boobs and light, wavy blond hair that she
kept off her face with large amounts of hair spray. She reminded
me of a conservative Dolly Parton.

"In the space of nine weeks you will be taught a routine by
two cheerleaders from the high school," Mrs. Evans said. "At
the end of nine weeks you will perform this routine at a special
assembly. There will be a second and final performance on the
last day of school."

A few of the girls started to murmur and Mrs. Evans held
up a hand.

"Now, you ladies have been selected to represent this school,"
she said, "and I expect you to take the work that's involved seriously, and to conduct yourselves with maturity."

She went on to lay out our drill team duties. We were expected to buy the uniform pattern and get it made, and to stay
after school for two hours every day except Fridays to rehearse.
I grabbed my lip gloss out of my Le Sports Sac and ran it over
my lips as Mrs. Evans finished up.

The bell signaling the end of the day rang, and filed out of the cafeteria. "Congratulations girls," Mrs. Evans called after us. "You're going to work hard *and* you're going to have fun!"

I sent away for the fabric and the pattern for my uniform the next day. As soon as it came in the mail I begged Mom to sew it right away so I could wear it around the house. She had learned how to sew as a teenager before she had money to buy clothes off the rack. Mom made a lot of my clothes when I was little, but dropped off when I got older and made it clear I'd rather wear clothes from a store. I wanted Jordache and Guess jeans. I wanted Izod shirts and button-down oxfords by Ralph Lauren. Mom indulged me sometimes, but I didn't have as many designer clothes as some of the other girls.

Mom didn't make clothes for herself anymore either. She loved to shop. She worked at a property management firm that was near the mall, and she spent her lunch hour looking for bargains. Once or twice a week Mom brought home bags of clothes that she tried on in her bedroom after work. She returned most of it. I liked to watch Mom try stuff on, guess at what she'd decide to keep and what she'd take back.

"How about this?" she'd say, modeling a dress for me as I lay splayed out on her Navajo-style bedspread. "Is this the right color for me?"

I'd wrinkle up my forehead like I was really studying her, but the truth was I liked almost everything. The stuff she decided to keep she hung up in the closet, and she draped the stuff she wanted to think about over the ironing board, which stayed unfolded in a corner of the bedroom. The clothes Mom didn't want went back in the bag. I felt sorry for the stuff she returned.

My mother was beautiful. Tall and curvy in all the right places, with the kind of coloring that people called striking. I inherited her pale skin but not her thick, black hair. Instead I got my father's dull, light brown hair, along with his wide mouth. It was too soon to tell if I had her legs, but I had my hopes up. Mom had great legs. Everyone said so, especially my stepfather. William liked to tell Mom that she had the kind of legs that looked good in high heels.

"I don't technically need my drill team uniform right away," I explained at dinner. "But it would be very good if I could practice wearing it."

William peered at me over the top of his glasses. "How does one practice wearing an outfit?" he asked.

"You just do. It's very important."

"And why is it important?"

William did this all the time. He said it kept me sharp. Mom said he had inherited his father's taste for ridicule and his instinct for being hard on people. Mom didn't like William's father, and I had the idea that he wasn't too thrilled about Mom and me either. We'd been living with William for six years, but when his parents came to visit each summer Mr. Hessler would act surprised to see us.

"Well, look who's here," he'd say.

"I have news for you," I told my father on the phone. I kicked my leg up and rested it on the frame of my white iron bed. "I got picked to be on the drill team at school!"

"That's great, honey," he said. "Can I drive up and see you perform?"

I lowered my leg from the bed frame and kicked the other one up. "I guess so. If you want to."

I wasn't sure parents would be invited to the drill team assembly. Even if they were, I thought I might tell Dad it was just for the students. I didn't want to be in the same room with Mom and Dad if I could help it. I had only a handful of memories from when they were together, and they mostly involved whispering and then shouting and then whispering again. When he came to visit me Dad didn't come inside, and Mom didn't go outside. And Dad hadn't met William. He didn't even act like he knew I had a stepfather.

"Now, what are you going to be doing, exactly?" Dad asked. "Will you be marching with flags?"

I snorted. "No! That's what a marching band does. We're going to be dancing in special outfits."

"And you do this at halftime? I didn't know your school had a football team. What're they called?"

"No, it's just us. We're inside. In the gym."

Dad cleared his throat. "Well, I can't wait to see you in action, honey. Just get me the dates and I'll take it from there."

"There's only one date. Well, two. But the main thing's in April. It'll be at school during the day, so."

"Oh. You'd think they'd hold it on the weekend, to make it easier for parents."

I balanced the phone on my shoulder and scratched at a scab on my elbow. Charlotte was a seven-hour drive. He would have to take a day off work. I thought of Dad's hands on the steering wheel of his Mustang. Dad had long fingers and thick palms, and dark hairs that grew just below his knuckles. Sometimes I had trouble picturing him, so I'd zero in on the parts of him that I remembered.

I was five when Dad moved to Charlotte. He took only his clothes, his golf clubs, and his fishing pole. I often imagined him golfing or fishing in Charlotte, though he never mentioned either. After Dad left, Mom sold our house in Reston and we moved to an apartment complex called Twin Oaks, not far from our old house. I didn't even have to change schools. I associated Twin Oaks with babysitters and microwave meals, and long afternoons in front of the TV. We moved in with William when I was seven, and Mom married him when I was eight.

• • •

"Polly, come try on your uniform," Mom called down the stairs a few days later.

I was doing my pre-algebra homework at the kitchen table. I ran upstairs and snatched it out of her hands.

"Come back and let me see you in it," Mom said as I hurried down the hallway to my room.

I studied myself in the full-length mirror. The uniform was beautiful: royal blue with white piping and pleated from the waist to just above the knee. I kicked first one leg out and then the other, imagining a crowd full of admiring faces. I thought of Tommy Ward in particular, watching from the back row.

Tommy was in my second-period social studies class, which was held in a trailer beside the school because of overcrowding. He sat in the second to last row of the trailer and I sat in the middle, so I had to turn around in my seat to look at him. Tommy's hair was longer than the other boys', and he was skinny with pointy features and red lips almost like a girl's. He didn't talk to anyone in class, and he didn't go to the roller rink on Fridays, so I couldn't talk to him there either.

Katie and I had been going to the Reston Skateway since the beginning of sixth grade. The Friday night seven to ten P.M. skate was for grades six through eight. Not officially, but that's who was there. The Skateway was open during the day, but it was different then. The lights were bright and it was full of little kids. On Friday nights the roller rink was kept dark except for flashing disco lights, and the music was louder.

Katie and I wore our tightest designer jeans and rugby shirts with the collars turned up. The boys wore the same shirts we did, but their jeans were looser and they wore gold chains around their necks. The girls wore their hair layered and curled back like Farrah Fawcett's. The boys feathered their hair back, too, but they didn't use curling irons. Everyone kept a comb in their back pockets. The girls wore white skates, and the boys black. Katie had blue and white pom-poms on her skates, but I didn't wear any. That was the one thing Katie and I did differently.

There were benches that lined the rink and spread into the locker area. A lot of people made out there. I never had. Neither had Katie. We waited for boys to come over, but the right ones never did. Katie said only the goobers liked us.

There was a place in the center of the rink where the show-offs could skate, but most people just skated the regular way. The best skaters could skate backward and do spins and go down low with one leg stretched out. Sometimes I would skate really fast around a corner or go backward on the straight part and pretend that Tommy Ward was there watching.

The DJ played Michael Jackson and Foreigner and Van Halen and Journey and the J. Geils Band. He played "Gloria" by Laura Brannigan and "Let the Music Play" by Shannon and "Don't You Want Me" by The Human League. He sat in a small room at the end of the roller rink, behind mirrored glass. There was a sign on the door that said IF YOU DON'T WORK HERE, DON'T KNOCK. The DJ didn't take requests, but he made announcements about birthdays sometimes. I pictured him old, at least eighteen, with high cheekbones and dark hair like Rick Springfield.

At the end of the night the parents lined up in their cars out front, and Katie and I pretended they were limousines. Kids raced out in groups of two or three, piling inside the cars before the parents had a chance to get out. We all lived in fear of a parent coming inside the roller rink. People made out there, people swore. There were stories about couples doing it, but I didn't see anything any more than heavy kissing or the occasional hand outside the shirt.

Across the street from the roller rink was the bowling alley, where the high school kids hung out. When we wanted a break from skating Katie and I sat outside and watched the older kids going in and out of the bowling alley, laughing and shouting and pushing one another around. Sometimes couples came out of the bowling alley and got into their cars and stayed there for a long time. I couldn't wait to be in high school. I'd have boobs and lots of friends and a driver's license. Maybe Katie and I would be cheerleaders with boyfriends who were best friends, too.

It turned out Katie didn't care that I made the drill team and she didn't. It was the least of her problems. Her mother had announced she was getting a part-time job. She was thinking about becoming a school bus driver.

"I would die," I said when Katie told me.

"She said it would be good because of the hours," she said. "I told her I'd quit school, and then she called me a snob."

Mrs. Ryan wouldn't recover from a single trip on the junior high bus. She wore a long skirt 365 days a year and thought Katie's eye makeup was shocking. She was not equipped to listen to kids cursing and talking about sex all the time. The boys on the bus were always taking some girl's name and singing the same song: "Missy Flannigan is so tight, you can't get in with dynamite." The boys picked a new girl to humiliate every day. Katie and I didn't really get the song, but we knew we didn't want her mother to hear it.

The first day of drill team practice arrived.

"Maybe Tommy will see me when we perform," I told Katie on the bus ride to school. I had my blue and gray pom poms with me. I liked the *shoosh* sound they made when they moved, and the way the other kids looked at me as I carried them down the aisle to my seat.

"You have to act like you like him if you want Tommy to know who you are," Katie said. She said this every time I brought Tommy up.

I pulled at the dingy, yellowish padding that poked through the torn brown vinyl bus seat. "I can't just *act* like I like him," I said. "I've never even said one word to him in my entire life."

"Well, probably he'll at least say something to you after the drill team assembly," Katie said.

I didn't want to wait that long.

Practice started out with a lecture from Tina and Michelle, the cheerleaders from the high school. We sat on the gym floor while they paced in front of us.

"Don't think that because we're cheerleaders we don't know drill team," Tina assured us. "Drill team is focused on moving together as one symmetric unit to a song, and cheerleading is more about brief cheers that are a little more individual in nature. In cheering you create the song, and in drill team you complement a song that's already there."

"But they both fall under the umbrella that we call *dance*," Michelle said. She pressed Play on a giant boom box and the beginning notes of "Beat It" sounded. I nodded my head up and down. "Beat It" was one of my favorite songs to skate to.

Tina and Michelle performed the routine that we would eventually learn. Their arms shot out; their heads snapped from side to side as they moved. They had smooth, thick cheerleader legs and long, glossy hair. I had skinny legs and shaggy hair that I was growing out. When Tina and Michelle finished performing they beckoned us forward, lining us up by size.

"Perfect symmetry," Tina said, switching two girls in line. "We need perfect symmetry!"

• • •

Two weeks later, I wished that Michael Jackson had never been born. Tina and Michelle stopped the music every thirty seconds and singled out girls who were doing their steps wrong. They especially seemed to love correcting them in front of everyone.

"Come *on* people, get it together!" Tina would say, as Michelle yanked the latest offender out of line. Whenever I got something wrong, which was often, I shook with embarrassment as I was forced to try it again in front of the others on my spindly legs.

Tina and Michelle played favorites with certain girls, especially Stacy, Tammy, and Meagan, who were obviously benefiting from years of ballet and gymnastics. They didn't screw up any of their steps, and were pulled out of line only to show the rest of us how to do something right. All three of them could do the splits and kick their legs up to their ears. And unlike the rest of us, they didn't sweat or get tired.

My gym locker was next to Tammy's, and every afternoon I struggled to think of something to say to her. She ignored me, and came to life only when Stacy and Meagan appeared at her side.

"You seem like you're good friends with Tina and Michelle," I finally managed one afternoon after practice.

I said it so softly that at first I thought Tammy hadn't heard me. I tried again. "You seem like you've known those guys a long time!"

A couple of other girls on our aisle looked over.

"God, gimme a second, I heard you the first time," she said. Tammy kept her eyes on the inside of her locker, where she was pulling a pink and blue sweat jacket from under her bag.

"You just seem like you're, you know, *actual* friends," I said.

"Well, my older sister is really close to Michelle," Tammy said, a note of pride creeping into her voice. "They're cheerleaders together and everything." She still didn't look over at me.

"That's cool," I said. I dragged my Docksiders out of my locker and reached into them for my socks.

"Well, and my sister's in student government with Tina, so they're close and all, too." Tammy zipped up her sweat jacket, straightened the front of it.

"They're constantly over at her house," Stacy said, materializing beside Tammy's locker. Meagan stood close behind, nodding in agreement. Neither of them was smiling. I sat down on the bench behind them.

"Wow," I said. "So you already knew them and everything before drill team."

I slipped one of my Docksiders on my foot and yanked at the thick cord of shoestring.

"Yeah, duh." Tammy slammed her locker and the three of them disappeared around the corner.

Now that I had talked to Stacy, Tammy, and Meagan, I felt their eyes on me when I was pulled out of line. I'd imagine their smirks and my legs would get rubbery, making me screw up. I didn't look over at them. I didn't have to.

"What's the matter?" Mom asked when she found me crying in bed in the middle of the night. I was having one of those big cries, the kind that leaves your whole body sore and tired.

Mom switched on the light, and I pulled the covers over my eyes. I could make out her figure through the pale yellow of my bedspread.

"Just nothing," I said.

Mom sat down on the edge of my bed. I could smell the floral scent of her night cream.

"What's wrong? Did you have a nightmare? Are you sick?"

She put a hand under the covers and against my cheek. I pulled away and kept on crying.

"I don't like the drill team." I was glad to say it out loud. I hadn't even told Katie.

"Honey, why? I thought you loved it."

"I don't know, I just don't like it. It's just, it's just that I don't belong with them."

I had managed to stop crying somewhat, but my nose was running and my mouth tasted dry and salty.

"What do you mean, you don't belong?" Mom asked.

I poked my head out from under the covers. Instead of looking at Mom I focused on my two Go-Go's posters, which hung side by side over my desk. One was from the *Beauty and the Beat* album where they were wearing towels, and the other was from the *Vacation* album, where they were on water skis. Gina Shock was my favorite. When I grew up I wanted to be a drummer in an all-girl band.

"What do you mean?" Mom asked again.

"Everybody's mean and I hate it," I said.

My tears came back. The Go-Go's went blurry, and I scrunched up my face. Mom pulled me into her chest and put her arms around me. I cried some more, but not as hard as before.

"Sweetie, why don't you just quit?"

I peeked up at Mom to see if she was being sarcastic. I had begged for three years before she agreed to let me give up piano lessons. Maybe drill team was different.

"But my uniform," I said. "I don't think I'm allowed to quit."

"You don't have to give anybody an explanation. But if you must, we'll think up an airtight excuse."

She kissed the top of my head. I could hear William turning over in bed across the hall. I felt much better. Mom's body was warm around mine. I wanted her to stay there until I got back to sleep, like she used to do when I had nightmares, but I was too old to ask.

Quitting turned out to be easy. I told Mrs. Evans that the team was interfering with my piano lessons and soccer was going to start soon and I didn't think I could do all of it. Mrs. Evans pulled a folder out of her desk with the names of the alternates. She studied the list before telling me to see if Karen Bridges would fit my uniform.

Stacy, Tammy, and Meagan started up with me a few days later. At first it was little things, like when they saw Katie and me they made a big show of saying hi to Katie but not to me. Katie would roll her eyes and ignore them, like she had expected as much, but I was confused.

There was more. Dirty looks in the hallway. Brushing past me and giggling when I was at my locker. In the lunchroom they stared at me and then whispered to one another and laughed.

Whenever I saw them coming I pretended I was busy searching through my Le Sports Sac for something, or I made a beeline for the water fountain, or set my attention on a poster that outlined the dangers of smoking, all the time worrying that they were going to do something to me. I didn't know what they might do, exactly, but I knew it was only a matter of time before something awful and humiliating happened.

Two Fridays after I quit the drill team, Tommy Ward showed up at the roller rink. I saw him midway through "Angel Is a

Centerfold," right when Katie and I were singing the na-na part. He was standing with Ben Waters, who was in my Teen Living class. Mrs. Wood was always having to stop the class to tell Ben to stop talking and pay attention.

I grabbed Katie's arm and slowed down.

"Oh my God," I said. "Tommy Ward's here!" I pointed.

We skated off the main floor and over to the bathroom, being careful not to get too close to him.

"You have to go talk to him," Katie said, once we were safely inside the bathroom. She put a hand on the paper towel dispenser to steady herself. The strong scent of hair spray wafted over us.

"No way! I don't even know him! Plus, he's with Ben, and he's a total jerk."

"You have to," Katie said.

I peered at myself in the mirror. My hair was behaving for once, and I was wearing my favorite baseball shirt, white with royal blue sleeves.

"You say something," I said. Tommy and Katie had gym together, so she kind of knew him.

"Should I find out if he wants to slow-skate with you?"

A tall girl skated into the bathroom and up to the mirror. She pulled an eyeliner out of her pocket and went to work.

I lowered my voice. "Okay, but make sure he's not with Ben when you ask him."

Katie skated out of the bathroom, and I went into a stall. Someone had written SANDRA BELL CAN GO TO HELL! on the door. I smiled and hugged my ribs.

Katie was back so fast that at first I thought she'd chickened out. She hadn't. Tommy was going to meet me at the entrance to the main floor for the next slow song.

"He totally knows who you are," Katie said. "I just said 'Polly Clark'. I didn't even have to mention social studies."

The next slow song was the last of the night. For the thirty minutes that passed before it Katie and I ignored Tommy. He and Ben sat by the snack bar while we skated to every song without stopping. When I thought about what Ben might say to me in Teen Living class on Monday, I was almost sorry Katie had talked to Tommy in the first place.

"Polly loves Tommy," he would say, at the top of his lungs. Or "Polly Clark wants Tommy Ward *bad*." Everyone in class would know, and then the whole school would find out.

Finally the lights dimmed and "I've Been Waiting for a Girl Like You" came on. I skated over to the main floor entrance. Tommy was waiting there already. His white oxford shirt was unbuttoned at the top, exposing his gold chain.

"Hey," I said when I got up to him.

Tommy took my hand and we skated onto the main floor. He wore tan rental skates that had orange numbers stamped on them.

I had held hands with goober boys during slow skates before, but it had never been as thrilling—and my hands had never been as clammy—as now. Tommy wasn't a good skater, so we were uneven. I'd pull out in front of him and then coast until I was beside him again.

"Aren't you on the drill team or something?" Tommy said about halfway through the song.

I caught my breath and said, "I was, but I quit. It was sort of stupid."

"Yeah, it seemed kind of stupid to me when I heard there was gonna be a drill team in the first place," he said.

Kirsten Parker and Mark Wallace passed us. Mark was skating backward in front of Kirsten and they were kissing.

"I know," I said. "I don't know why I signed up at all, I mean, it was really dumb."

"Yeah."

We skated around the corner in silence. I searched my mind for something to talk about.

"How come I've never seen you here before?" I asked, instantly regretting it. Now he knew I'd been looking for him.

Tommy shrugged, which made him lose his balance. He pitched forward and I put my free hand on his shoulder to right him.

"I'm not the best skater," he said.

The song ended and the main lights were turned on. We dropped hands and skated to the edge of the floor in silence. Katie already had her skates off and was sitting on the floor near the entrance, putting her shoes on. Her lavender eye shadow had rubbed off of one eye.

"See you on Monday," Tommy said. He skated off in the direction of the rental counter.

As soon as we were settled on the couch in Katie's basement, our sleeping bags stretched out and Mrs. Ryan safely out of earshot, I filled Katie in on everything that happened while Tommy and I were skating. Especially the part about Tommy thinking the drill team was stupid.

"He probably doesn't like me though," I said when I got finished.

Katie took a sip of her apple juice, which we had poured into wine glasses.

"Tommy likes you," she said. "I can tell."

I looked at the block of wood that sat on top of the Ryans' television. If you looked at it the right way it said Jesus. Otherwise it just looked like a block of wood with a bunch of sticks glued to it. Katie's family was Catholic. She went to church every Sunday except for in the spring and fall, when we had soccer games. Sometimes when I slept over on Saturdays I went to church, too. I thought it was boring, but it was fun to get dressed up. My family didn't go to church. When I asked my mother what religion we were, she said, "If anybody asks, just tell them we're Christian."

Katie was a "blessing," as Mrs. Ryan liked to say, born after her older siblings had grown up and moved away. "'Blessing' is another way of saying 'accident,'" Katie told me in private. I didn't know if I was a blessing or not. Mom said she was constantly worried when I was a baby. I didn't sleep through the night for eight months and it hurt her when I breast-fed. Sometimes I cried for hours without stopping, no matter what Mom did. She was sure there was something wrong with me. She said good things, too, like how she could tell I had a sense of humor because I laughed whenever she said "Boom," but mostly Mom talked about how unprepared she was as a new mother.

"I bet Tommy kisses you by Friday," Katie said.

I clinked my glass down on the coffee table, causing my apple juice to slosh over the rim.

"Do you think he would try to kiss me in school?"

"I don't know. Maybe." Katie giggled.

I had seen some of the eighth graders kissing in school. The thought of a teacher seeing me kiss someone was too embarrassing to even think about. Not only that, but I didn't know how to French kiss. I had only regular kissed Ricky Stinson and then Derek Lindsey in the sixth grade. In seventh grade you were supposed to use your tongue.

Katie and I talked about kissing a lot. French kissing wasn't a sin, according to Katie. Since I didn't listen in church and I hadn't so much as opened a Bible, I had to take her word for it. According to Katie, anything up to intercourse wasn't a sin, but if you had sex before marriage you were a goner.

It scared me to think of the number of people who would trade an eternity in hell just to have sex. When people on TV had sex, they didn't talk about how they were going to hell. They just did it.

I was pretty sure Mom and William had sex before they

got married. They were already living together, after all. I told myself it was probably okay if you got married eventually. Mom and William had to wait to get married because Mom and Dad didn't bother to get a divorce until William came along. If getting married as soon as you could didn't make up for premarital sex, nothing would.

Monday after first period I found a note in my locker. The note had been pushed through the slots, and it was stuck partly behind my picture of Adam Ant. Katie's locker was three away from mine, and I waved the note at her.

"Is this from you?" We often left notes for each other in our lockers, but Katie usually pushed her notes through the space on the side, not through the slots in front.

"No," Katie said. "What if it's from Tommy!"

I unfolded the note. Katie slammed her locker shut and came toward me.

You can't seem to figure out why we don't like you, and you need to know for your own good.

I turned away from Katie and walked a few lockers down, focusing on the steady stream of people passing by to keep the tears from coming. This was worse than the time Tina pulled me out of the drill team line and said that I had obviously never taken a dance class.

Katie came up behind me, and I stuffed the note into my pants pocket.

"What's it say?"

"It's Tammy and those guys saying why they hate me," I said.

The bell rang. I looked over at my locker door, which was standing open. Kids were pushing their way around it, and it swung back and forth against the momentum of backpacks and arms. There was my picture of Adam Ant pouting into his microphone. Suddenly it seemed stupid to have a picture of Adam Ant.

"Let me see," Katie said.

"I have to go." I ran back to my locker and grabbed my backpack. I was going to be late, and I had to go to the trailer for social studies. I jogged through the crowd to the doors leading outside. It was cold, and I had forgotten my coat inside my locker again.

I reached my seat just as Mrs. Morgan began handing back the homework. I glanced over my shoulder to see if Tommy was there and then back before I could see if he was looking. I pulled the note out of my pocket and read the rest of it.

1. *You act like you think you're pretty but you're not.*
2. *A lot of people think you're weird.*
3. *It's embarrassing to be seen with you.*
4. *You still go to the roller rink like you're in the sixth grade.*
5. *Everybody knows why you're not on the drill team anymore.*

It was signed *Stacy, Tammy, Meagan and a lot of other people.* At the end there was a P.S. that said *Write back so we know you got this and understand why we hate you.*

I opened my notebook to a clean sheet and wrote *Go to hell!* in large block letters across the center of the page. How did Stacy, Tammy, and Meagan know I still went to the roller rink? Or what it was like to be seen with me? Or whether I thought I was pretty? Mrs. Morgan placed a U.S. map with the state capitals on the overhead, and I began to color in the block letters.

After I finished I turned around in my seat to look at Tommy again, but he was writing something down in his notebook. I didn't look again, and after class he left without saying anything to me.

I cut through the math wing to get to my Teen Living class so I didn't have to go through the locker commons. Ben Waters was out sick. It was the first good thing that had happened all day.

I hid out in the library with Katie during lunch ("I don't want to talk about it," I said when she pressed me about the note) and avoided the locker commons for the rest of the day. I told the teachers who noticed that I didn't have my books that I had accidentally left them at home.

I had managed not to run into Stacy, Tammy, and Meagan in the halls, but I had to go to my locker to get my coat and my books after last period. I was so busy barging toward my locker, hands clenched into sweaty fists inside my pants pockets, that I didn't even notice Tommy coming toward me. He raised a narrow forearm to stop me from plowing into him, and I jumped back.

"Hey, Polly," he said.

"Hi." I pretended to be interested in two eighth graders who were stomping on a Hershey bar a few feet away.

Then he just said it, really fast: "Will you go with me?"

The final bell of the day rang just as I said yes, drowning me out, but he seemed to understand.

"Okay," Tommy said. "See you later."

Just like that it was over and he was walking away, his light blue ski jacket flapping open behind him. I ran the rest of the way to my locker, forgetting about Stacy, Tammy, and Meagan. Katie was there, waiting.

"Tommy just asked me to go with him! I'm going with him now!"

Katie squealed, and we jumped up and down together.

"I thought you liked spaghetti," Mom said at dinner.

Instead of eating I was twisting my napkin in my lap. "I'm not hungry, I guess," I said. "I don't know why."

William picked up the salt. "What's going on?" he said.

I wasn't sure if I was anxious because I was going with

Tommy or if it was because of the note. I decided I'd rather tell them about Stacy, Tammy, and Meagan.

"These girls on the drill team are being mean to me." I shoved a forkful of spaghetti in my mouth.

"Why?" Mom asked. "I thought you quit."

"I *did* quit. They just hate me now, I guess."

"Don't talk with your mouth full," William said.

"What are they doing?" Mom said.

I swallowed. "They pick on me in the halls. And today they wrote me a note." My voice broke on the word *note*, and I ate another mouthful of spaghetti.

William had stopped eating. "Can we see it?"

I looked down at my balled-up napkin. "I don't have it."

"Honey, those girls don't mean anything," Mom said. "They're just jealous of you."

I shook my head no, keeping my eyes down.

"There's only one way to deal with people like that," William said. I looked up. He was leaning toward me across the table, his fork in his right hand. "You ignore them."

"I can't. They go wherever I go."

Willam's voice picked up speed. "They want you to pay attention to them, so you just ignore them. They want you to give them power, so you take it away. You pretend like they don't exist, and soon enough, they won't."

"Maybe," I said. The lump in my throat had gone away.

"If they do anything more I want you to tell us," Mom said.

I nodded.

Two days later another note showed up in my locker. I didn't read it, but instead made a show of tearing it up and throwing it away in the big trash can in the center of the locker commons, right in front of Stacy, Tammy, and Meagan. I was afraid to look over at them, but I hoped I came across like I didn't care what they thought.

Things with Tommy remained relatively unchanged, except now we walked back from the trailer together after social studies. And Friday we planned to meet at the roller rink.

I wore my purple corduroys and Katie's pink Izod shirt, and took my time with the curling iron. I put on purple eye shadow to go with my corduroys. In the car I rubbed at the black scuff marks on my skates. I wanted everything to be perfect.

Tommy was waiting at the door to the skating rink. Ben Waters wasn't with him. I had thought about Tommy all day, pictured us talking and laughing like the other couples I saw at the roller rink. But now that he was in front of me I didn't know what to say. I followed Katie to a bench to put on my skates while Tommy waited in the rental line.

"This is all kind of embarrassing," I said.

"Pretend you don't like him," Katie said, lacing up one of her skates without bothering to look. "Or pretend you're me. I'm not nervous at all."

Tommy wobbled up, and together the three of us made our way out onto the floor. Katie and I got on either side of Tommy and gave him some pointers.

"Don't try to stand up too straight," Katie told him. "Keep your knees bent."

"Keep your eyes on where you're going—don't look down at your skates," I said.

Two hours later Tommy was skating without any problems. He wasn't ready to skate backward with me during the slow songs, but he wasn't threatening to fall down anymore either. He even managed to skate over to the snack bar and pay for a soft pretzel without losing control.

"Let's get out on the floor, everybody. Three more songs

and we're out of here," the DJ blared as we were finishing up
at the snack bar.

We stood up. Katie hurried over to the floor, and I started
to follow. Tommy tapped my elbow.

"Can I talk to you in private for a second?"

We skated over to the locker section as the dread gathered
in my stomach. Two older boys I didn't recognize were standing next to the lockers spitting dip onto the carpet, which
already smelled like feet as it was. Tommy paused in front of
them and then led me around the corner to the back of the
lockers. My skates stuck on the carpet as I followed him into
the corner.

All at once Tommy swung around and kissed me. He was
taller than most of the other seventh graders and I was shorter
than most kids, so he had to really lean down to get to me. At
first I wasn't sure if it was going to be a French kiss, but then
I felt his tongue on my lips. I opened my mouth and frantically
moved my tongue around.

After a minute Tommy straightened up and nodded at me.

"Okay," he said.

"Okay," I answered.

We lurched back across the carpet to where it was floor
again. Tommy took my hand as we made our way back onto the
skating floor, but dropped it once we got going, since it was a
fast song. I couldn't wait to tell Katie.

Monday before first period I found Meagan standing outside
my classroom. Her shoulder-length black hair was feathered
back into two perfect wings that met in the back of her head.
I thought I might be able to slip by her, but she turned around
to face me just as I got up to her.

"Me and Stacy and Tammy think you should read our notes,"
she said.

Meagan held out another note, and I took it from her. She was wearing a thin gold bracelet that hung down several inches from her wrist.

I dropped the note into the trashcan Mrs. Gold kept by the door for gum. I started into class, and Meagan's arm shot out in front of my chest.

"You better read it, Polly," Meagan said.

A couple of kids looked over at us, and I felt my face get hot. "I don't feel like it," I mumbled. I pushed through Meagan's arm. I marched to my desk, fighting the urge to look back and see if Meagan or anyone else had picked up the note. Meagan followed me inside and stood at my desk. The other kids stared.

"You better think about what you're doing to yourself," she hissed.

The bell rang. I lowered my head, and Meagan disappeared back into the hallway.

Three weeks went by and there were no more notes, although they continued to give me dirty looks whenever they saw me. Katie joked that maybe someone else had quit the drill team, and there just wasn't enough time to harass both of us. I knew that nobody on the team would quit now. The assembly was only a couple of weeks away.

Tommy continued to meet me at the roller rink on Fridays, and we stayed after school together a few times. We went out by the ball fields to French-kiss in private. I was glad that Tommy wanted to kiss in private instead of in the hall or in the locker commons.

He told me about his dog, Chance, a black Labrador mixed with some other kind of dog he didn't know. It was Tommy's job to walk Chance after school, but on the days we stayed after, Chance waited.

I told Tommy how Ben was always getting thrown out of Teen Living class and having to sit in the hallway for a time-out. Ben rode Tommy's bus, and Tommy said that Ben was obnoxious but he was funny, too. I said I guessed that Ben was funny but I didn't mean it.

Tommy didn't like school, and he hated homework more than anything. Whenever I tried to talk about social studies, like how we should quiz each other on the state capitals we had to memorize, he got bored.

When we wanted to kiss we leaned up against the school between windows so nobody inside could see us. Sometimes we sat next to each other on the ground with our legs stretched out. We kissed at the roller rink, too, in the booths near the snack bar. It was easier to kiss at the roller rink because there wasn't much of a chance a grown-up was going to catch us.

I was sure Tommy had noticed that I hadn't started growing any boobs yet. I was sore under my nipples though, which I took as good sign, and I had pubic hair. Even though I didn't have boobs I wore a bra like everyone else in gym class. Mom wanted me to wear an undershirt over my bra to help prevent colds, but I put my foot down. Undershirts were for little kids.

Two days before the drill team assembly I found a piece of notebook paper taped up to the outside of my locker. Written on the paper in blue magic marker was *Tommy can't get to second base.* Underneath in bigger letters it said *Polly Prude!!!!!!!* Someone else had added *She's flat anyway* in ballpoint pen.

I ripped the paper down, my heart banging against my chest. I hadn't been to my locker in two periods. I prayed that the paper hadn't been there that long. I dialed my locker combination through my tears. I was afraid to look up. I didn't want to know if I was being stared at or if people were laughing at me.

I was certain that Stacy, Tammy, and Meagan were somewhere nearby.

In Teen Living Ben Waters passed by my sewing machine and sang, "Tommy can't get no, Satisfaction," and some of the other kids laughed. Pat Barker shouted "Polly Prude" at me during gym, which I pretended not to hear. Derek Lindsey greeted me with my new name as I got on the bus.

"Shut your face, shorty," Katie said, as I threw myself down next to her.

The next day Tommy came up to me after social studies class like nothing was going on.

"Can you stay after?"

"No," I said. I rushed out of the trailer without looking at him. He called after me once, but didn't catch up to me.

The next day was the day of the drill team assembly. Tommy tried to block my way as I came into the social studies trailer. I kept my head down and walked around him. He followed me to my desk.

"I didn't tell anybody you were a prude," he said.

Somebody behind us snickered. I pulled my social studies book and notebook out of my backpack and put them on my desk.

"I didn't do anything," he said.

I opened my book and looked down at a drawing of Abraham Lincoln. The caption underneath said, *Abraham Lincoln wrote the Gettysburg Address on the train to Gettysburg.*

Tommy went back to his desk, and after class I took my time getting up. By the time I got to the door of the trailer he was gone.

• • •

The drill team assembly was held during last period. I filed into the gym with the rest of my class and sat down in the metal bleachers. I didn't see Katie or Tommy anywhere. Tina and Michelle, dressed in their cheerleader uniforms, were standing off to the side, chewing gum and surveying the crowd. They looked bored. I could see their bright blue eyeliner all the way from where I was sitting. I hunched down in my seat, hoping they wouldn't notice me.

"Beat It" started, and the drill team filed out of the locker room in two purposeful rows. Everyone clapped. A boy on the other side of the bleachers shouted, "Beat Me! Beat Me!" and some people around me laughed. I smiled, even though I didn't get it.

Fresh pangs of rejection ran through me. The routine looked neat from a distance. Twenty girls raised their knees high in front of them, like I remembered being shown. They held their arms straight at their sides, pom-poms hanging limply, and when they reached the center of the gym their arms began to mechanically move up and down, like they were independent of their bodies. Then they broke into two rows, weaving around one another. After that they went back into one row and flipped their pom-poms over their heads one after the other, so they were doing a wave. I was impressed.

Stacy, Tammy, and Meagan were together in the center, smiles frozen on their faces. Just as "Beat It" ended, the group dropped their pom-poms into two neat lines and shot their hands up into the air. Everyone clapped and cheered.

The drill team stayed perfectly still while the crowd thundered around them. Stacy's and Tammy's and Meagan's high, swinging ponytails were the only movement in the line. It seemed like they were smiling right at me.

two JASON

Reston, Virginia, was a thirty-minute drive from Washington, D.C., a planned community sold to families not as a small city or a big town, but a "place."

Reston was a place of public pools, community tennis courts, soccer fields, and tree-lined paths. Schools were designed to blend into the landscape, along with shops, libraries, post offices, and grocery stores.

We lived on Sunwood Court, between Trailleaf Court and Robinbend Court. We lived at the bottom of Sunwood, which sloped downward and was a perfect place to sled when we had a good snow. As in all Reston neighborhoods, there were plenty of kids to play with and, later, to babysit.

I wore braces for a year and a half. I permed my hair. I got promoted to the "gifted and talented" program at school. I grew nine inches in four years. Katie transferred to a Catholic school when ninth grade started, and I didn't come out of my room for three days. We stayed best friends, but by the following summer it began to feel like an effort and we saw less and less of each other.

I redecorated my bedroom. I got my period. I became obsessed with the Ramones. My skin broke out. I learned to drive. I got drunk for the first time. I took up smoking. I went to my first rock concert, Iron Maiden. I let a boy I barely knew, Tom Jacobs, get to second base with me at a party. I cried for no reason once. Twice maybe.

I wished I had bigger boobs. I wished I had a boyfriend. I wished I were shorter. I wished I wasn't so skinny. I wished I had blue eyes. I wished I looked like Michelle Pfeiffer in *Grease 2*. I wished I had a sibling.

I took French. *"Quelle heure est-il?"* I asked at the dinner table.

"Don't they wear watches in France?" William asked.

"Don't listen to him," Mom said.

We were going to the movies. I was wearing my Megadeth T-shirt, the one with the skull that said KILLING IS MY BUSINESS on the front and BUSINESS IS GOOD on the back.

"I'm not leaving the house with her in that," William said.

"Don't listen to him," Mom said.

I got a B+ on an English paper about *MacBeth*. We read the play aloud in class for two weeks, and I wrote about the scene where Lady MacBeth couldn't wash the blood off her hands.

I didn't think Lady MacBeth was crazy. I thought Shakespeare
was just trying to show us what happens when you push people
too hard. If you make someone else commit a crime it's the
same as if you commit the crime, I wrote.

"It's not an A," William said.

"Don't listen to him," Mom said.

I hated high school. I didn't play a sport or go see any sports. If
you didn't want to go to the homecoming dance, if you didn't
listen to Prince and wear Forenza sweaters, if you didn't tease
your bangs up and fold your jean cuffs in tight, you didn't belong. Even if you did these things, sometimes you still didn't
belong. I made friends with other people who didn't belong.

Herndon High School was large—more than three thousand
kids. The popular kids were called bops. Cheerleaders were
bops, members of the student government were bops. The
jocks doubled as bops off the field.

Then there were the grits, who were also known as rednecks, or sometimes freaks or burnouts. The grits spent most
of their time in the school parking lot, smoking Marlboros and
listening to Lynyrd Skynyrd or Led Zeppelin in their pickup
trucks. The grits wore jeans and denim jackets, and kept their
hair long and shaggy. Beards were optional for grits, but they
could all grow them with the ease of a thirty-year-old man.
Grits tended to have Southern accents.

Everyone was afraid of the grits, except for the bamas. The
bamas were tough black kids who listened to rap and were
rumored to carry guns. Not all of the bamas were black. The
Hispanic bamas were called spamas. Asian bamas were chamas.
White bamas were whamas. The bamas carried boom boxes and
yelled profanities at passersby.

Then there were the surf punks. The surf punks missed even
more school than the grits did. The surf punks wore shorts in

every season, bleached their hair, and did a wide variety of drugs. The surf punks had nicknames like Kicker, T-Bone, and Boomer. The surf punks liked to talk about wave conditions, even though Reston was several hours away from the ocean. All the surf punks were male, and they had a reputation for using girls.

There were skaters and deadheads and new wavers and metalheads and punk rockers and band geeks and drama geeks and regular geeks and art fags, but none of these groups, with the possible exception of the band geeks and the drama geeks, had the sheer numbers that the grits, bamas, bops, and surf punks did.

Fistfights were common at Herndon. The jocks fought the surf punks, the grits fought one another, the bamas fought everyone. No matter how many fights I saw, they always gave me the same sick feeling in my stomach and caused my legs to shake and my head to pound. Unlike most of my friends, my instinct was to run away from the fighting instead of toward it.

The first time I saw Jason Wilson, he was getting out of the backseat of Eric Graham's car. It was January of junior year, and Theresa and I had come out to the parking lot to sneak a cigarette before first period. We shivered in our sweaters and shifted from foot to foot in the cold.

Eric introduced us. Jason was wearing motorcycle boots and a leather jacket over a Slayer T-shirt.

"Hey," Jason said.

I didn't know how I could have missed him before. It was his hair that I liked the most: blond, shoulder-length, stick straight, messy in places like he wasn't aware of how great it was. His hair reminded me of the guitarist from Iron Maiden's hair.

"Do you know that guy?" I said once Jason and Eric had gone inside.

"Who, Jason?" Theresa said. She tapped an ash to the ground with one of her long, red nails. "He's a total dumb ass. I mean seriously out of it."

"He's cute," I said. Theresa shook her head.

I didn't see Jason again for a week. When I finally spotted him, walking by himself down the corridor, the same strong, quavering feeling that had washed over me the first time I saw him returned. It was like being at a rock concert, in that moment when the band first takes the stage.

As he got closer to me I saw recognition dawn on his face. I marveled at how his pale hair lay against his even lighter skin. When he came up alongside my locker he slowed down and pointed his finger at me and said my name, "Polly," before continuing down the hall. Clinging to my locker door, I watched the back of his Venom T-shirt fade into the crowd.

This was what I had been waiting for. This unbearable moment; this boy slowing down in the hallway and pointing at me, saying my name. I felt like my real life—the one I was supposed to be living—was finally starting.

Theresa told me Jason was sixteen, the same age as us but a grade behind. I caught a glimpse of him crossing the parking lot from the window of my third-period trigonometry class. I watched him pull a pack of Marlboros out of his pocket as he wandered under the stadium bleachers. It left me feeling desperate and weak.

I wrote long entries in my journal about how I couldn't believe he existed, right at my school. Songs that normally would make me switch radio stations became treatises on my behalf. "I can't live, with or without you," Bono sang, and I felt his starved resignation, understood how these things could come to be.

I made up fantasies about seeing Jason. He'd come up behind me in the hallway, get my number. In my daydreams he didn't

ask for it, he just said, "Give me your number." In my daydreams he felt the same way I did, felt the connection between
us when he said my name in the hallway that time. I varied my
daydreams so that sometimes I ran into him in the parking lot
or the lunchroom, but he always ended up with my number.

Mom must have felt this way when she met Dad. It was
strange to think of Mom looking forward to seeing Dad the way
I looked forward to seeing Jason. My parents met when they
were biology lab partners in college, fell in love dissecting frogs
and pigs. I wondered if Dad asked Mom for her number, or if
he just looked it up and called her. Maybe he made an excuse
when he called her, asked her something about biology lab.

My parents got married in the campus amphitheater. There
was a photo album from their wedding that I kept in my closet
on the top shelf, under my yearbooks. Mom didn't know I had
it. I found it when we were unpacking when we moved in with
William. I worried she would think it was weird if she knew
how much I liked to look at the pictures. There were questions
I wanted to ask her, like how Dad proposed and how long they
were engaged, and where she got her dress and what kind of
cake they had. But I didn't think she would want to talk about
it. Or else she would make a big deal over wanting to know
how I felt about the photo album.

My mother wore a peasant dress and no veil. My father
wore a white oxford shirt with a wide collar, which he wore
unbuttoned at the top. Mom had long hair then, and she wore
it loose and wavy against her pale skin. She looked beautiful.
My father had long hair too, almost touching his shoulders. But
it wasn't like Jason's. Dad's long hair made him look like one
of the Bee-Gees.

Two weeks went by before I broke down at the lunch table and
asked Theresa to tell Eric Graham that I liked Jason.

"Oh God," Theresa said. "Don't you want to at least talk to him first, before you get started with *liking* him?"

"Please. I'm freaking out," I said.

Sunday night he called. I was in the kitchen spooning ice cream into a bowl, and didn't get to the phone until the third ring.

"Do you know who this is?" he asked.

Instead of saying I didn't know I said "Jason," in a voice that came out high and thin. I sank down to the linoleum, still holding my ice-cream bowl, embarrassed about how I sounded, grateful that he couldn't see my grin, and glad I was alone.

He told me that he got my number from Eric, who got it from Theresa in case I was wondering. I struggled to think of a response.

"That's cool," I said.

I pushed a spoonful of ice cream into my mouth. There was a sharp click followed by the short, angry beeps of a phone number being punched in from another extension.

"Oh, honey, I didn't realize you were on the phone," my mother said. "Would you mind calling your friend back?"

"I guess," I said.

I scribbled Jason's number on the back of a notice from the Reston Association about dog leash policy. Mom picked up the receiver again in time to hear Jason tell me that I could call him as late as I wanted.

I danced through the kitchen and leapt over the vacuum cleaner in the hallway. I trotted upstairs, pausing to smile at the framed black-and-white pictures of my grandparents that hung in the stairwell. When I arrived in Mom and William's bedroom, Mom was propped up on the bed, holding the phone to her ear. The walls in their bedroom were painted white except for one wall behind the bed, which was deep blue. Mom called it an accent wall.

"How much is the shipping?" Mom said. She was holding a pad of paper in one hand and a pen in the other. William was stretched out beside her, reading the newspaper. They ignored me as I pranced around the perimeter of the bed.

"Let me know when I can have the phone back," I said.

I skipped across the hall into my room and sat down at my desk. I made a list of things to talk about with Jason: *records*, *bands seen live, going into the city*, and *people we both know*.

I didn't need the list. To my great relief Jason was the talkative type. He told me that Marlboros were his favorite brand of cigarettes, that Big Red was his favorite kind of gum (when he wasn't smoking, he was chewing gum), and that acid was pretty much his favorite drug to do (but lately he was just doing it on special occasions).

"Like if I'm with somebody I haven't seen in a long time, I'll do some acid," he said. "Like I won't seek it out, but if someone offers it to me I might do it."

I piped up once in a while. I mentioned that I only smoked cigarettes sometimes, that I wasn't addicted or anything. I told him that I had never done acid, and had only smoked pot one time with Theresa when we went to see Iron Maiden.

"I was at that concert," Jason said. I wondered how I could have missed him, even in a crowd of thousands.

Jason called me every day after school for a week. Each afternoon I raced off the bus and down the street to my house. Reaching my room, I'd drop my books on the floor and throw myself on my bed, ready to snatch up the phone as soon as it rang.

Once I saw him outside in the parking lot smoking with a couple of surf punks. Jason waved but didn't come over. I guessed he must be shy in public.

On the phone we talked about everything. Jason told me stories about his older brother, Todd, who had dropped out of school the year before and was locally famous for punching somebody on the bus for a dollar. He told me where the best places to smoke at school were and where he hid out when he didn't feel like going to class. I loved listening to Jason talk. His voice was thick and deep, with the faintest trace of a Southern accent.

We talked about music a lot. We liked the same bands. I had started listening to metal toward the end of junior high, when Quiet Riot was big. After Quiet Riot came Def Leppard, followed by Iron Maiden, which made me stop listening to Quiet Riot and Def Leppard. I liked the fierceness of metal. The speed of the guitars and the jump of the drums, the screaming voice. Jason and I agreed: the faster the band, the better.

Jason told me about a construction site between the school and his house where he hung out some afternoons. It was a good place to drink beer because it was right near the woods, which made it easy to hide if the police showed up.

"A couple of weeks ago these fuckin' cops turned up and I was like, fuck, I'm fucked," he said. "But I bolted into the woods, and then guess who was fucked."

I giggled.

"Lost my beer though," he added. "You should come check it out after school tomorrow maybe."

When we hung up I pulled my best jeans out of the laundry and sniffed under the armpits of my favorite black wool sweater.

The site was really just a muddy clearing with a couple of bulldozers, a crane, and concrete blocks here and there. Jason was there when I arrived, sitting on one of the concrete blocks.

"Welcome to my home away from home," he said, throwing a hand up.

"Nice place you got here," I said.

It was cold out, but there was no wind and it was sunny

enough so you could stand it. Jason climbed up onto one of the bulldozers and I followed him. I put my foot on the tread where he had and accepted a hoist onto the ledge next to the cab, feeling the distinct charge of his grip on my arm. I assumed he would have beer, but there didn't appear to be any stowed anywhere.

"It'd be cool to drive one of these sometime," Jason said, handling one of the gearshifts.

"Yeah."

He put his hands on the bulldozer's steering wheel and turned it. I looked away, inhaling the strong scent of upturned earth, then stole another glance at him. His face was round and flat as a dinner plate, and he was broken out around his mouth.

Jason lit two Marlboros and handed me one. We sat quietly, smoking, blinking into the sun. I thought of how we might look from the ground, a couple enjoying a cigarette together. I'd wanted to be a smoker ever since I'd seen *Grease* when I was eight. When I smoked I didn't feel like the girl who excelled in math and French, I felt like someone who might dye her hair a strange color or wear black leather pants or run away from home. Jason and I were Sandy and Danny on the bulldozer or, better, Rizzo and Kenickie. We were the rock star and his girl-friend lounging on the tour bus before the show.

Jason slipped an arm around my shoulders, and my breathing became labored.

"You have to try acid sometime," he said.

"It sort of scares me."

He described different things he had hallucinated on acid. A melting car, a dancing beer can, a little man running up and down his arm.

"I was like, man, there's a fucking troll on my fucking body! It was fucking freaky, even though he wasn't any bigger than my thumb."

"It sounds like *Gulliver's Travels* or something," I said.

A puzzled look passed over Jason's face as he inhaled on his dwindling cigarette.

"Maybe we could trip together sometime," he said.

"Maybe. Okay."

He flicked his cigarette over the front of the bulldozer, and I threw mine down after it. A knot had formed in his hair just over his ear, and I scooted over and tugged at it.

"Yow!" Jason pulled his head away.

"I'm just trying to fix your knot."

"Maybe I should just let it dread."

He leaned his head in my direction and I worked my fingers through his hair. My wrist touched his ear and I left it there, enjoying the feel of his skin against mine. He smelled of cigarettes and Tide and something slightly sour.

The knot came untangled, and I let my fingers go still in his hair. Jason reached a hand up and placed it on the back of my head, pressing our foreheads together. I felt my insides crumple up as Jason put his cold lips on top of mine. His hand moved up and down the back of my head in time with his tongue. I reached an arm around his shoulders. Under his leather jacket he wasn't that much bigger than me.

When we stopped kissing Jason stuck two more cigarettes in his mouth and lit them. As he handed me mine he said he guessed we were going out now. I wanted to scream.

Back at home I lounged on my bed, reading *The Scarlet Letter*. I had to have the first three chapters down for a quiz in English, but my mind kept wandering back to Jason. How we had kissed. How he was my boyfriend.

There was a knock on my door. "Enter," I said.

William opened the door but didn't come in. "Your mother's in the hospital," he said.

Tears came to my eyes just like that.

"She's fine," William said. "She's had a miscarriage."

I stood up. "Are we going?" My voice was shaking.

William nodded.

The waiting room smelled like Ajax and coffee. There were a few people sitting in yellow plastic chairs. I couldn't tell if anything was wrong with any of them. Mom was sitting close to the door, her hands folded on top of her purse in her lap. Her lipstick was gone.

"I thought it would take longer," William said.

"Well, it didn't," Mom said.

In the car Mom started to cry. Not big sobs, but little chokes that sounded like she was trying to hold back. William put a hand on her leg and changed lanes. Mom moved her leg away. I couldn't see her face. I rolled down my window partway, and the sound of the wind filled the car.

Mom was twenty-two when she married Dad and twenty-three when she had me. Now she was thirty-nine. It hadn't occurred to me that she might have another baby. William was thirty-seven, two years younger than Mom. He teased her about it sometimes, called her his old lady. When he said it Mom would make a bored face that meant she wasn't really bored but annoyed.

When we got home Mom went straight upstairs to their bedroom and shut the door.

William took off his glasses and looked at them. "Your mother needs to rest," he said.

"Okay," I said. After a minute he put his glasses back on and went upstairs after her.

Mom hadn't so much as looked at me since I'd gotten to the hospital. I thought maybe she was embarrassed. I was embarrassed, too, but I wanted her to talk to me. I wanted her to tell me why she'd kept her pregnancy a secret from me. A part of me had nursed the childish idea that Mom and I were closer than she and William. But now I could see it wasn't like that. I knew I was too old to be jealous of William, but I let myself feel it anyway.

I heated up two hot dogs in the microwave. I cooked them too long, and they split and puckered. I didn't bother with mustard or a bun. I put them on a plate and ate them with a knife and a fork. I drank orange Kool-Aid instead of milk. While I ate I sat at the counter and watched a *M*A*S*H* rerun on the small kitchen TV. Frank Burns was trying to get switched into a new tent without Hawkeye finding out.

William came in, opened the refrigerator, got something out, and shut it again. I kept my eyes on the TV while he carried whatever he had gotten back upstairs to Mom. After *M*A*S*H* was over I left my dirty dishes on the table and went up to my room to finish the first three chapters of *The Scarlet Letter*. There wasn't any noise coming from their bedroom. When the phone rang, I let it ring. We all did.

Over the next couple of weeks I met Jason regularly at the construction site. I still didn't see him around much in school, but he left notes in my locker, telling me when to meet him. He wrote *Dear Sweaty*, but I knew he meant *Sweetie*. I saved his notes in a folder that I kept in my desk at home.

Although there weren't any workers around when we were there, a foundation for something had begun to form at the construction site. A dirt pit with a concrete floor emerged. We walked to 7-Eleven and back when we needed more cigarettes, but mostly we hung out on the bulldozers and made out.

I told Jason how William was hard on me about stupid shit. It didn't matter that I got good grades. Nothing was good enough for him.

"It's no different than when I was younger," I told him. "When I was little William would get up and leave the dinner table just to make a point about me not blowing bubbles in my milk with my straw. Now he makes a big show of not leaving the house with me if I'm wearing something he deems unacceptable. He's always trying to teach me some lesson."

Jason grunted.

"My mother just sits there and watches us like we're on TV," I continued. "She doesn't give a shit. She tells me to ignore William, and she tells William that I'm just going through a phase. That's her answer for everything. I could start knocking over liquor stores and she'd say it was just a phase."

Jason put his arm around me. We kissed, and I stopped thinking about Mom and William.

"I don't know how to tell Jason I'm a virgin," I told Theresa over the phone.

"So don't tell him," Theresa said. She was chewing gum.

Theresa lost her virginity the summer she was fourteen, when she was visiting her aunt and uncle in Pennsylvania. Paul was a neighbor, two years older with dyed black hair and a great record collection. Now Theresa reminded me that she didn't tell Paul that she was a virgin.

"I sort of want Jason to know," I said. "Besides, it'll probably be obvious."

"Please. Boys don't know shit."

By the beginning of March the skeleton of a house grew at the construction site, and the bulldozers disappeared. I wished Jason were in school more so that we could walk down the hall together or eat lunch like normal couples. Sometimes on the phone I would mention wanting to go into the city on the weekend, and Jason would say that sounded fun, but nothing ever came of it.

"Theresa calls you the phantom boyfriend," I said one gray afternoon at the construction site, after we had finished making out. We were sitting on the outer wall of the house, which was about three feet high.

"Whatever," Jason said, exhaling cigarette smoke.

"She says you're too freaked out to come up to me at school."

Jason shrugged. "I'm hardly ever in school."

"I know. That's what I said. But Theresa still thinks it's weird we're never, you know, seen together."

"Theresa sure spends a lot of fucking time thinking about me," he said.

"Not really," I said. "It's just like when I bring you up that she talks about you. Like when I told her I was coming here today she told me that if she didn't know better she'd probably think I was lying about going out with you."

"Well, fuck Theresa then," Jason said. "Why doesn't she mind her own fucking business? Fucking bitch." He jumped down to the ground, landing with a thud.

"God, she's just joking," I said. I jumped down after him. "And don't call her a bitch. She's my friend."

Jason stalked toward a pile of two-by-fours.

"Why don't you just break up with me," he shouted over his shoulder, "and go hang out with that bitch Theresa?"

"God, what's your problem? It's not that big a deal!"

I spun around and headed toward a group of trees at the edge of the clearing. It was almost time to walk back to school and take the last late bus home.

I heard Jason's boots on the dirt behind me. I felt his hands on my shoulders, and the weight of him caused me to stagger forward and nearly fall. He pulled me around to face him, kissing me with a force I wasn't used to.

"You're freaking me out," I said.

"I love you," he said.

"I love you, too." His hand felt heavy on the back of my head.

"I wasn't sure if you loved me yet," he said.

"Me neither."

I grinned at him. I wanted to have more misunderstandings so we could make up and say *I love you* again and have more kisses like these.

On the night we'd been officially going out for six weeks it snowed five inches. School was canceled for the next day. Jason called and said that I should come over to his house if the public bus was running. His father and stepmother were still planning to go to work, and his brother hadn't been home in days.

"We could be alone," he said.

"I've never taken the public bus," I stammered.

Jason was all business. "You can get it right near you, I'll find out where. It usually still runs when it snows. It stops right at the end of my street."

"Okay," I said. "I can probably figure it out."

When we got off the phone I lay on my bed and listened to the radio. I was too lazy to put a record on. A DJ was interviewing an ecstatic caller about how many hours a day he listened to the station.

"Man, you should see my electric bill!" the caller exclaimed.

"We've got a WCXR fan on our hands, you better believe it," the DJ answered.

Maybe this would be it. I got up from the bed and stripped naked. I studied myself in the full-length mirror. I saw myself naked every day, but now it was different. I wanted to see what Jason would see.

I put my right foot on my wicker laundry basket. The basket was low and wide, and looked like the sort an Indian snake trainer would use. I looked at my tiny, A-cup boobs. Maybe I could convince Jason to keep the lights out while we did it. He'd already felt me up enough times to know what he was in for, but I still wished I could somehow grow some curves overnight. Every other girl in my school was trying to lose weight, but I hated how skinny I was. My hips were nonexistent. My elbows were sharp. My wrists were like a child's. I wore long johns under my jeans to thicken my legs, but people still stared. I looked like a boy.

I tried to look on the bright side. I had pubic hair; that was something. I'd gotten my period three years ago, but since then it only came once in a while. I loved it when my period came, cramps and upset stomach and all. It reminded me that even if most of my body refused to cooperate, I was still technically a woman.

I pulled my T-shirt and sweatpants back on. Maybe sex would be great. I thought about calling Theresa and grilling her, but I didn't want to tell her about tomorrow yet. I wanted tomorrow to be just mine, at least for a while.

Before William, when Mom and I were living in Twin Oaks, I woke up once in the middle of the night to the sound of someone bumping against the hall table, where we kept extra place mats and candleholders. After the bump I heard a deep voice swearing. I was scared, but then I heard Mom giggle and say in a loud whisper, "Be quiet, you'll wake my daughter."

I didn't know that Mom had a boyfriend, and he was gone when I woke up the next day. I met some of her later boyfriends, but William was the first one Mom let me see her hold hands with. Gradually I saw him kiss her on the cheek. Then on the mouth. It wasn't too long after that that I heard them say *I love you* to each other.

Sometimes on the weekends Mom and William went into their bedroom in the middle of the afternoon and locked the door. When we were first living together, when I was still young enough to ask, I wanted to know what they were doing in their bedroom in the middle of the day. Mom told me the truth: they were having sex. She told me that they were in love, and when you were in love you had sexual intercourse.

"But what's sex?" I asked. I knew it had something to do with a boy and a girl, something dirty. I'd heard kids at school talking, and I knew that sex was the same as fucking. I didn't want Mom to know that I knew the word *fuck*.

"It's when the man puts his penis into the woman's vagina."

I gasped. "That's gross!"

Mom smiled. "Someday you won't think it's so gross."

The next morning I was both excited and dismayed to discover that the roads were mostly cleared and the bus was running. Mom waved at me through the windshield of her Honda, the wipers straining against the snow. I stood in the doorway and waved back at her, the garage door groaning shut between us.

I called Jason for the directions to his house. He rattled them off, as if he had given the route between our neighborhoods some thought.

"See you soon," he said before he hung up. He sounded nonchalant. I couldn't tell Jason the truth about me. I was probably the only virgin over the age of fourteen in Reston.

I dressed mechanically, pulling my tall, red leather boots over my jeans. I loved these boots. No one else at school had them and they actually made me feel cool, like I stood out, but not too much. I brushed my hair for a long time and put on makeup, but not so much that Jason would notice I had done anything different.

I got off the bus a stop early and walked the extra few blocks to Jason's house. I had the directions folded up in my coat pocket, but I had memorized his address: 1347 Rainwash Way. I watched my red boots darken as I crunched through the snow. It had warmed up, and the snow was already melting. School would be back in session tomorrow, and I would be there like always. But I would be different, even if nobody knew it but me.

Jason opened his door right away, as if he had been waiting on the other side of it all morning.

"You made it," he said.

There was a plastic mat by the door. I pulled my boots off, hopping around to keep my balance. My socks had gotten wet, too, but I left them on. I could see the living room from where I was standing. There was a floral-print couch with a glass coffee table in front of it, and beyond that a TV in a blond wooden cabinet.

How much trouble could go on in this living room, where the tan drapes picked up the darker brown shade of the rug? I was confused. Why didn't Jason come to school more? Why hadn't his brother been home in days?

"Let's go listen to records in my room," Jason said.

I followed him upstairs. My wet socks pressed against the carpet. One of Jason's belt loops had separated from his jeans on the bottom. It was frayed at the end like someone had taken a lighter to it. I had an urge to pull on it.

The only furniture in Jason's room was a single bed, a dresser, and a stereo that was set up on the floor. Next to the stereo there were two orange crates full of records. There was a KISS poster hanging on the wall above the bed, along with a lot of flyers and record inserts from bands like Minor Threat and the Clash.

I sat on the edge of his bed, which was unmade. Jason crouched down in front of his stereo. He removed *Licensed to Ill* from the record jacket and placed it on the turntable. There was a heap of clothes in the corner near the closet. A black backpack I had never seen before hung from the doorknob. The music started, and Jason began nodding his head. I crossed my legs and stretched a hand out behind me. I was going to lose my virginity to the Beastie Boys.

Jason came over and sat beside me. Then we were kissing and then we were lying down, and it was just like at the construction site only on a bed, and then Jason took off my sweater and my T-shirt, instead of just rooting around under them like he usually did.

He unhooked my bra. I turned my head and kissed the place where Jason's neck met his shoulders, just above the collar of his T-shirt. I couldn't remember if I had ever kissed him there before. I didn't think so. I kissed him again, further up on his neck.

He was lying flat on top of me now, one arm over my head and the other hand brushing against my hip. My stomach growled. Neither of us said anything. His bedspread felt thin and scratchy underneath me. Not like my own down comforter at home. Jason grunted and shifted his weight, and then he sat up and took his shirt off. He was almost as skinny as I was. He had a zit on his shoulder, a blackhead in desperate need of popping. Maybe last night Jason had looked at himself in the mirror and worried that I would notice it.

It came out before I had time to think about it. "I'm a virgin."

Jason looked at me for what seemed like the first time since I got there. "I thought maybe you were," he said.

"You did?"

"I love you no matter what," Jason said. "I hope you know that."

"I know," I said.

We made out some more. I liked the way it felt to have our chests pressed together with no shirts on. "All the fly ladies are on my jammie," Adrock whined. Maybe it was Mike D. I got them confused. I felt Jason's fingers unbuttoning my jeans. I raised my hips slightly to make it easier for him to pull them off, keeping two fingers crooked around the waistband of my panties so they wouldn't slide down with my jeans.

Jason pulled his own jeans off and shoved them onto the floor on top of mine. He rested on top of me for a moment in his boxers, which were blue and white striped and much too big for him.

"I have a condom," he said.

"Okay." My voice sounded normal enough, in spite of the fact that my heart was pounding and my legs were shaking.

He left the room and came back a few seconds later with a condom and a ratty blue towel.

"I had to get it from my brother's room," he said.

I assumed he meant the condom. I wondered what the towel was for.

Jason gestured for me to move over and laid the towel on top of his sheets.

"You should lie down on this," he said.

I got on the towel. I shut my eyes as he took off my underwear. The overhead light bored through my eyelids. I felt like a patient on the operating table. I opened my eyes to a squint and watched Jason unwrap the condom. It had a strong smell, kind of like a swimming pool. I shut my eyes again when Jason got on top of me. His boxers were gone.

I stopped shaking. Everything slowed down. Jason's movements became deliberate, the guitar riff on "No Sleep Till Brook-

lyn" lengthened, and my breathing dragged to a halt. I felt the
push of him against my vagina. It hurt, but in a bearable way.

Jason grunted and pushed. The pain got less bearable. He
was moving back and forth, and I wondered if I should be moving back and forth, too. I tried to lift my hips up, but it was
impossible with him on top of me.

He pulled away. "This isn't working right," he said.

I felt the blood drain out of my head all at once. I tried to
read his face, but his expression was blank. "Maybe you could
try again," I said.

He climbed back on top of me. This time I tried pushing
back and widening my legs, which resulted in a splintering jab
of pain. There had to be something else I was supposed to be
doing, something I hadn't heard of. I thought of the song the
boys used to sing on the bus in junior high. *Polly Clark is so tight,
you can't get in with dynamite.* Maybe there was something really
wrong with me.

The record ended. Jason rolled off me and onto his side.

"Maybe we should just do oral sex," he said. He sounded
irritated.

I sat up on my elbows. Tiny beads of sweat had formed at
his temples, and I could hear his soft breathing now that the
record was over. I felt a lump in my throat. I couldn't tell Jason
that I didn't know how to give a blow job. That I hadn't laid
eyes on a penis before today.

"It's okay. You don't have to," he said, less irritated now.
He put a hand on my calf and stroked it.

"What do I do?" I asked.

Jason showed me. His same smell was down there too, but
stronger, more pungent and salty. After only a few seconds he
shuddered and placed both hands on my head and raised me off
him. I thought I must have done something wrong until I felt
his stuff on my neck and chest.

"Sorry," he said. He dabbed at me with the towel. "I didn't think you'd want me to come in your mouth."

I stared down at myself. It was all milky and sticky, like what a baby would spit up. I took the towel from him and pressed it to my chest. Jason put his arms around me and I let myself hug him as hard as I could.

We got dressed and went downstairs to the kitchen. Jason heated up canned chicken noodle soup in a pot on the stove. I sat on a tall, wooden bar stool at the counter. The kitchen was immaculate.

We ate at the kitchen table while we watched *The Price Is Right* on a little TV that was on the counter. During the commercial break I mentioned that a bus was coming soon.

"I guess I should get back, so my parents won't start freaking out," I said.

Jason ran upstairs to get his leather jacket out of his room while I sat on the floor by the front door, pulling my boots on.

The sun outside was so bright we had to squint to see. Jason shook two Marlboros out of his pack and lit them both before handing me one. Puddles had formed where the street dipped, and Jason plowed his motorcycle boots into them, spraying water up into the air. It was still cold despite the strong sun, and his ears had gone red. I took a deep drag on my cigarette and fingered the dollar for the bus in my pocket with my other hand. I felt closer to him now. I tugged the sleeve of Jason's jacket and he smiled around the cigarette that was clenched between his teeth.

He waited with me until the bus came, telling me a story about the time he almost got caught shoplifting at the mall.

"I never ran so fast in my life," he said. "I fuckin' outran that security bitch by a hair. She must've been some kind of a marathon runner or some shit."

• • •

My bedroom was just as I left it, oblivious to the great changes
I had undergone. I was glad to have the house to myself. My
bed was unmade, my comforter spilled halfway onto the floor.
I took off my boots and jeans and climbed under the covers. I
wasn't sure if I was still a virgin or not. I didn't feel like a virgin. I pulled the bedsheet halfway up my face and peered out.
There were two empty wine bottles sitting on my dresser, one
green and one brown. They were left over from a dinner party
Mom and William had held a month earlier. I planned to soak
the labels off and put candles in the necks, but I hadn't gotten
around to it yet. Light streamed in from the window, and the
bottles glowed.

Mom and William knew I had a boyfriend named Jason, but
that was all. We'd had only one conversation about him, soon
after Jason and I had started going out, at the dinner table.

"This Jason who keeps calling the house—is that your boyfriend?" William demanded out of the blue.

I shrugged, smiling into my plate. "I guess so."

"When is he going to come over and meet us?"

Never, I thought. "I don't know," I said.

"Give her some privacy," Mom snapped. "It's none of your
business."

Privacy was one of Mom's things. She refused to open William's mail, even if it was just the electric bill, and became
angry if anyone so much as looked at her junk mail. She and
William were exceptionally clean—you could perform open-
heart surgery on any of our floors, and there was never so much
as a newspaper out of place. But Mom stayed out of my room,
even though she hated the mess and complained about it.

Mom pretended that my love life was none of her business,

but I had the feeling it made her uncomfortable. And William wanted to know only so he could ridicule me. If I told him about Jason he'd tell me that I could do better or—worse— he'd act like Jason wasn't important.

I imagined myself at the dinner table tonight, asking how everybody's day went and then casually announcing that I'd lost my virginity.

"You know that boy who calls here? Jason? We had sex for the first time today."

Grinning, I pulled the covers over my head and let out a scream. That's when I noticed that I smelled like him. I sniffed my forearm. It was faint, but there it was—cigarettes and Tide and that specific sourness I loved. I rested my arm on my face and inhaled. I fell asleep like that, breathing Jason in.

I didn't see him at school the next day. I felt sore whenever I sat down, which made me feel strangely proud. I couldn't bring myself to tell Theresa everything, but I told her about the soreness. She groaned in sympathy.

"It'll stop hurting eventually," she said.

I decided if it didn't work between Jason and me the next time, I would ask her what I was doing wrong.

He was waiting at my locker the next morning before first period. I smiled and sped up as soon as I caught sight of him through the crowded hallway. He didn't smile back. At first I thought he didn't see me, but as I got closer I could see that his face was purposefully solemn.

"Is everything okay?" I asked. Out of habit my fingers fell upon my locker and I dialed the combination.

He held up a folded up piece of paper as I yanked open my locker door.

"I thought I should give you this in person," he said.

I took the note from him. All around us was the roar of other conversations as people passed back and forth in the hallway, backpacks dangling from their shoulders.

"What's going on?" I asked.

The five-minute bell rang. Jason pointed at the note and backed away from me. "Just read it," he said, the crowd closing in around him.

I unfolded the note. *Dear Polly*, he had written (not *Sweaty*, I noted), *I'm sorry but its not working out. Things have gotten too intense. We should just be friends. —Jason*

I found Theresa at her locker. We went out to the parking lot to share a cigarette. I kept expecting to cry, but my whole body had gone numb.

"What a rotten prick," Theresa said. She brought her cigarette to her mouth. Her nails were cut short and painted a pale, funguslike green.

I shook my head. "I just don't get it. I mean, yesterday we were fine."

"I swear, once they get laid it's all over," Theresa said, like she knew. "That's why I'm not touching anyone at this fucking school."

"Jason's not like that," I said. "There must be something else wrong."

I considered the possibilities. Maybe he was upset with me for leaving his house so abruptly. Or maybe he was hurt that I hadn't called him. In the back of my mind I knew better. I was bad in bed. That was all there was to it.

"Maybe I shouldn't say this to you so soon," Theresa said. "But you might be better off without him."

I stared down at the slush at my feet. "I don't feel better off."

School went by even slower than usual. When Mrs. Prigman called on me in analytical functions class it was all I could do

not to jump out of my chair and run screaming into the hallway. I found myself thinking about junior high and Katie. I'd
gotten over being separated from Katie—we rarely even talked
anymore—but now I wished Mom had let me go to Catholic
school, too. Then Katie and I would still be friends, and I
wouldn't have met Jason. I wouldn't have to feel this way.

By the end of sixth period I had made up my mind to confront him. It was only fair. He couldn't just break up with me
without an explanation. Maybe there'd been a misunderstand-
ing, something I could explain. Maybe he wanted me to come
after him, so we could make up like the day he told me he
loved me at the construction site.

I dialed Jason's number as soon as I got home from school,
but hung up when he answered. Now that I had seen his house,
his room, I could picture him in it. I paced around my bedroom. I picked up the phone again, set it down. I had to think
about what I was going to say.

From my desk I grabbed the green spiral notebook I used
for an address book and picked up the phone again. I called my
father in North Carolina and hung up when I got his machine.
I hated the singsongy way he said, "This is Bob Clark, leave a
mess-age."

I dialed his work number. He wasn't at his desk, but the
receptionist paged him when I told her who I was.

"Polly, what's happened?" he said when he got on the line.
He sounded out of breath.

"Nothing," I said. "I just wanted to say hi." I could hear
people talking in the background. I knelt down on the rug in
front of my mirror and studied my face. My expression was as
somber as Jason's had been when I'd seen him this morning.

"You about scared me half to death," Dad said. "When Sarah
said it was you, I was sure something horrible had happened."

"I'm sorry," I said. "I'm just saying hi."

I could hear Dad's smile. "Well, things are sort of busy around here, but I always have time to take a phone call from my baby."

I picked up some of the fray from the edge of my rug and started to braid it. "I was thinking maybe I could take the bus down to see you some weekend," I said into the mirror.

Dad cleared his throat. "What does your mother think?"

"I don't know. I haven't asked her."

"If it's okay with your mom, it's okay with me."

"I'm sure she wouldn't mind. It's just a weekend."

Dad was silent. In the mirror my eyes filled with tears, and my reflection shook. Maybe if they hadn't gotten divorced it would be easier to talk to him.

"Yeah, well," I said.

After a lengthy pause I told him I'd better get started on my homework.

"You call me anytime you want to talk," he said in a bright voice just before we hung up. I promised him I would.

I decided I would wait until I saw Jason to talk to him. Make him deal with me in person. But I didn't see him. Days went by, and calling and hanging up on him became habitual. He was usually home, but when he wasn't I felt a scraping pain in my chest. He was probably at the construction site without me.

I was constantly on the verge of crying, but I couldn't quite bring myself to let it out. It was like a part of me had known that this was going to happen. The worst thing about my depression was that it felt ordinary and natural.

When I finally did see Jason again, weeks later, enough time had gone by that I was as shocked as I would have been if he had subbed for one of my teachers. I was walking past the main office on my way back from lunch when I spotted him slumped over in a chair, staring stone-faced at the floor. His hair fell in thin clumps straight down across his face, and I wasn't sure if he had seen me. I slowed down as I approached him, grateful that we were alone.

Jason didn't move. In the end I just walked by, willing him to look up and speak to me, to say something, even just hi. He didn't.

A couple of days later Theresa told me that I probably saw Jason by the front office because he was dropping out of school. That's what Eric Graham had told her. I wrote a poem about it during government class:

You're gone
There's no hope
You were my answer to light
And now it's only night

I added the poem to the folder in my desk where I kept Jason's letters.

If Mom and William noticed my vacant behavior, they chose not to address it, although they must have thought it was strange that I'd lost interest in talking on the phone. At dinner they talked about work, pausing only to ask me the occasional question about school or offer me more food. My appetite had come back a couple of days after the breakup, and I now considered dinner to be one of the few bright spots in my day. I stopped being picky. I helped clear the table and load the dishwasher without being asked, and then I returned to my room and melted back into my mourning.

When I wasn't at home sulking or at school, I was with Theresa. Theresa lived with her mother and stepfather and her little sister, Amelia, who was ten. Amelia and Theresa had the same red hair and the same spray of freckles across their forearms and noses. Theresa didn't want anything to do with Amelia, but there was no getting rid of her. She would listen in on our conversations and then bring them up at dinner.

"What does seduce mean?" she asked one evening, pointing a forkful of mashed potatoes at us. "You were talking earlier about someone trying to seduce someone else at school."

"It means tease," Theresa said. "Like if someone is teasing you at school you can go ahead and tell the teacher that they're trying to seduce you."

"That's not quite right," Theresa's mother interrupted.

Theresa's stepfather poured gravy over his meat. "Amelia dear, you might consider looking it up."

I liked Theresa's family. They didn't shock easily. Nobody criticized her when Theresa painted a wall in her bedroom black, and she was allowed to smoke in her room if she opened a window. She didn't have a curfew; she just had to be home when she said she would. She was allowed the occasional glass of wine. Theresa told me that her parents were like that because of their left-wing, socialist politics. I wished Mom and William were more left wing. My curfew was midnight.

Theresa's mother insisted that I call her Liz. This made me uncomfortable, so I made it a point not to address her. Liz had a thing for houseplants. They were everywhere you looked, as if the older ones had mated and were now raising plants of their own. Theresa's house had high ceilings, and Liz had put a potted plant as large as a tree in the foyer. It towered past the stairwell, the branches creeping close enough to the banister to reach out and touch on your way upstairs.

"I pride myself on not being able to identify a single plant by name," Theresa told me once, as if it was the one thing she didn't know.

Theresa's father and stepmother lived in Reston, too. Theresa and Amelia went over to their house for dinner once a week and spent one weekend a month there. I met Theresa's dad only once, when he gave me a ride home on their way out to dinner. He had red hair, too, but darker than his daughters. According to Theresa, both sets of parents were friendly with each other, though she detected a faint rivalry between Liz and Linda, her stepmother. Liz criticized everything from Linda's Toyota ("That model is notorious for breaking down") to the presents Linda gave them ("Theresa's totally beyond J. R. R. Tolkien, and Amelia's not quite there yet"). I wondered what it would be like to have a stepmother. It could happen. Maybe she'd be someone I could be friends with. We'd go out to dinner and talk about girl things. Maybe I could tell her about Jason.

"Sex changes everything," I told Theresa at the lunch table for the millionth time. I wasn't sure what I meant exactly, but I knew it was true.

"Sex with morons changes everything," Theresa said. "And every single guy in this school is a fucking moron, so."

She was applying a thick layer of black lipstick while she talked. When she was finished she handed the tube to me. I'd been drawn to bleak colors since Jason dumped me. My red boots had been relegated to the back of my closet.

"Look," Theresa said after I wondered aloud whether it would be too obvious for us to hang around the 7-Eleven near Jason's house after school. "It's time for you to go out with another guy."

I stopped chewing my sandwich.

"I can't!" I was still calling and hanging up on Jason at least three times a week.

"Why not?" Theresa said. "At this point a little scamming around might seriously help you."

I started chewing again, took a gulp of my grape juice.

"Like it's that simple," I said. "What would you have me do? Just grab the nearest jock and straddle him?"

"Well, it's not exactly hard to make out with the rejects at this school. You don't have to have a *relationship* or whatever."

I wrote another poem after lunch.

Sex is beautiful
Sex is painful
Sex is meaningful
Don't tell anyone.

I wished I could sing and play the guitar so my poems could be lyrics. I had a terrible singing voice and I didn't own a guitar, but I still hoped maybe someday my poems would turn into something.

I went to a party the next weekend with Theresa. A surf punk named Bone was selling acid for five dollars, and Theresa and I bought a tab. I was surprised by the size of it, tinier than a stamp, with a music note printed in the center. We went into the bathroom together to take it.

"Do you really want to?" I asked. I was scared.

Theresa nodded. Her face was serious. I could tell she wouldn't do it unless I did. "Do you?" she asked.

"Just don't leave me."

I carefully folded the tab in half before I tore it down the middle so I could make sure we got equal amounts. When we had it on our tongues we stuck them out and looked at ourselves in the mirror. We giggled at our reflections and went back to the party.

Tripping was fun, although I didn't see any little men running up and down my arms or any furniture melting like Jason had. I laughed at everything Theresa said and paid close attention to the trails from the cigarettes I continuously smoked. I spent the night over at Theresa's, but I didn't fall asleep until dawn. I hoped that Jason would hear about how I had done acid—there were a few people who knew him at the party—and maybe call me and ask me about it.

Spring set in and there were more parties. And boys, lots of them all of a sudden, as if Theresa had handed out flyers about me being available.

Mark Preston kissed me at a party after he finished telling me about the time he went to a gun show. He was drunk and sweaty and not like Jason at all.

Steve Swanson tilted his head really far over to the side when he kissed me and slid his tongue in and out of my mouth like he was doing it for exercise. When Steve slipped a hand in my pants I told him I wasn't over my old boyfriend yet. He didn't ask who my old boyfriend was. He just pulled his hand back out and kept kissing me. Andy Porter tried to kiss me in his car but I pushed him away, reeling from the smell of his Polo cologne. That same night Theresa gave Billy Henderson a blow job at a party. On the phone we discussed how long it had taken Billy to come versus Jason. Billy took longer.

I made out with Kurt Ridley one night on the golf course. The soggy grass seeped through our clothes while the wind hissed through the trees around us. When I told Kurt I wouldn't have sex with someone I didn't love, he gave me a long kiss and then told me he loved me. I pried him off me and asked him for a ride home.

In my journal I cataloged them. This one was short. That one had hairy forearms. Another one was a slow kisser. After a while I got bored. None of them were doing what they were supposed to be doing. None of them made me forget about Jason.

• • •

It was a band that finally took my mind off Jason, at least for a brief, welcome spell. They were called Dag Nasty, and they were playing at the 9:30 Club in D.C. Sean Hanson, a boy Theresa was "kind of but not really seeing" drove us in his beat-up green hatchback. Sean kept his hand on Theresa's thigh the whole ride, while she stared out the window and smoked. I stayed quiet in the backseat. I could tell Sean wished I weren't there.

"You're gonna like Dag Nasty," Theresa told me as we pulled into a parking lot around the corner from the club. "They're fast."

I shrugged. I didn't care whether I liked Dag Nasty. I was just glad to be in the city. D.C. made me feel sophisticated and worldly, especially at night. Even though Mom knew exactly where I was and what time I'd be back, I felt myself getting more independent and confident as we crossed the bridge from Virginia. Someday I'd live in D.C., in my own apartment. Maybe Theresa and I would be roommates.

There were kids our age and a few years older hanging out in the parking lot, slamming car doors and bumming cigarettes from one another. A couple of them had cans of beer, but not many. Most of them were male. Even though they were dressed more like Theresa and me than the drunken rednecks I was used to seeing at metal shows, I still found them intimidating. There was something predatory and tense about the boys who went to rock shows, like they were seconds away from fistfighting at all times. More kids were loitering outside the club, looking up and down the street like they might be missing the real action.

Inside the club more boys waited around in clumps of three

or four. The few girls I saw wore heavy black eyeliner and scowled at the ground as we walked by. As we paid for our tickets I felt myself shrink into my scuffed-up boots and my oversized black sweatshirt. I wanted to be invisible.

Theresa was just the opposite. She threw her shoulders back and straightened her spine as we moved farther into the club. I was used to Theresa being the coolest-looking girl at school, but I was surprised that she was also the coolest-looking girl here. Her blue eyes were rimmed with black like they were supposed to be. The black streak she'd put in her hair last fall was growing out, and she had it tucked behind one ear. Her leather motorcycle jacket was unzipped so you could see the rise of her cleavage through her thin black sweater, and boys watched her out of the corners of their eyes. She was wearing her wool houndstooth miniskirt that she got at a thrift store and her black tights that she'd ripped on purpose. I knew all of Theresa's clothes by heart.

Sean touched his sparse chin hair with one hand and rested his other hand on the small of Theresa's back. I lit a cigarette, wishing that we had brought someone else for me to talk to in case Theresa and Sean disappeared somewhere.

Dag Nasty started, and suddenly it got crowded. A few people pushed in between Theresa and me on their way to the stage, and a pathway was established. Kids poured between us, until I was at least six feet away from Theresa and Sean. I shook my hair out of my face, lit another cigarette. Theresa looked over and I waved. She'd tied a thin black leather strap around her neck, and I could see her freckles on either side of it.

Most of the people in front of me were slam dancing. Every few seconds a wave of bodies would come toward me, and everyone in my vicinity would put out their arms and push them in the other direction. Soon I found an opening, and seconds later I was knocking against everyone, inhaling the collective sweat of the crowd. Theresa had told me about the pit. I pushed a careening body aside, and my head bounced against someone's shoulder. One guy after another jumped up onstage with the band and hurled himself into the crowd, who threw up their arms to catch him.

After five songs I was too tired to go on. I staggered out of the pit and toward the back of the club. My right shoulder was throbbing and the heat was starting to make me feel faint, but I was happy. I had the content, exhausted feeling I used to get playing outside in the neighborhood until dark.

I couldn't get the show out of my head for days. Theresa taped me her Dag Nasty record, along with some records by a few other hardcore bands she knew. I listened to them over and over again. Hardcore bands were real. The lyrics weren't about the devil and evil, but about stuff that I thought about. Like how fucked-up the world was, and how nobody in charge gave a shit. There were other people who felt the way I felt. Frustrated and angry and rejected and furtive and raw.

I wanted to go to every hardcore show there was. And I didn't want to just be in the audience; I wanted to be onstage. To have fun and be angry at the same time. After school I'd dress up and pretend. I was the lead singer. Sometimes I played guitar and sang, other times I just sang. Shut in my bedroom, I'd change into a pair of fishnet stockings that I bought at the dance store at the mall. I'd put on my pleated black wool skirt and a black tank top. I'd move one of my bra straps over so that it was showing. I'd take off my watch and replace it with a silver cuff bracelet I'd had since eighth grade but never worn. I'd put on my crucifix necklace and over that the necklace I had made from a safety pin and a strip of black chain link I had bought from the hardware store.

Then I'd go to work on my face. I'd start with loose white powder. Once my face was as pale as my palms I'd put black eyeliner on so thick I'd have to sharpen the liner halfway through. I'd tease random pieces of hair until they stood straight out, keeping them in place with a large amounts of hair spray that made my face sticky. The cheap, sweet smell of it crept into my nostrils and stayed there.

The Bad Brains record was my current favorite out of the albums Theresa had taped for me. The first song would start and I'd grab my round brush off the dresser and jump in front of the mirror. I'd shake my head with the drums and wind my hips around with the guitar. I was singing, and Jason had come to my show.

I'm in here
You're out there.

Jason was staring up at me, full of regret.

Loading up the streets
Synthetic sounds so sweet.

After the show Jason would tell me how much he had missed me. Sometimes he would jump onstage and kiss me. Other times I did a stage dive and landed in his arms.

I was midway through a performance one Saturday afternoon when I spotted my mother's reflection in the mirror behind me. She was holding the laundry basket in her arms, a smile spread across her face. I spun around and dropped my brush. Mom laughed.

"That's a serious load of makeup you've got on," she shouted over the music. "You look like a vampire."

I went over to the stereo and turned it down. "What are you doing in here? You're supposed to knock."

"I'm sorry to interrupt your game, honey. I was just wondering if you had anything for a white load."

"It's not a *game*. And you're supposed to knock!"

"I did knock. You didn't hear it over that racket."

She went over to my laundry basket and dumped my dirty clothes out onto the carpet. I bent down and helped her sift through my clothes for the white things as fast as I could. Other than a few pairs of socks and my underwear, there wasn't anything white.

"Your wardrobe is getting blacker and blacker," Mom said.

"If it offends you so much I can always do my own laundry."

"Why would I be offended? It's just a phase."

I heaved a sigh, willing her out of my room. Mom stood up, leaving the laundry in a pile on the floor.

"I've been meaning to talk to you about my pregnancy," she said.

For one stomach-plunging second I thought Mom was pregnant again, but then I realized what she meant. I wanted to ask her why she had wanted a baby in the first place. Instead I said, "Are you feeling okay?"

"I'm fine," Mom said.

"That's good." The truth was, her miscarriage seemed like it had happened years ago.

"I don't want you to think that William and I were keeping it from you. We'd only just found out when it happened."

I hoped she was telling me the truth. "That's okay."

Mom kneeled down and picked the laundry basket up. She held it in front of her and wrapped her arms around it like a barrel. "Is there anything you want to talk about? You can, you know."

I let myself ask. "Are you trying to have another baby?"

Mom looked over my shoulder, toward the window. I'd drawn the blinds so none of the neighbors would see me dancing. She drew her mouth into a thin line before she spoke. "I don't know," she said. "I don't think so. Not right now anyway."

There were creases on either side of her mouth that hadn't been there before. Tiny lines at the corners of her eyes and on her forehead. It was faint, but her face was definitely changing.

"Well, maybe this baby stuff is just a phase," I said. "Maybe you'll outgrow it."

Mom didn't laugh. "Is that something you would like?" she asked.

"For you to have a baby?"

"Yes."

"I haven't really thought about it," I lied.

When she'd gone, I picked up my brush and began working at the sprayed knots in my hair. A small part of me was curious to see what it would be like if Mom had a baby, but most of me hated the idea. I had fantasized about a sibling when she and Dad were getting divorced, and then when it was just the two of us living together. But now it was too late. I was almost grown.

I wondered if Mom ever thought about what it would be like if she had never married Dad, never had me at all. If instead she had met William five years sooner and had a baby with him. How much better it would have been.

Everybody heard about the party that was going on the afternoon of the last day of school. Stephanie Kenning's parents had gone out of town, and she was getting a keg. Theresa and I didn't really know Stephanie, but everyone was going. Even the people we didn't associate with, like the bops.

We got a ride with Sean, who was sulking because Theresa

had finally admitted that she didn't want a boyfriend. We had to park well down the street from Stephanie's because there were so many cars there. People were spilling out onto the yard and the driveway, all of them holding blue plastic cups.

"I give this party about an hour before it gets busted," Sean said as we got out of the car. He bent over and adjusted one of the cuffs of his camouflage pants.

It had finally gotten warm enough that we didn't need jackets, and Theresa and I were dressed identically in black T-shirts and black jeans.

"Here come the dykes," a jock shouted.

"Why don't you go date-rape a cheerleader or something," Theresa shouted back. "Make yourself useful."

We crossed the yard and opened the front door, which was decorated with a wicker wreath with a banner affixed to it that said, MAY ALL WHO ENTER HERE COME IN PEACE.

"Stephanie must have got that special for the party," I said. Theresa snickered.

We made our way through throngs of people to the kitchen where the keg was. Prince's "Little Red Corvette" was blasting throughout the house. In the doorway of the kitchen Theresa struck a Prince pose, thrusting her hip out and turning her head in the opposite direction. Sean shook his head and stepped past her.

I stopped dead. Jason was sitting on the counter behind the keg, talking to Kurt Ridley. His head was shaved bald, but there was no mistaking his wide face. Dumb, wild panic spread through me, and I snaked a hand toward Theresa's arm. We backed out of the kitchen.

"What?" said Theresa. I dragged her past bunches of people until we were in the foyer, next to an empty wooden umbrella stand. The stand was sculpted into the shape of a lion. The umbrellas went into a hole in the top of the lion's head.

"He's here!" I whispered.

"Who?"

"Jason! He's in the kitchen with Kurt."

"Where? I didn't see him."

The front door opened and five or six people came in, and I put a finger over my lips. "He better not know about Kurt and me on the golf course," I whispered.

"Whatever. It's not like he can say anything to you about it," Theresa said. "Kurt probably doesn't even know you guys ever went out. I mean, God."

Theresa stalked off. After a minute I followed her. I hated when Theresa pretended like she didn't know how important Jason was. I sucked in my breath and stepped back into the packed kitchen. Jason was laughing at something Kurt was saying.

Theresa was standing by the keg with two cups in her hands. She raised an eyebrow at me and I scowled and looked down at the linoleum floor. The off-white tiles were streaked with dirt and spilled beer.

Jason tapped me in the side with his boot. I turned around.

"Oh. Hey," I said.

"Hey Polly." His face had gone red from drinking. Even the top of his head was flushed.

Kurt hopped down from the counter without acknowledging me and wandered over to the keg.

"You shaved your head," I said.

"Yeah." He smiled and raised his hand up to touch his scalp. His hands were thick and strong-looking, just like I remembered.

"It took only about five minutes to get rid of all my hair," he said. "I got it saved in a plastic bag at home."

Theresa came up beside me and handed me a cup of beer. I kept my eyes on Jason.

"I heard you dropped out of school," I said.

"Yup. And I'm moving to Richmond in a month."

"What's in Richmond?" A lump began to form my throat.

"Not much. I'm gonna live with my mom. Get a job and shit."

I nodded. I couldn't remember if I had known that his mother lived in Richmond. "That's cool," I said.

Jason's gaze wandered over my shoulder, and I fought the urge to turn around and see what he was looking at. I took a sip of my beer, which was warm and had too much foam in it.

Kurt came back and said that he heard another keg was coming. Jason leaned over to say something to him and I followed Theresa out of the kitchen. We walked down a narrow carpeted hallway into the living room.

"I can't believe he shaved his head," I said.

"Yeah, he looks gross like that," Theresa said.

I drained my beer. "I'll be right back," I said.

When I got to the kitchen Jason and Kurt had disappeared. I refilled my beer cup, lit a cigarette, and arranged myself against the counter where Jason had been. After a minute I went back into the living room to find Theresa. She was sitting Indian style on the tan shag rug with Sean and Mark Preston and Billy Henderson. They were passing a bowl around.

"Want some?" Theresa asked.

Before I could answer Stephanie ran in and said, "I said no pot and I mean it!"

Stephanie was wearing a stretchy black tube dress and no shoes, and her voice had the loud, hysterical ring of too much alcohol. It reminded me of something Mom said about my father once. "Alcoholics can hide a lot of things, but never the voice," she said. I saw my father so rarely I mainly knew him by his voice, and he always sounded the same to me.

I had only one memory of Dad being drunk. It was an afternoon in the middle of winter. Mom locked Dad in the backyard, and I watched from my bedroom window as he staggered around, waving his arms at the door and saying things I couldn't make out. After a few minutes, he fell to his knees and vomited. I was scared enough by the sight of him to run downstairs and tell Mom that Daddy was sick.

Stephanie fixed a glassy eye on me and said, "You have to smoke your cigarette outside." She pointed at the sliding glass door that led to the backyard.

Sean stood up. "Come on, I'll go with you," he said.

Jason was standing at the edge of the yard, smoking and talking to Kurt. We walked in the opposite direction while Sean said something about failing his chemistry final. I made a sympathetic noise. When I finished my cigarette I was going to talk to Jason. For real this time.

"You seem like you're pretty drunk already," Sean said. "Like you're kind of out of it."

I started to protest, but then I saw two policemen coming around the side of the house and into the yard where Jason was.

Sean yelled, "Cops!" and I tossed my beer and my cigarette behind a nearby bush.

All around us people were running and cars were starting. One of the policemen had Jason by the arm and was dragging him back around the side of the house. Another cop had Kurt. I started after Jason, but then Sean grabbed my hand. He pulled me toward the woods that divided Stephanie's yard from the next development. I let go of Sean's hand and we sprinted toward the trees.

Once we were safely in the woods we sat down, both of us out of breath. Then we were laughing, and Sean said that was scary, and I said I hoped Theresa was okay, and Sean said I shouldn't worry, that Theresa could figure her way out of anything. Then he kissed me.

I let Sean lower me all the way to the ground and stretch out on top of me. He kissed me again, and I shut my eyes. I thought of Jason's head being shaved, his hair falling out of his scalp in pieces, floating toward the floor to rest there, impossibly light against the tile.

three MIKE

William adopted me the summer before my senior year, when I was sixteen. It had been in the works for months, but as usual I hadn't known. It turned out my father had been behind on his child support for years, and it was the only way to keep the state from taking action against him. As of July 1, 1987, I was no longer Polly Elaine Clark. I was Polly Elaine Hessler. William was my legal father.

"It doesn't mean anything," Mom said. "Bob is still your father."

I cried the whole way through it: when Mom told me, in the lawyer's office, alone in my room. Dad called me every day for two weeks, but I wouldn't talk to him.

"Now that he's not my father I don't have to do these stupid, obligatory father–daughter phone calls," I said to Mom. "Tell him I said that."

I could hear Mom on the phone telling him that everything

would be okay, that I just needed some time to get used to things. But I didn't want everything to be okay. I wanted Dad to feel bad for once. I wanted him to regret that he didn't have a daughter anymore.

Mom let me cancel all my babysitting jobs and take the rest of the summer off. William, my new father, put thirty dollars on my dresser once a week without saying a word. It was like they were afraid of me. I couldn't stand it.

I stayed out of the house as much as I could. Theresa and I went to see bands: Seven Seconds, Ignition, UK Subs, Scream, Government Issue, Black Market Baby . . . I liked some bands better than others, but after a while the shows became a blur.

I became familiar with the crowd. I was able to distinguish between skinheads, and I'd notice when someone's hair went from platinum to black. Theresa and I didn't talk to anybody, though, unless someone from Reston happened to turn up. We kept to ourselves, sitting on the floor smoking cigarettes until the bands started.

I was still Polly Clark. Mom and William had agreed that it would be easier if I kept Clark until college, so I didn't tell anybody about my change in dads. Not even Theresa.

We met Carrie in early August, at a rickety half pipe some skaters had assembled from wood they stole from construction sites. Carrie was friendly and sarcastic. She had olive skin, long dark hair and dark eyes, and wore lots of jewelry, like a teenage Cleopatra. She dressed all in black, smoked Camel Lights, and had a boyfriend named Lyle. Lyle was six feet tall and his legs were covered with scabs from skating. Lyle was funny, and you could tell he was in love with Carrie. Theresa and I agreed that Lyle was unusually cool for his age. Carrie was a year behind us, and Lyle was only a sophomore.

Now that we were seniors Theresa had sworn off boys, especially high school boys. She had instead devoted herself full-time to "the cause of music" and had accumulated the largest record collection of anyone I knew. She advised me on which bands were worth seeing and which records I should buy, while Carrie took over on topics like boys and clothes. Carrie and Lyle had been going out for six months, which made Carrie an authority on relationships. The first week I knew Carrie I learned that Lyle had told her he loved her after only two weeks of dating, but that she had made him wait another two weeks after that to have sex.

Carrie was my only friend whose parents were still married. The Thorpes were the most conservative family I knew, Baptists from South Carolina. I felt vaguely ashamed in their presence, like they might quiz me on the Bible or ask me to say grace and find out I didn't know anything.

Mr. and Mrs. Thorpe vehemently objected to most of Carrie's wardrobe. They lectured her on the color black and banned miniskirts all together. She took to hiding clothes in her car and changing into them once she was safely out of her neighborhood. When her clothes got dirty she gave them to me to wash. Mom and William thought it was funny. I think it made them feel superior to know they weren't the kinds of parents who would forbid clothing outright. Just the occasional item here and there.

"Teenagers are supposed to express themselves through their outfits," Mom said when I explained why my laundry had doubled. I hated the way she made me feel like she had me all figured out.

After Jason, Mike Franklin was the first one who counted. He was a junior, part of a group of skaters I knew from the hallways at school. I got to talking to him over at Keith Toole's house, where people had been congregating for two weeks while Keith's parents were in Myrtle Beach. Keith lived a mile away from me, on a street where the houses were so identical that every time I went over there, I worried I would knock on the wrong door.

Keith's house hadn't suffered much damage in his parent's absence, considering. The kitchen floor was badly in need of mopping, the sink was full of dirty dishes, and a permanent cloud of smoke hung in the air, but the police hadn't been summoned a single time. Unlike the parties that were thrown during the school year, Keith's were mellow, with the stereo kept at a neighborly level, and not more than ten or fifteen people present at any one time. It was late August, and there was a bored, languishing quality to everybody, owing to the fact that school was only days away.

I hadn't seen Mike all summer, but on the second-to-last day before school there he was, in Keith's living room, sitting next to Adam Schreiber on the couch. I'd hated Adam Schreiber ever since sophomore year, when he'd called me a poseur for wearing a Metallica shirt to school the day after the show. Theresa said that Adam was the worst kind of music fan. He was angry and contemptuous toward people who liked the same bands he did.

Mike had a red glass bong clasped between his legs, and his long fingers were curved casually around its neck. His hair had grown out from the skater cut I remembered him having the year before, the one that made all the skaters' heads look like lightbulbs. It was shaggy now, like he'd stopped caring about how he looked. He'd definitely gotten cuter, even if he was hanging out with Adam.

"Can I have a bong hit?" I said from across the room.

"Sure. C'mere."

Mike held the bong up. It was tall and decorated with a skeleton sticker. I perched on the edge of the coffee table, lifting the bong from his hands and nestling it between my knees. Someone had put Jimi Hendrix on the stereo instead of the usual hardcore, and MTV was on with the sound off. Adam and

Mike's stoned silence made me feel scrutinized, even though I knew they were staring over my head at the television, at a Squeeze video.

I found the shotgun hole in the back of the bong and put my finger over it. I had used a bong only once or twice, and I hoped I could remember how to do it. Keeping the rest of his body perfectly still, Adam rolled his head back and forth to the music. Jimi Hendrix made me think of Mom and William. The first couple of years they were together, they spent a lot of evenings in the living room in front of the stereo, drinking wine and listening to Hendrix, Neil Young, and Bob Dylan while they told stories about when they were young. I was allowed to be in the living room with them until my bedtime, but I usually got bored and wandered off.

"This is a pretty impressive bong," I said, taking my finger off the shotgun and exhaling.

"I just bought it," Mike said, coming out of his stupor. "It's a Toke-Master."

"He's got mucho spending money now because his parents are getting a divorce, so his mommy is spoiling him," Adam said. He pronounced it "dee-vorce."

"I remember that phase," I said. "Only I was five, so I got Barbie paraphernalia instead of drug paraphernalia."

Mike laughed and Adam took his eyes off the television long enough to sneer at me. His right eyetooth was discolored. I sneered back at him. The pot was beginning to creep through my body like an extended yawn.

"My mother's not exactly aware that I own this bong," Mike said. "We don't have that sort of rapport."

I giggled. I was sure Jason didn't know the word *rapport*. I handed the bong back and sat down on the couch on the other side of Mike.

Carrie appeared in the doorway and signaled that it was time to go. The clock on the VCR said 10:45. Carrie was the only one of my close friends who had a car, so I was forced to put up with her early curfew.

I stood up. "Well, it looks like I gotta go," I said. "Thanks a lot for the bong hit."

"Yeah, good to see you, Polly," Mike said. He smiled up at me in what I hoped was a significant way. "Sorry you gotta take off so soon."

"Me, too."

I followed Carrie out of the house with a stoned grin stretched across my face. I could see Theresa's and Lyle's orange cigarette tips glowing from inside Carrie's car.

Even though we didn't have any classes together, before the end of the first day of school I had memorized the location of Carrie's and Theresa's lockers and staked out a table in the lunchroom. I didn't have any classes with Carrie because she was a year behind me. I didn't have classes with Theresa because I was good at math.

When I did math it was like I was in a trance. I wasn't good at it in a creepy, child-prodigy kind of way, I was just good enough for the teachers to notice. It started with pre-algebra in the seventh grade, then algebra I in the eighth grade, advanced geometry in the ninth grade, and algebra II–trig in the tenth grade. In eleventh grade I took advanced functions first semester and analytical geometry second semester. Now that I was a senior I was taking calculus. I knew that math wasn't supposed to be easy. Even Theresa hated math, and she got good grades.

My math classes were small, considering the size of the school. My classmates were mostly male nerds, with a few girl nerds here and there. All the girls in class except me were openly ambitious—they clearly had something to prove. Their hands shot up faster than the teachers could finish questions, and they scored the highest on tests. They ignored the boys, and talked only of test scores and getting into college. They ignored me, too.

Thanks to math I was placed in accelerated English and history, though I didn't deserve to be in those classes. I did okay, but it wasn't like math. Being good in school made everything easier. When my friends skipped class, the front office called their parents. When I told my teachers I had a doctor's appointment or a head cold or bad cramps they believed me.

Adam Schreiber was the first one to find us at our lunch table. His head had been freshly shaved since Keith's party, and there were nicks here and there. It looked like he'd shaved it himself.

"Mike will be here in a second," he said, plopping down next to me.

"That's nice," I said. I wondered if there was already a rumor going around that I liked Mike. I looked over at Carrie. Her face was blank.

Just then Mike lowered himself into the chair across from me, his lunch bag in one hand and a copy of *High Times* magazine in the other.

"Hi, you guys," Mike said. He threw the magazine down on the table. Theresa snatched it up and began thumbing through it, her red hair bouncing against her shoulders.

"Check it out," Theresa said, spreading the Bud of the Month Centerfold out on the table. Everyone leaned forward. It wasn't much to look at. Just a giant pile of pot leaves.

"I would be so stoked if I had that," Mike said. He was wearing a baseball hat backward. It made him look about twelve.

"You'd rather check out a weed centerfold than a *Playboy* centerfold," Adam said.

"Shut up." Mike pulled the saran wrap off his sandwich and balled it up. His cheeks had gone red.

"*Playboy* is cheesy," Theresa said.

Mike called me that night. When I answered the phone he just said, "Hi, Polly. It's Mike," and then I said, "Oh, hi," and then he said he was just calling to say hi, and then we were silent for a minute or so. My bedroom window was open, and I could hear a dog barking somewhere in the neighborhood.

"God, my mom," I finally said. "She, like, expects me to come home from school and do my homework and then immediately begin doing chores like I'm some extra sister on *Little House on the Prairie* or something. And then my stepfather, he keeps trying to limit my television time because he thinks it's going to cut into my *real existence,* whatever that means. And I'm sorry, but it's my life and I'm kind of sick of them butting in all the time, you know? Not to mention that it's the first week of school. I mean, God. It's not like I've got a test tomorrow."

I wasn't sure why I was telling him all this. In fact, my household duties were minimal, consisting only of keeping the upstairs bathroom clean and picking up after myself.

"Yeah, I hate that parent bullshit," Mike said. "Hey, you want to hear something I'm learning on the guitar?"

"Sure."

Mike put the phone receiver by his guitar. I couldn't really make out what song he was playing. I stretched the phone cord over to the window and gazed out at the smooth, dark pavement of my street and the perfectly arranged clusters of trees. I was careful not to look over at my backpack, which I had shoved behind the laundry basket. I had physics homework to do. My teacher, Mrs. Fern, seemed intent on making her class the challenge of her students' lives. "Physics is tough stuff," she had announced at the start of class. I resented Mrs. Fern already. Senior year was supposed to be easier in the accelerated program, so we could focus on our SAT scores and getting into a good college. Apparently Mrs. Fern hadn't gotten the memo.

Mike played me a few songs. Then he announced it was time for him to have dinner. After I hung up I put on Minor Threat and danced in front of the mirror for three songs straight.

"Maybe you can drive a wedge between Mike and Adam," Theresa said when I told her about Mike calling me. "Once you get close enough."

I looked down at my Bad Brains T-shirt. At lunch Adam had sneered, "Nice shirt," and rolled his eyes at me. Later he made fun of Carrie for liking New Order. "New Order's a fag band," he said.

"If Mike likes Adam's personality as it is now I don't see how I'm going to change his mind," I said.

I pictured myself as Mike's girlfriend. I would be Polly, otherwise known as Mike Franklin's girlfriend. I just had gotten used to not thinking of myself as Jason's ex-girlfriend. It had been two months since I had let Jason dissolve in my mind— that's what it had seemed like, a television dissolve edit—and up to now I had thought of him only occasionally to fill the space that having no one to like created.

The next week at the lunch table, Mike and Lyle began plotting their new band. Lyle didn't play an instrument, but he had a microphone stand and a couple of amps his older brother had left in his basement. Lyle was going to be the singer, and Mike would play guitar. All they needed was a bass player and a drummer. Plus more equipment. Even though nobody had any money, Carrie agreed to drive them to the mall to look at band stuff after school.

Mike caught up with me as I was throwing my lunch trash away.

"Are you gonna come with us today?"

"Is this your way of telling me you need a roadie? Because I'm not very strong," I said.

"Come on," Mike said. "You can help me decide which amp looks the coolest. I think I can talk my mom into buying me one."

"Okay, but I get final say," I said. Mike grinned. I tried to keep my return grin a normal size.

Adam was the first person at Carrie's tan Ford Escort after school. I watched him as I crossed the parking lot. He was sitting on the hood, staring down at the yellow lighter in his hand. He flicked it over and over again. As I got nearer, I could hear the hiss it made each time he ran his thumb over the spark wheel.

"Got a cigarette?" he asked when I got up to him.

I pulled my pack out of my jacket pocket and handed it over.

"You used to go out with Jason Wilson," Adam said, blowing smoke. He said Jason's name in the same tone of voice he used when he talked about New Order.

"Yeah, so?" I said.

"I know Todd, Jason's brother. He told me about you and Jason."

I was surprised Jason's brother knew who I was. "I've never even met Todd," I said.

Adam smirked. "Well, he sure seems to know all about you."

I took my pack of cigarettes off the roof of the car where Adam had left it and put it back in my pocket. I wanted to ask what Todd Wilson had said about me. If Adam knew about my failed attempt at sex with Jason, Mike knew. I hadn't even told Theresa.

Over Adam's shoulder I spotted Mike across the parking lot. He was wearing an army-green corduroy jacket that looked stiff and new. The boys' soccer team jogged out of the school and toward us, on their way to practice. They swarmed around Mike, a mass of sweatshirts and running shorts and thick legs. Three or four of them carried soccer balls. They turned toward the stadium just as Mike reached us.

"I used to play soccer," Mike said, gazing after them.

"It's never too late to be an idiot jock," Adam said.

"I used to play, too," I said. "Until ninth grade. What position did you play?"

"Mostly defense."

"I was a half-back. Right side. I liked throw-ins."

"I kind of sucked," Mike said. "I'm not really cut out for team sports."

I swooned. "Me neither."

"I was a goalie," Adam said. I tried to picture his skinny frame and scraped bald head in a soccer uniform, diving for the ball, not wanting to let down the team.

In the car, Lyle sat up front with Carrie. I sat in the backseat between Mike and Adam, my feet resting on the center hump. My legs were longer than Adam's, but it was worth the discomfort so I could sit next to Mike. The pink shirt that Carrie had changed out of that morning peeked out from under her seat, near Mike's feet.

"Sweet Child o' Mine" came on the radio. We groaned. I swayed back and forth in my seat and wagged my head in my best Axel imitation.

Mike flashed me a quick smile. "You're retarded," he said.

I smacked him in the arm. "Am not!"

We merged onto the highway, and Carrie sped up. We were out of Reston now. We passed the auto parts store and

Woody's Driving Range. William went to the driving range once in a while, even though he didn't play golf. He said it relaxed him. When he was teaching me to drive I would take William to Woody's and drink a Coke while he hit balls. This was before I ran into a NO PARKING sign and snapped it in two, and William announced that he didn't want to ride in the car with me ever again.

I exaggerated my Axel impression, twisting my upper body right and then left.

"Where do we go, where do we go now," Carrie and I sang. Mike grabbed my arms and pulled them behind my back, knocking me into Adam. I squealed and jerked an arm free.

"Fuck, man, cut it out," said Adam.

I poked Mike under his armpit. He flailed in his seat and pushed me into Adam again.

"Fucking cut it the fuck out," Adam said.

We continued to struggle. Soon Mike had both my arms pinned at my sides. I tried to wriggle away, and then all at once he kissed me. His lips were softer than I expected.

"Ai yai yai yai yai yai yai yai," Axel screeched over our kiss. Mike loosened his grip on my arms, and I felt the corduroy collar of his jacket against my collarbone.

The music stopped and I heard the click of a tape going into the deck. Adam sighed and said, "Get me out of here," and just like that we stopped kissing.

The mall loomed up in front of us. Carrie braked and threw her cigarette out the window. Mike had his arm around my shoulder. We both stared straight ahead.

The next day Mike came by my locker after third period and gave me a drawing of a skater going over a waterfall. There were curvy lines coming off the skater in every direction. At the bottom of the drawing the curvy lines turned into the words *To Polly From Mike.*

"I drew this last night when I was high," he said.

Bethany, the girl who had the locker next to mine, looked over at us and then away again. She was wearing a turquoise Converse sneaker on one foot and a red Converse sneaker on the other foot, part of the standard drama geek uniform. She kept a *Guys and Dolls* playbill taped up inside her locker, and boys wearing fedoras and trench coats regularly stopped by to say hi.

Bethany had long, fluffy brown hair that she was constantly shaking around. I had seen her in the math wing once. When I said hi, Bethany gave me a bewildered look, like a fearful celebrity cornered in a public place. Now we ignored each other.

"I wish I were high right now," I said, loud enough for Bethany to hear.

"Do you want to come over after school?" Mike said.

Carrie and Lyle gave us a ride. Mike lived in a subdivision of town houses that had just been built. The neighborhood looked barren, the newly planted trees small and scraggly along the street. Mike didn't invite Carrie and Lyle in.

Mike's sister was lying on the floor in the living room, propped up on her elbows in front of *General Hospital.*

"This is Caitland," Mike mumbled. Caitland twisted around and regarded me before turning back to the television. She had the same thick dark hair and large brown eyes that Mike did.

His bedroom looked exactly as I expected. Band flyers covered the walls, and stereo components were piled next to cratefuls of records. There was a narrow bed and a tall dresser with skate stickers all over it. The only thing that distinguished Mike's room from Jason's was the black electric guitar lying across the foot of the bed. I sat down next to the guitar while Mike put on Dag Nasty. Then he pulled his bong out of the back of his closet.

Mike sat down on the bed beside me as smoke filled my chest. He took the bong out of my hands just as I exploded into a coughing fit. I coughed all the way through Mike's bong hit and into the next Dag Nasty song.

"Are you okay?" he asked when I had stopped.

"Yes. Now I am."

Mike took another hit and offered me the bong back. I shook my head no. "I'm good," I said.

He set the bong down on the rug, which matched the forest green wall-to-wall rug in the hallway.

"So tell me about when your parents got divorced," Mike said.

His question startled me. I tucked a foot under my thigh and said what I was used to saying. "I was pretty little. My dad drank a lot and they fought all the time, so."

"Do you still see your dad?"

"Yeah, a couple times a year maybe. And we talk on the phone. He's in North Carolina."

"Mine just got divorced last spring," Mike said. "I haven't seen my dad since he left."

"Really?" I felt sorry for him.

"Yup." He picked up his guitar and strummed it.

"Do you know where he is, though?"

"Yeah, he lives in Annandale. He calls here sometimes. I don't want to see him, though. He punched me right before they broke up."

"God. How come?" Nobody in my family had ever hit me.

"He told me not to get this haircut I wanted. When I got it anyway he freaked out and hit me. Mom threw him out, and we sold the house and moved here."

"What was the haircut?"

"It was like shaved on the sides."

Mike lowered his head over his guitar. He was hard to hear since he wasn't plugged in, but I was enthralled by the way his hair flopped over his eyes and how his fingers flew up and down the fret board. I scooted back on the bed and leaned against the wall, where I could see out his window. The view was of the sidewalk out front and the adjacent row of parking spaces that were only about a quarter filled. I studied the way the still, late-afternoon sun shone on the tops of the cars as the pot tingled through me. Mike's mom had stuck up for him. I didn't know what my mom would do if William hit me. When I was twelve I kept forgetting to lock the front door when I went out and William got so angry he ignored me for a week. Mom acted like nothing out of the ordinary was going on, even though he was absent at dinner and came home from work without acknowledging my presence.

"I'm actually not talking to my father right now either," I said.

Mike stopped playing guitar. "How come?" he asked.

I told him my secret. How I wasn't really Polly Clark, but Polly Hessler. I told him that even though my dad had a college degree and a job, he still couldn't support me. "It's probably because he's an alcoholic," I said. "He spends all his money on liquor."

Mike was quiet, and I worried I'd said too much. I held my breath as he rose from the bed and carefully set the guitar back on its stand. Then he crossed back over to the bed and swooped down on top of me. He reminded me of a seagull. He was on his hands and knees, and I had to strain my neck up to kiss him. He was a seagull, and I was a crane. We stayed like that, kissing, until without any kind of warning he pushed himself up into a kneeling position and began unbuttoning his pants.

I propped myself up on my elbows. I could see Mike's paisley boxers peeking through his fly. I was confused. He hadn't

even been up my shirt yet, and here he was taking his pants
off.

"What are you doing?" I asked.

Mike took me in with bloodshot eyes. "I don't know."

He lay back on top of me. I could feel his warm breath on
my neck. He didn't seem to have an erection. It was hot underneath him, and a puddle of sweat was forming in the center of
my bra. I wriggled down so we could kiss some more.

The next day we were walking from my locker to first period
when Mike pulled another drawing out of his backpack. This
drawing was abstract. He had used green, brown, and orange
markers, and each shape he had drawn blended into the next.
The edges of the paper were saturated with color. I was impressed.

"You're really good," I said.

After class I hung it up in my locker. I borrowed some
tape from Bethany, who inexplicably kept masking tape hanging
from one of her locker's coat hooks. She peered around the
edge of her locker door at the drawing. I could tell she wanted
to ask about the picture but didn't.

In the weeks that followed I fell into a pattern of going over
to Mike's after school to get stoned and make out. He didn't
try to have sex with me. Instead, I gave him blow jobs. It was
the easiest way to put off sex, especially after what had happened with Jason. The best part was I didn't have to take off
my clothes. I was hoping Mike couldn't tell what kind of body
I had. There wasn't anything I could do about my face, but I
liked to think that my body was my secret. I had a dark, oval
birthmark on my lower back, about an inch long. Mike didn't

know about it. My T-shirts and sweaters were baggy, and my posture was slightly stooped. I liked to think people couldn't tell whether I had boobs. I longed to wear my combat boots with short skirts, but my legs were still too skinny. Instead I wore my boots under my jeans like a guy.

Carrie and Lyle dropped us off each afternoon, and William picked me up on his way home from work. I would have preferred for Mom to pick me up—having William do it was embarrassing—but she worked in the opposite direction and Mike's house was on William's way. Mom and William didn't make much of a fuss over "my new friend," as Mom referred to him. William didn't even see Mike when he came to get me; he'd just honk his horn at 5:15 and I'd run out, half an hour before Mike's mom was due home. On the ride home William listened to NPR and bitched about Reagan.

"Trickle-down economics! Give me a break! Anti-missile weapons in outer space! Jesus H. Christ!"

I didn't respond. He wasn't talking to me.

I waited for Mom and William to grill me about Mike, but they left me alone. At the dinner table, they talked about work. Mom was frustrated. She was nothing but a glorified secretary at her property management job. She was one of the most knowledgeable people in her office, but the sanctimonious men above her didn't care. William was supposed to be spending his time designing software, but the idiots he worked with bombarded him with stupid, unrelated computer questions all day. He got more done at home in two hours than he did all day in the office.

When they got finished complaining about their jobs they'd pause to watch Dan Rather, who droned from a miniature TV on the counter. Then they'd start in on politics, venting about Iran-Contra and Ollie North. I hated him, too, for his military haircut and his self-important, bully's face.

"He looks like an older version of the meanest jocks at my school," I said, which made them both laugh.

After dinner I'd go up to my room to do homework and think about Mike. I'd lent him my Bad Brains T-shirt, and he'd given me a bracelet he made out of fishhooks. I had to take the bracelet off to shower because it got caught in my hair when I washed it, but otherwise I wore it all the time. I even slept in it. And Mike was there at my locker every morning, waiting to walk to first period together. We were obviously a couple for anyone who cared to notice. I pretended that everyone did.

On the days that I didn't go over to Mike's I went over to Lyle's basement to watch their band practice. They had decided on the name Massive Hemorrhage. Lyle's basement was full of boxes with labels like UPSTAIRS LAMPS, SKI STUFF, and GRANDMA'S THINGS, and Carrie and Theresa and I had to squeeze between them to get to a couple of scratchy, worn-out couches. I loved Lyle's basement. Like my house, his was built on a hill, so the basement had a sliding glass door that led to the backyard. Other than that it was nothing like my own basement, with its rust-colored rug and big TV and spotless furniture. My mother was not one to waste space on storage. She gave so much stuff to Goodwill that they called whenever their truck was going to be in the neighborhood. The night before a pickup she'd roam through the house with a trash bag, looking for things to get rid of.

"Do you really think we're going to use this waffle iron again? Who makes waffles in this house?"

"These hand weights are just cluttering up the laundry room!"

I lost my old Barbies that way, and my Shawn Cassidy and Olivia Newton John records.

• • •

Massive Hemorrhage's songs were fast and short. I liked them. Sometimes they would stop for a four-beat in the middle of a song and then start again, even faster than before. Lyle was tall and skinny like Joey Ramone, and he leaned far over the microphone while he shouted the lyrics. Mike was the opposite. He leaned back when he played, shutting his eyes and nodding his head during his brief solos. When they did the stop-start parts Mike would lift his guitar up until it was nearly even with his shoulders and then sling it back down when he started to play again. I would dig my back into the itchy couch and push my feet against the floor, willing him to look over at me.

They had found a drummer and a bass player at school, sophomores who were both named Chris. They were best friends. Chris L. was the drummer and didn't talk much. Chris S. talked, but only about music. The Chrises were straight-edge: they didn't drink or smoke or do drugs. Shortly after joining the band the Chrises started eating lunch with us.

Carrie and I were smoking in one of the bathroom stalls at school when she asked me if I wanted to go on the pill with her. She said it like she was asking if I wanted to go to the mall.

I tapped an ash into the toilet. "Um, I don't think so," I said. "I mean I don't really need to or anything."

Carrie rolled her eyes. "Polly, I don't know why you have to act like it's such a big secret. Mike told Lyle two weeks ago that you guys were doing it. I mean Theresa and I were both wondering why you're being so closemouthed about it. You guys are going out and everything, it's not a big deal."

"I was going to tell you," I lied.

"Whatever. So we should go to the doctor together and get on the pill."

The fifth-period bell rang and we threw our cigarettes into the toilet. I put my foot on the handle and flushed.

"I just don't know if I want to go on it yet," I said as we made our way out into the hallway.

In Mrs. Fern's tough-stuff physics class, I wondered if Mike told Lyle that we were sleeping together out of the blue, or if he was warding off questions in the same way I was forced to with Carrie. I would have to ask him about it. The next time I was over I would bring it up. Before we got stoned.

"Tell me about your high school girlfriend," I said to William that afternoon on the ride home from Mike's. I was rolling down the window in an effort to get the pot smell out of my clothes.

He looked over at me. His tie was loose, and there was an ink stain on his shirt. Dark stubble colored his chin. "What is it you want to know?" he said.

"I don't know. You know. What was her name?"

William shrugged. "There were a few, as I recall. No one significant if that's what you're asking. That didn't happen until college. It wasn't like it is with you and your friends."

"What do you mean, like it is with me and my friends?"

"In my day we didn't travel in packs on the weekends. We went on proper dates, and things weren't serious. You might go out with one person on Friday and another on Saturday. There was none of this relationship stuff."

"Two dates in one weekend? You've got to be kidding me."

William braked and downshifted. "I'm certainly not. And from what I can tell, it beats your system."

He changed his mind and sped up to get through a yellow

light. I felt myself begin to get irritated. I was trying to talk to him about something real. Something important.

"There's no *system,*" I said. "And I don't always go out in a group. For your information, I spend plenty of time alone with Mike."

"Let me ask you something," William said. "Do you think of yourself as being in a relationship with this guy?"

I crossed my arms. "Do you mean, Is he my boyfriend? Yes."

"And yet he doesn't care to take you out on any real dates."

"What do you mean, real dates?" I said. "You just said that nobody in my generation goes on dates."

"Well, the full extent of your relationship seems to take place at his house after school. That's not what I would call dating."

I couldn't tell if William was in a bad mood or if he was genuinely concerned. "That's not true. I see him at band practice," I said.

William gave me a smirk as we turned into our development. At the top of the street Jimmy Porter, who was four years old, was standing in his front yard. A blue stuffed bunny lay at his feet. As we passed by Jimmy raised a stiff hand and moved it back and forth like he was riding atop a parade float. I waved back.

"You don't even know Mike," I said.

"My point exactly!" An excitability had crept into William's voice that I was all too familiar with. This was the voice he used to talk about my reluctance to study for the SATs, my lack of interest in chores, and the amount of time I spent on the telephone.

"You're right, I don't even know him!" he continued. "And why is that? You should be going places—he should be taking you places! He should be picking you up at the house, coming in so your mother and I can meet him!"

He pulled into the driveway and jerked the car to a halt. I ran upstairs to my room without my usual thank you. I had only wanted to know if he'd had a girlfriend. Maybe something bad had happened with a girl when William was my age, and he was taking it out on me. Or maybe Mom was his first girlfriend. Maybe everyone else had rejected him.

I rushed through dinner, which was meat loaf. I hated meat loaf. Mom and William talked about work, as usual. I took my plate to the sink and scraped my leftovers into the garbage disposal when they were only halfway through. I had some homework to do, and then I wanted to call Theresa.

"In case you're wondering, you may be excused from the table," William said.

I went upstairs and shut my bedroom door. I sat down at my desk and switched on my fluorescent desk light. It came on with a hiss. I opened my notebook. I wasn't ready to do homework yet. I drew a treble clef and then I started on a guitar. As I shaded it in I heard Mom and William's voices drifting up from the vent in the kitchen. I couldn't make out what they were saying, but I could tell they were having a fight. I pushed my chair back and crept into the hallway in my socks. I sat down at the top of the stairs, where I could hear them better.

"She doesn't listen to a word I say," William said.

"We've had this conversation enough times."

I was surprised to hear Mom say that. Someone turned on the water in the sink and then turned it back off again. I heard a dish clatter into the dishwasher.

"Fran, listen to me! She's going to wind up pregnant, or dropping out of school, or in jail, or in a drug rehabilitation center, or God knows what!"

"Would you just stop with this? She's a good kid. Look at her grades."

I heard the water go on again and then more dishes rattling. I was glad Mom was sticking up for me.

"What do you think she's doing over at Mike's house? Studying? She gets into the car reeking of pot!"

I felt a pit of dread begin to form in my stomach. I wished I'd been nicer on the car ride home.

"What would you have me do, force her to break it off with that boy? Ground her for the rest of the school year? We're not talking about anything out of the ordinary here. She's not stealing cars or shooting heroin, for God's sake."

There was a long pause. I waited. "What do you mean, what would I have *you* do?" William finally said. "Don't I have any goddamn input around here?"

"Judging by the way you're overreacting, I think it's best if you don't have any input, actually."

The phone rang. I started to stand up to get it, but then thought better of it. Mom went around the corner to pick it up, and her voice became muffled. I was sitting under a framed 8 x 10 photograph of my ninth-grade school picture. I had a perm and braces, and I was so skinny that you could see the bones jutting out of my face. I had told Mom repeatedly that I wanted her to take it down. She thought it was cute. I told myself that I would invite Mike over to meet them as soon as they took down the picture.

I heard William's voice again. "She dresses like a lunatic, she never comes home after school, and she sleeps until after lunch on the weekends! Is this what you consider normal?"

"She makes her curfew. She's not breaking any rules."

"Fran, she doesn't have any fucking rules!"

I heard my mother's quick footsteps coming toward the stairs. I darted into my room, slamming the door behind me and locking it. I plugged in my headphones and threw the needle onto the turntable. It was the Bad Brains. I lay flat on my bed, letting the music blare into me. I hadn't heard William use the word *fuck* before.

I remembered the time when I was little when William had

taken me to a carnival just off Sunset Road. It was shortly after Mom and I moved in with him. We were on the way home from my piano lesson, and William and I were alone in the car. I had been too shy to do anything but point out the carnival as we drove by, but William pulled over into a makeshift parking lot that had been created in a neighboring field.

"How about a couple of rides before dinner?" he said.

It was just getting toward dusk, and the carnival was very nearly empty, the workers hanging out in clusters between the rides they were supposed to be running. I was quiet as I walked beside William, trying to match his big strides with my own.

I slowed in front of the Tilt-A-Whirl. I hadn't been on the Tilt-A-Whirl before, but it looked promising. The large, hollowed-out, red-painted eggs were suspended on a gentle incline that appealed to me. I was scared of things that went up high, like roller coasters and Ferris wheels. But this looked like something I could have fun on.

William bought two tickets and we climbed into one of the eggs. Since it was still early we were the only two people on the ride. The worker flipped a switch and carnival-sounding music started up. We jerked forward, and I grabbed on to William's arm with both hands. The ride was faster and scarier than it looked. The problem with the Tilt-A-Whirl wasn't heights, it was spinning. Nausea began to take hold of me as we were yanked from side to side. Our egg went into a never-ending fast spin, and I stifled the urge to cry out. I vowed that no matter what, I would not throw up in front of William.

William yelled things like "Hey, stop!" and "Slow down!" at the operator. But the operator didn't understand William over the music. Instead of slowing down he hit a new switch and the thing sped up even faster. It was no longer possible for me to move or make a sound. William waved one hand at the man whenever he came into view, and kept the other tight around me. "Don't worry," he said, over and over. Finally, the ride came to an end. Our egg hung at the top of an incline, slowly swaying to a stop.

"She's only seven years old!" William barked at the operator as we climbed down a set of rusty steps to safety. The operator shrugged at us and turned away to light his cigarette. A few people had shown up at the Tilt-A-Whirl, and they clamored past us onto the ride. I was embarrassed that I had been such a baby in front of William, but I felt closer to him, too, like we had been through something together. At dinner we told Mom about it like we had narrowly escaped something exciting and dangerous, like a rock slide or a burning building.

"Lyle and I tried to have anal sex," Carrie confessed over the phone a few days later.

I was alone in my bedroom, but I was still blushing. Being Carrie's friend meant sitting through recounts of things like how long it took Lyle to get his erection back after sex, and how he liked to have her blow him for a minute or two before they did it. Not that I wasn't interested. But Carrie was graphic, and she was talking about Lyle. It was impossible to think of Lyle, the gangly lead singer of Massive Hemorrhage and the most sarcastic guy at the lunch table, as the star of Carrie's sex stories.

"Have you and Mike ever tried it?" she asked me.

"No," I said. "I would tell you."

"Well, let me tell you, I don't recommend it," Carrie said. "I don't see why people do it. I really don't."

"Well, thanks for the warning."

"Just hope Mike doesn't ask you for it. He probably won't. Unless maybe if Lyle tells him about it," Carrie said.

She moved on to the topic of lubricant. I opened my English lit notebook. I wrote my name in bubble letters in the margin of my notes on *Heart of Darkness* by Joseph Conrad. *Heart of Darkness* was the first good book we'd read in English all year.

I liked it so much I'd already finished it, even though we had another week before it was due. It took place a long time ago, but it was haunting and scary and deep. In class we talked about evil and human nature. Mrs. Mason said that everyone had a dark side. I didn't have any trouble believing that.

When I finished writing my name in bubble letters I started on Mike's name. I connected the *Y* in Polly to the *M* in Mike. Carrie and Lyle were at the stage where they were experimenting. Mike and I, for reasons I didn't understand, had a monotonous routine. Not that I wanted to try anal sex. But I couldn't remember the last time Mike had even bothered to feel me up. I still hadn't asked him why Carrie and Lyle were under the impression that we were sleeping together.

It wasn't really sex I wanted, though. I was still kind of afraid to have sex. I wanted other things. Boyfriend things. I wanted Mike to rest his hand on my thigh when he sat next to me, like Lyle did with Carrie. I wanted him to miss me when I wasn't there, or at least tell me that he did. We'd been going out for three months. I wanted him to tell me that he loved me.

Mike and I were different from other people. We didn't fit in at school. We had the same sense of humor. We didn't like sports or school dances or extracurricular activities. We were loners in black clothes, poets imprisoned in the suburbs. We loved cities and hated nature. We loved vintage cars and hated acid-washed jeans. We were fans of punk rock music and John Waters movies. We detested bops and Christians. We loved our mothers and hated our fathers. We didn't belong in Reston. We were lucky to have found each other.

I broke up with him over the phone a few days later. It wasn't something I planned. Mike wanted us to take acid and watch *The Wall* over at Adam's house. One of my relationship rules was that I didn't go over to Adam's.

"I'm not doing that." I said it like he had invited me to a square dance at his church.

"Why not?"

I sighed. I could hear his guitar. "For one thing, I've already seen *The Wall*."

"But every time you see it, you notice more things," Mike said. "And you have to see it on acid. Have you ever seen it on acid?"

 "Maybe we could do something else instead," I said.

"Like what?"

"Like go out to dinner or something."

"You want to trip and go out to eat? I can never eat when I'm tripping. And I can tell you right now Adam's not gonna wanna do that."

I stared out my bedroom window. Next to the streetlight a calico cat I didn't recognize was stretched out on the roof of our neighbor's pale green Honda. William was right.

"Mike?"

"What?"

"Do you want to just be friends or something?"

He stopped playing guitar. "Is that what you want?"

I sat down on my bed. My stomach felt like it was full of clay. "I'm asking you," I said.

"Yeah, I guess," he said.

We were quiet. I could hear Mike's breathing. I unclasped the fishhook bracelet from my wrist and threw it across the room. It made a pinging sound against the mirror and fell into the laundry basket. He hung up without saying good-bye.

I made an X with my arms and legs on the bed. My hands and feet dangled off the sides, and I waited for the blood to rush there. The clay feeling in my stomach had gone away, and now I felt like I had gotten the wind knocked out of me.

I sat up and called Theresa. "I'll be right over," she said. "I'll tell my mother that I need help with math."

I went downstairs to the basement and told Mom and William that Theresa was coming over to get help with math. They were watching a British mystery on PBS.

"Okay, honey," Mom said. I lingered in the doorway. I couldn't decide whether to tell them about Mike. It felt rude to interrupt their show, and PBS didn't have commercials. I waited for one of them to ask me what was wrong. I wanted it to be like when Mom told me I could quit the drill team. All I had to do was burst into tears, and she would take care of me.

On TV a scruffy, nerdy investigator was questioning a red-faced, overweight housecleaner. "And how long have you known about Mrs. Shervington's previous marriage?" he demanded. I went back upstairs and put on my coat and hat.

When Theresa showed up we headed for the neighborhood playground. It was deserted, and the jungle gym looked naked, like some sort of modern sculpture instead of something kids played on.

I lowered myself into a swing and kicked at the sand underneath me. "God, this place is just like one giant cat box," I said.

Theresa leaned over to light my cigarette. Her gloves smelled of tobacco. When I lifted my cigarette to my mouth, I noticed that my wrist felt lighter without the fishhook bracelet.

"There's something to be said for being free," Theresa said. "I like it."

"I know," I said. "But I liked being Mike's girlfriend, too."

"That's weird."

"What?"

"What you said. That you liked being Mike's girlfriend. Not that you liked Mike."

"You know what I mean."

"Why'd you break up with him, then?"

I thought about it. "I don't know. It was just like all of the sudden it seemed like things had gotten so . . . pointless."

"Yeah. I can see that."

"Did it seem that way to you?"

"Pointless?"

"Yeah."

"God. I don't know. How would I know?"

"Well. We weren't exactly Carrie and Lyle material."

"You say that like it's a bad thing."

"Well."

"Oh please," Carrie said when I told her I didn't want to sit at the lunch table anymore. "Everyone is as much your friend as Mike's."

We were at my locker, which was decorated with several of Mike's drawings. I hadn't decided what to do with them yet.

"You can sit by me. Everybody will think I've got two chicks," Lyle said. He put one arm around me and the other one around Carrie. I laughed. Carrie gave Lyle a look. Lyle took his arm away and said he was just kidding. I slammed my locker shut and followed them into the lunchroom.

The stench of cafeteria food and the closeness of the lunch crowd was almost too much to bear. I kept my head down as I made my way through the food line. I wasn't hungry in the least. I finally settled on a soft pretzel and a grape juice.

"That's not much of a lunch," the lady at the register said as I paid her.

"I have an eating disorder," I muttered. I felt faint. Mike was already at our table, chatting away with Adam. He was wearing a navy blue sweater I hadn't seen before, which unnerved me.

I sat down at the end of the table, as far away from Mike as I could get. He picked up his sandwich and came over next to me and sat down. He was having his usual sandwich, tuna salad that he brought from home.

"How are you doing?" he said.

I got up and moved next to Chris L. and Chris S. Mike followed me. I got up and moved, and he followed me again.

"Come on, I know you still like me," he said, loud enough for everyone at the table to hear. "Let's at least talk about it."

The sick feeling I had carried around with me all day was going away. "I don't want to talk to you," I said.

"Come on, Polly. I know I'm an asshole sometimes."

"Are you kidding?" I said. "This is a joke, right?"

"Look. I said I know I'm an asshole. So will you just drop this and be my girlfriend again?"

"Is that a new sweater?"

"Come on. I'm asking you to get back together with me in front of everybody."

I stared down at my soft pretzel. This was the last thing I had expected.

"Don't fall for it, Polly," Theresa said.

"At least go to another table or something," Adam said.

Mike pushed his chair back and stood up. "Polly, I'm ordering you to get back together with me right now!" His hands were flung wide, and his cheeks were red. He was acting like one of Bethany's drama boyfriends.

I beamed. "Okay, you win," I said.

"I thought you'd wised up about that twerp," William said when I called him for a ride home from Mike's.

"I have wised up," I said. If I hadn't broken up with him, Mike wouldn't have been so affectionate in the lunchroom. It wasn't like Jason. This time it was going to work out.

Friday night Massive Hemorrhage practiced. This was a better practice than usual, as Lyle's mother was out of town with her

boyfriend and we'd gotten a case of beer. I basked in the faint
scent of damp boxes mixed with the more generic scent of
Lyle's house, a smell as familiar to me now as the harsh overhead lighting and the scratchiness of the couch.

After practice was over Mike squeezed himself next to me
on the couch and kissed me on the lips. He was sweaty from
playing, and his T-shirt stuck to him in places. I set my empty
Milwaukee's Best can on the floor. Mike put his arm around me
and I rested my head on his shoulder.

"Good practice," I said.

"Yeah, some of it," Mike said. "We need more songs before
we play out, though." I held his hand in my lap and ran my fin-
gertips over his calluses while he drank his beer with his other
hand. He wasn't stoned tonight. I liked him this way.

There was a rap at the sliding glass door. Lyle turned down
the stereo and yanked the curtains aside. It was Adam and a boy
I didn't know. The boy was wearing a leather motorcycle jacket
and his short bleached hair was spiked up like Billy Idol's.

"You guys know Todd," Adam said when they stepped inside.

"Hey," Todd said. His voice sounded familiar.

Lyle turned the stereo back up and everyone started talking
again. I watched as Todd crossed the room to the case on the
floor and helped himself to a beer. He straightened back up and
walked straight over to Mike and me. He cracked his beer open
and stared down at us. I was getting a bad feeling.

"What's going on, Todd?" Mike said.

"Are you Polly?"

"Yeah."

Todd's eyes raked over me. "You're the one who fucked my
brother," he said.

Todd didn't look a whole lot like Jason. Their coloring was
similar but Todd was taller and his nose was slightly larger and

more crooked. He had a cruel, dominant air about him that Jason lacked.

"Jason and I broke up a long time ago," I stammered.

"I guess I should thank you, 'cause Jason was a virgin." Todd's voice was tinged with ridicule. "I thought he was gonna die a virgin."

Adam laughed. "Who wants a smoke? " he said.

I felt myself redden as Todd's words sank in. Jason had been a virgin like me. And still I hadn't been good enough.

Todd followed Adam outside and I made myself look over at Mike. He had grabbed his guitar from the side of the couch and was busying himself over a broken string.

"Well," I said. My voice cracked like a boy's. "That was weird. What a fucking jerk."

I waited for Mike to say something, but he just shrugged and pulled at his string. He didn't look angry. I crossed one leg over the other and sighed. Mike knelt in closer to his guitar. I got up to get another beer before it was time for Carrie's curfew.

It happened Monday, as we were walking from my locker to first period. When we reached his classroom Mike paused in the doorway.

"I think we should break up."

I'd been talking about how I thought Massive Hemorrhage was ready to play a real show. Now I looked down at the floor, coming to focus on a silver gum wrapper.

"Why?" I asked.

"I don't know, it just seems like it's stupid for us to keep going out. I mean, let's face it. It's not like we have something important going on here."

I forced my gaze to his face.

"Oh," I said. The bell for first period rang, and a boy with

hair the same auburn color as Carrie's squeezed his way in between us and into the classroom. Two others followed him.

"Well, see you later then," Mike said.

It wasn't until he turned around that I realized that he was
wearing my Bad Brains shirt.

"Hey!" I called after him. He walked to a desk in the back
row and sat down, sliding his backpack to the floor.

Instead of going to class I went upstairs to the second floor.
The final bell rang, and the hallway abruptly emptied out.
Doors slammed shut. I inched along, pausing to look through
each classroom window for Theresa.

She was sitting in the far corner of the last classroom on the
hall. Her head was propped up on her elbow, and her wavy
hair spilled onto the desktop. I waited at the window until she
looked up and saw me.

four JOEY

I thought about my father a lot after Mike and I broke up. I still wasn't taking Dad's calls, which came less and less often. I hated how I was supposed to accept his alcoholism, like a stutter or a lazy eye. I hated that he expected me to be nice to him—to make room for him in my life—just because he was my father. It was easy for Mom to be nice to him. She had William.

I thought about Dad's love for the Beatles, F. Scott Fitzgerald, and the Three Stooges. And the thing he loved most: scotches with just a touch of water. I thought about his deep, scratchy voice that had taken on a slight twang the last few years. The slow, deliberate way he had of speaking. His stooped posture and disheveled light brown hair that was just like mine. His watery blue eyes. I thought about his indecipherable handwriting inside my birthday cards. He sent me childish cards, oversized and pink, illustrated with puppies and balloons.

In college Dad had been a psychology major and a biology minor. Now he worked at the airport. He loved planes, he said once, as if that explained it. I knew he couldn't be making much more than minimum wage. He drove a white 1969 hardtop Mustang he'd inherited from his father when he died. It constantly needed work, but Dad hung on to it like it was the only thing he cared about. When I was younger he'd drive up and we'd go for rides. I loved the white leather seats, the chrome detailing on the glove compartment and the gearshift. There wasn't a stray mark anywhere on the car, inside or out.

Now that Mike and I were over, I didn't have anyone to talk to about Dad. We were supposedly still friends, but we avoided each other as much as we could. We sat at opposite ends of the lunch table, and I didn't go over to Lyle's for band practice anymore. We broke up in February, and I didn't stop moping until April, when I met Joey.

I was at a Dag Nasty show, and he was staring at me from behind the T-shirt table. His whole face was thin—narrow, crooked nose, small mouth with nonexistent lips, little eyes close together, eyebrows so dark they called attention away from his puffy, crayon-red hair. He was cute, in a clownish kind of way. I was in the bathroom line, and at first I hadn't been sure he was looking at me. But as the line moved his gaze followed me. I smiled and looked down at the floor. I wasn't used to being looked at.

Dag Nasty's set started as I was coming out of the bathroom. I hurried toward the front of the stage, snaking my way through the pit. Even though the T-shirt guy couldn't see me from where he was sitting, I still had the distinct sensation of being watched.

Theresa came up beside me during "Thin Line."

"That T-shirt guy likes you!" she shouted.

I rolled my eyes and turned my attention back to the stage. A skinhead was standing in front of the singer, preparing to dive. The crowd rolled back into us, and we put our arms up and pressed back. I could feel the sweat under the shirt of the boy I braced myself against, could see his shoulder blades moving up and down before he disappeared back into the pit and someone else replaced him.

"That guy selling T-shirts told me he likes you," Theresa said after the last song was over. Her voice had the far-away, muffled tone that engulfed everything after a show. I lifted my sweaty hair off my neck and looked back over at the T-shirt table. He wasn't sitting there anymore.

The crowd had bottlenecked at the exit, and we waited to get outside, inhaling the scent of perspiration and cigarettes. I could see Carrie, Lyle, and Adam waiting just outside the door. My legs were tired; I wanted to sit down. As the throng in front of us began to move again the T-shirt guy appeared before me. Theresa widened her eyes and surged forward with the crowd.

I waited for him to say something, but he stood rooted where he was, staring into my face. His hair was an even brighter red up close. He was taller than I would have thought, and so skinny he looked fragile. I felt myself flush, and let the crowd carry me past him. When I was almost by he tugged my sleeve and handed me a folded-up piece of paper. I took it without looking at him and pushed myself the rest of the way outside. I jogged across the parking lot to catch up with the others. Halfway to the car I checked over my shoulder to see if he'd followed me outside. He hadn't.

"What happened?" Theresa asked when I got to the car. Carrie already had the engine running.

I unfolded the paper, which was part of a flyer for an upcoming Verbal Assault show. In a boyish scrawl he had written, "I think your beautiful."

"Oh, God," I said. "How embarrassing."

I put the note in Carrie's outstretched hand while Theresa told everyone in the car how he had stopped her and asked about me. I pretended not to be interested.

"He wanted to know if you had a boyfriend," Theresa said.

"What did you tell him?" I asked.

"Duh, I told him you didn't."

"I've seen that guy around," Adam said. "He hits on everybody."

"Even the boys?" Theresa said.

"He spelled *you're* wrong," said Carrie.

"Can you try to look at the road while you're driving?" Lyle said.

"He could have talked to me," I said. "He didn't have to write me a note."

I kept the note in my backpack. When my classes got boring I studied it. His handwriting was small and overly slanted; I thought he might be left-handed. He'd written only one measly sentence. I could forgive the spelling error, but why hadn't he signed his name? Maybe the whole thing was some sort of a joke. I wasn't a girl that strange boys approached. My mother was the sort of woman you'd call beautiful, but not me. I was skinny and gangly. I had bad posture. I was flat-chested. My face was too long. I had dry, limp hair, and most of the time I had dark roots showing under the bleached parts. Still, I couldn't help hoping that his note was sincere.

I thought I might get teased about the note at the lunch table, but even Adam neglected to ridicule me. Instead he ridiculed the band that opened for Dag Nasty. Mike sat in his regular seat next to Adam, nodding at everything Adam said.

"You weren't even there, Mike," I said, after he agreed that it was lame for the opening band to play an encore.

Mike didn't answer me. He had buttoned the top button of his flannel shirt, which gave him a boyish look that I found adorable.

The Saturday of the Verbal Assault show, I deep conditioned my hair and took my time shaving my legs. I wore my coolest outfit—blue-and-green-plaid miniskirt, black tights, combat boots, and my black hooded sweatshirt. Carrie came over early so she could trim my bangs and help me put eye makeup on. She was an expert, thanks to her strict parents. She could apply eyeliner while she was driving.

Verbal Assault was playing at an old church in southeast D.C., in a black neighborhood we hadn't been to before. I saw him as soon as we got inside. He was behind a folding table, handing a shirt to a skater kid who looked about twelve but for the hairy legs sticking out of his baggy shorts. Sick with fear, I followed Carrie and Lyle and Theresa in the opposite direction. I was glad Adam and Mike weren't with us.

We settled near the front of the stage. Beside us three heavily made-up skinhead chicks stood in a knot, casting dirty looks this way and that as people filled in the spaces around them. I hoped they weren't in the mood to fight, or at least not in the mood to fight us. The skinhead guys were violent, but the skinhead chicks were worse. The skinhead chicks beat up people and took their leather jackets and Doc Martens. They reminded me of the grits at school, single-minded and predatory, waiting for the opportunity to punch someone. Only the grits at Herndon didn't hit girls.

"Was that him selling shirts?" Carrie asked. She craned her neck to get a better look.

I glanced over. Now he was talking to a girl with long, blue-black hair. He bobbed his head from side to side and waved his hands in front of him. Maybe he hadn't seen me yet.

The first band wasn't any good, so we went back to Carrie's car to drink the six-pack of Michelob that Theresa had stolen from home. I was careful not to look over at the T-shirt table as we filed out.

"You're gonna regret it if you don't talk to him," Theresa said once we had settled back into the car. She handed me a beer.

"Maybe I should wait for him to come up to me," I said.

"Polly, please," Carrie said. "Just get it over with."

A police cruiser swung into the parking lot. "Five-Oh," Lyle said. We scrambled to hide our beers at our feet. After a cursory circuit of the lot, the cop car pulled back out onto the street and we picked our beers up again.

"I can't just go up to him," I said.

"If you drink enough you'll be able to do it," Lyle said. "That's what I did with Carrie."

"That's sweet. I didn't know you did that," Carrie said.

Once we were back inside I just did it. Before I could talk myself out of it, I let the others get ahead of me and then turned around fast and rushed over to the T-shirt table.

"Hi," I said, clutching the edge of the table. I was out of breath.

He beamed and stood up while I panted in front of him. "I thought I might see you here," he said. His voice was different than I expected. Nasal and high-pitched.

"I was just wondering if you had any Verbal Assault shirts," I said.

Behind us Government Issue started to play, and he gestured for me to lean toward him.

"Verbal Assault sells their own shit," he shouted into my ear. "I just got Government Issue shirts tonight."

"Oh!"

He straightened up and pointed at an empty folding chair beside his. I shrugged and walked around to his side of the table,

my heart threatening to burst out of my chest. I sat down and
smoothed my skirt out on the chair.

"I don't believe we've been formally introduced." He held
out his hand. "I'm Joey."

I could barely make out what he was saying over the music.
"I'm Polly," I said. His hand felt warm but not sweaty. Some
people came up to the table and Joey got up to help them. I
fished around in my sweatshirt pocket for my cigarettes and lit
one. Joey's black, shapeless pants were cinched around his waist
with a silver-studded belt, and he had rolled up the cuffs so
that they rested at the top of his combat boots. He looked like
a punk-rock Ronald McDonald.

Joey sat down and put his hand on my knee in one smooth
motion, like we'd been going out forever. I yanked my leg
up and he took his hand away. Seething with embarrassment,
I watched a fat guy wearing one of Joey's Government Issue
shirts in yellow play air guitar by the bathroom. I wanted Joey
to put his hand back on my leg, now that I was expecting it.

I turned toward him and he shocked me again, this time
by kissing me lightly on the mouth. He kissed me without his
tongue, the way a friend of my mother's might greet me. Before I could respond more people arrived at the table, and Joey
stood up again. I wished Government Issue would hurry up and
finish so we could talk.

Just then Todd Wilson appeared before me, squinting and
sneering, and I felt my chest get tight. I hadn't seen him since
he'd humiliated me at Lyle's. Adam came up beside him, an
unlit cigarette hanging out of his mouth.

"What's up?" I yelled.

Adam looked over at Joey and rolled his eyes, and I screwed up
my face in what I hoped was a hostile expression. Todd grinned.
His lower front teeth were crooked, but in a good way.

Adam pointed at my lighter and I handed it over. Todd kept
right on smiling at me, like we were in on a joke together. I

supposed we did share an inside joke, in a way. The inside joke of Jason. Once Adam got his cigarette lit they wandered back into the crowd. I glanced over at Joey, but he was still waiting on customers.

When he sat back down I was ready. I leaned in close to his ear.

"So, how'd you get into the T-shirt business?"

"Just one of those things, I guess," he shouted.

I smiled and pulled my chair closer to his. I wanted him to see that I wasn't afraid of him.

"I guess you might say I turned being a punk-rock kid into a career," he continued. "One minute I was seventeen, seeing as many bands as I could, and the next thing I know I'm twenty-two, with an apartment full of T-shirts and equipment."

I opened my mouth to respond, but Government Issue had finished, and a crowd instantly assembled at the table. Joey was up on his feet again, running this way and that, taking money and handing out shirts. I had to move my chair out of the way twice to let him get to a box of shirts at my feet.

"Thanks, sweetie," he said the second time I had to move. He gave me a wink. He was officially the most forward boy I had ever met.

I stood up. Joey was negotiating over a stack of shirts with a guy with a tangled mohawk, so I slunk away without saying good-bye.

I found Carrie and Lyle and Theresa in front of the stage. Carrie had Lyle's leather jacket balled up under her arm, and all three of them were sweating.

"So, what happened?" Theresa said.

"He kissed me, and he's twenty-two!" I said. Theresa's mouth went round.

Verbal Assault ran out onstage and started up. Everybody began knocking into one another. The four of us were pressed into the stage. The singer also played bass, and was alternating between jumping up and down in front of the microphone and leaning out over the crowd. I got that feeling I loved, of being anonymous but part of something at the same time. My body felt loose and fluid. I didn't think about Mike or Joey or Todd or my parents or anything else. Just the wham of the music going through me.

I made it through four songs before my adrenaline ran out. Carrie and Lyle had left the pit a song before me and Theresa wanted to stay up front, so by myself I worked my way through knot after knot of sweaty guys. I tried to ignore the feel of their slimy skin against mine as I squeezed past them.

The crowd thinned, and I squatted down in a relatively empty space at the back of the church. I tried to imagine what the room would look like with pews and a pulpit where the stage was. It was hard to picture. I unwrapped my sweatshirt from around my waist and felt in the pocket for my cigarettes and lighter.

Just as I realized that Adam still had my lighter, I felt a tap on my head. Joey was standing beside me. I stood up. I had forgotten how tall he was. He cleared my five-seven by almost a foot.

"I got somebody watching the table," he shouted into my ear. "Let's go check out the band from the balcony."

He took my hand and led me over to a wide, curving staircase that I hadn't noticed. Near the top of the stairs we dropped hands and stepped around a girl with multiple ear piercings on both sides. She was studiously rolling a joint in her lap.

"I hope she doesn't get caught with that," I said.

"Nah, the bouncers don't come up here that much," Joey said. "There's too much shit going on downstairs."

It wasn't nearly as crowded in the balcony. I leaned over the railing and watched the sea of bodies in front of the stage. The guitarist had stopped playing for this part of the song, and he was jabbing his fist out over the crowd. A hundred fists jabbed back at him. Out of the corner of my eye I could see Joey's narrow wrists on the railing next to mine. I wondered if he was ever teased like I was for being too thin, or if that didn't happen at his age.

When the song ended I turned away from the railing to ask Joey if this was his first time seeing Verbal Assault, but before I could speak he bent down and kissed me. For real this time. I raised my hand to the back of his head. His hair felt like cotton between my fingers and he had a smell of sweat and leather mixed with something faintly chemical.

When we stopped kissing Joey placed his hands on either side of my face and smoothed my hair back. His expression was serious, almost quizzical. I couldn't help smiling.

"What?" I said.

"I know I'm too old for you but I can't help it."

I started to scoff but then stopped myself, realizing how girlish it would look.

"You're not too old," I said. I didn't want to tell him how old I was. Not yet.

Joey took his hands away from my face and led me down the length of the balcony to a corner where there was a different, shorter set of stairs. They led down to a room that was too dark to see into. There was a chain across the head of the stairs with a DO NOT ENTER sign hanging from it. Joey stepped over the chain. Then he reached back and lifted me over. The ease with which he lifted me sent a dull thrill through my body. He was stronger than he looked.

"I didn't know these stairs were here" was all I could think to say.

He led me down a few steps, until we were in relative privacy, and then he carefully leaned me against the wall, like I was an expensive painting he had just brought home. We kissed some more. The roar of the band below pounded around us. I put my arms around Joey's waist and moved them up until my hands were between his shirt and the inside of his leather jacket.

I liked the smoothness of the jacket's lining against my skin, and the way he felt pressing against me. I was vaguely aware that downstairs a song had ended and another had begun. Still kissing, we lowered ourselves down until I was sitting on the stairs and he was kneeling in front of me.

"Wait a minute," he said.

Joey slid his leather jacket off and wadded it up in his hands. He tucked it between my back and the stair behind me before leaning into me again. It was too dark to see him clearly; he was just a figure flashing before me. His hands seemed not to touch me exactly but to flutter around me, inside my shirt and on my legs and up my skirt. It was exciting, being hidden away on these stairs with him. He was a stranger, older than me, capable of any number of thoughts and urges that were beyond my grasp.

He helped me undo his pants and pulled them down partway. He wasn't wearing any underwear, which gave me a queasy sensation that I managed to put aside. I didn't want to think too much about what I was doing.

Joey kissed me, and then he guided my hand to his penis. I shut my eyes and pressed my face into his shoulder while I moved my hand up and down. I was grateful that he didn't try to take my skirt off, didn't try to have sex with me, even though I knew that if I were older he probably would have. After he came Joey kissed me again, and I wiped my hand off on the inside of my skirt. I had that feeling I got when a boy came because of me. Kind of like triumph but not exactly.

Joey pulled his pants up. "Do you have a boyfriend?" he said.

I laughed. "Isn't it a little late for that question?"

I started to stand up but Joey pulled me back down and kissed me again.

"Come over to my place," he said.

I lowered my head. "I can't. I have to go home," I said. The rest came out in a rush: "I'm in high school. I still live with my parents."

Even though he couldn't see me that well, I rolled my eyes, as if to tell him that I, too, thought my age was tiresome.

"I figured you were in high school," he said. He smirked. "How old are you exactly?"

"I'm seventeen, but I'm a senior," I said, as if that somehow made me older. "I'm graduating this year."

He nodded, kissed me again. "Are you sure you can't come home with me? Tell your parents you're at a friend's?"

I giggled. "Yes. I'm absolutely totally sure I can't come home with you."

We stepped back over the chain. Verbal Assault had finished, and more people were coming up to the balcony. Joey took my hand, and I felt the new scrutiny of having him beside me. I jutted my chin forward as I walked, a smile playing across my lips. I wanted Todd Wilson to see me now.

The black-haired girl I had seen Joey talking to earlier was sitting at the T-shirt table.

"Thanks a lot, Joey," she snapped as we walked up. "You said you'd just be a minute."

"This is Tiffany," Joey said, dropping my hand and grabbing a pen off the table.

"Hi," I said. Tiffany glared at me. Her nose was slightly hooked and she had small eyes, a combination that, along with her hair, gave her a witchy look. But a pretty witch, saved by a wide, full mouth.

"I better go find my friends," I said. I knew Theresa and Carrie would be looking for me by now, and I didn't want to make introductions.

"Hold on a minute." Joey tore off the edge of a flyer that was sitting on the table and looked up at me expectantly. "Tell me your number."

He wrote my number on one half of the flyer and then scribbled his on the other half.

"Will you come over to my place soon?" he asked.

"Maybe."

He called me Sunday night.

"Hi, Polly. Guess who," he said when I answered.

"Hi, Joey." There was no mistaking that high, nasal voice.

"I bet you weren't expecting me to call this soon."

"I don't know. I hadn't really thought about it." I settled myself on my bed, propping a pillow at my lower back like Joey had done on the stairs with his jacket.

"Are you in your bedroom?" he asked.

"Yes."

"On your bed?"

"That's right," I said. "And are you at your apartment?"

"Uh-hunh. What are you wearing?"

"You sound like an obscene phone caller."

"I am an obscene phone caller. When are you coming over to visit me?"

A wave of panic passed over me. "I don't know. Maybe after school one day."

"It's cute that you're still in high school," he said.

"I'm glad you think so. I find it demoralizing."

"And are you going to college soon?" He said this like college was something amusing a toddler might do.

"Yes. I don't know where yet, though. I'm still waiting to hear."

"So you're a good student. That's cool."

"Pretty good."

"So when can you come over? I'm dying to see you."

• • •

Joey called every night that week. At school I felt newly confident. I breezed by the cheerleaders and the jocks without looking at their jeering, snotty faces. I didn't care about them. Joey was part of my life now. Joey who was dying to see me, Joey who thought I was beautiful, Joey who had nothing to do with high school, nothing to do with Reston. I thought of Joey making T-shirts in his apartment—which I pictured as Lyle's basement minus the band equipment—waiting for me to get home from school so he could call me.

"I hope he's not some sort of weird stalker guy who's going to end up killing you or something," Theresa said at the lunch table.

"He's not," I said, immediately worrying that he was.

Mike looked over at me like he'd just now remembered I existed, and then he went back to his tuna sandwich. It was all I could do not to stand up and cheer.

Saturday morning I told Mom I was going to the mall with Theresa. I had to take a bus and a subway to get to his apartment. It was my first time going into the city by myself, and I was excited. Joey had given me careful directions, so I didn't have any trouble finding his place, but it still took me twice as long as driving. His apartment was in the basement of a modest brick town house, in a better part of town than I expected. He had his own entrance around back. I checked the address in front and walked back down the driveway, my footsteps louder than I wanted them to be on the loose gravel.

There were two cars parked in back. One was a green sedan, and the other was a beat-up brown station wagon that looked like it hadn't been started in years. I wondered if one of these cars was Joey's and, if so, why he hadn't offered to drive out and pick me up. Not that I was anxious to introduce a twenty-two-year-old man with dyed red hair and a studded leather jacket to Mom and William.

I tapped on the door, and a moment later Joey stuck his neon head out.

"You're late," he said. He was all eyebrows and sharp limbs and clown hair, and I suddenly felt shy.

"Public transportation is hard to predict," I said.

"That's all right, darlin'," he said, putting on a country accent. "Come on in and put your dawgs up. I'm awful glad to see you."

"Thanks," I said. I stepped past him into the apartment.

It was bright outside, so it took a few seconds for my eyes to adjust to the dimness. Joey guided me past a couple of large, heavy-looking machines to the far corner of his apartment, which was really just a big, L-shaped room. Against the wall that made up the shorter part of the L there was a metal desk. Next to that was a TV, VCR, and stereo stacked on a shelving system made out of boards and cinder blocks. It looked like it was about to fall down.

Once my eyes fully adjusted I took in the most interesting aspect of Joey's apartment. Nearly every inch of wall space was covered with horror movie posters. There was a black-and-white still from a movie called *The Hills Have Eyes,* which showed a grimacing bald man in profile, brandishing a small knife. The bald man was wearing a fur vest and a dog collar. On another poster, for a movie called *Deadly Blessing,* a woman was stretched out on her stomach with her eyes closed and her mouth open. A menacing pair of hands encircled the woman's head. Next to these were posters for *Chamber of Horrors* and *Dr. Terror's House of Horrors,* among others. I hadn't heard of any of them.

I pointed at a poster for a movie called *Horror High,* which featured a skeleton cheerleader in a blond wig and the words

KILLER TO THE LEFT. KILLER TO THE RIGHT. STAND UP. SIT DOWN.
FRIGHT! FRIGHT! FRIGHT!

"That one's my favorite," I said.

"You've seen it?"

"No. I mean the poster."

"Yeah, I like movies about freaks," he said. "'Cause I can relate."

He let out a high-pitched laugh, and I gave him a polite smile. My eyes had come to rest on the oversized mattress that took up most of the floor space. His bedding was strewn around, exposing the bare, yellowish exterior of the mattress here and there. I lowered myself into the only other place to sit, a faded gray chair that looked like it might once have been blue.

Instead of stabbing me or wrapping his hands tight around my neck, Joey produced a Milwaukee's Best from a small refrigerator that doubled as a nightstand—there was no kitchen that I could see—and I accepted it with relief. He knelt down on the floor in front of me and tugged on one of my bootlaces as I opened my beer.

"Are you nervous to be here?"

"No," I said. I glanced over at the mattress. "I mean, should I be?"

"Of course not. I just want you to be comfortable is all."

"Your hair seems brighter today," I said.

He shrugged. "I did it last night. I touch it up every month or so."

Raising my beer to my mouth, I tried to picture him bent over a bathroom sink, dabbing at his roots. When I took the can away from my face Joey kissed me, softly, like he had the first time at the T-shirt table. I inhaled his salty, leathery smell. He helped me out of the chair and onto the mattress. A few minutes later I was down to my skirt and bra.

"There's one thing you have to know," I said, moving his hand off my skirt. "I can't sleep with you. You know, not yet."

He kissed my chin. "I know, honey, I'm not expecting that. There are other things we can do."

"Like what?" I asked. My mother called me honey.

"You know what."

After Joey came I asked him if it was okay for me to smoke. He got an empty beer can out of the trash and put it on the floor next to the mattress. I was on my stomach, like the woman in the *Deadly Blessing* poster.

"I can't believe you don't have a boyfriend," he said.

I thought about Mike. The thing I missed the most was the way he used to look at me when I said something funny. Like there was no one he liked better than me. And how he laughed at my jokes even when no one else did. Mom said that having the same sense of humor was one of the most important things in a relationship.

"I can't believe you don't have a girlfriend," I said.

"And here we are," Joey said.

"Yes. Here we are."

On the way home I thought about Frank, one of Mom's old boyfriends. Frank had a beefy upper body with comparatively skinny legs. He was a fireman, and he liked to make jokes about his name and my mother's: "It's Frank and Fran!" he'd shout when they came home from a date to find me and the babysitter waiting for them. On the phone he'd say, "It's Mr. Frank, calling for Miss Fran." At the time I thought he was funny. Frank brought me a fireman's hat and promised to take me to the station so I could slide down the pole, but before we had a chance to go my mother broke up with him.

Mom didn't have very many boyfriends that I remembered, just Frank and the guy I heard in the hallway and William. There might have been more. I wondered now what made Mom break up with Frank. What made Frank not even worth dating, but William worth marrying? Was it his sense of humor or something else? Mom and I didn't talk about those kinds of things much, but I thought maybe I'd ask her.

I knew that when you were older you had to think about more things when you were dating someone, like whether they liked your kids or had a good job. Maybe in the end love wasn't even a factor when you were choosing someone to marry, although Mom and William still held hands in public and kissed when they got home from work. I knew they loved each other, but as far as I knew, Mom might have loved Frank, too. She had seemed happy enough to see him when he came to the door.

I still wasn't sure if I had ever been in love. I had thought that Jason was my first love, but now I preferred to think of it as infatuation since I didn't feel like I loved him anymore. I was hanging on to the idea that real love lasted forever. With Mike it seemed like we were in love—or at least that we were about to be in love, but then he broke up with me. Maybe there was just something wrong with me. Maybe I would never find what I wanted.

Monday after third period I slipped outside to call Joey from the pay phone in front of the school. After four rings he answered, his voice scratchy from sleep.

"I didn't mean to wake you," I said. Through the doors of the school I could see people opening and shutting their lockers, navigating their way around one another.

"That's all right, honey," he said. "I'm glad to hear your voice. What time is it, anyway?"

"Ten-thirty. I thought you'd be up. I'm sorry."

"Don't worry about it, sweetie. I'm your boyfriend, after all. Just try not to call me before noon, okay? I always get up late."

"Okay."

I hung up. Joey had used the word *boyfriend*. Joey was my boyfriend. I was late for government class, but I took my time in the hallway and swaggered to my seat a full twenty seconds after the bell rang. I imagined Joey walking me down the hall in front of the bops and surf punks and grits and bamas. People would talk about the weird older guy and the girl they'd never noticed before for days.

It turned out Joey wasn't kidding about being my boyfriend. We saw each other as much as we could. He taught me how to make T-shirts on his machines, which smelled like burning rubber when they were turned on and issued a low, rumbling hum not unlike my family's dishwasher. He bought me a studded belt with a small black heart on the buckle. He gave me a lot of T-shirts, too, but the belt was special. I wore it every day.

I found out that neither of the cars parked out back belonged to Joey. He didn't drive.

"One of the reasons I live in the city is because I hate cars," Joey told me. It hadn't occurred to me that a person could hate cars. I liked that about him. Maybe I hated cars.

I spent less and less time at home. William nagged Mom and Mom nagged me. I told her as little as I could get away with.

Once in a while Theresa and Carrie and Lyle and I would cut last period and drive over to Joey's. We'd listen to music and drink beer, and then Theresa and Carrie and Lyle would walk down to the record store while Joey and I rolled around on his mattress. We always stopped short of intercourse.

"I'll wait until you're ready," Joey said. "You just tell me when it's time."

I thought I'd wait for a sign. If I got an A in my tough-stuff physics class, I'd have sex. If I got into every school I applied to, I'd have sex. If Mike Franklin found a new girlfriend, I'd have sex. Maybe then.

The majority of our relationship was conducted inside Joey's apartment, but we ventured out once in a while. We went for walks in his neighborhood, drinking beer out of Burger King cups and making out in public. When we went to see bands I sat behind the T-shirt table, helping Joey fold shirts and make change. I waited on people with the studied aloofness of a record store employee. And I handled the money even better than Joey.

"You sure can subtract fast," he told me, kissing the top of my head.

"You should see me add," I said. "And fractions, look out."

"You're the smartest person I know," Joey said, and I believed him.

Carrie and I were sneaking a cigarette in the back parking lot near the tennis courts before lunch. The courts would be packed in fifteen minutes, but they were empty between classes.

"I feel like I haven't talked to you in, like, years," Carrie said.

"What do you mean?" I said. "I talk to you all the time."

"You know what I mean," Carrie said. "All you do is hang out with Joey."

"That's such bullshit," I said. I touched the heart on my belt buckle. "I'm lucky if I see him twice a week. You don't know what's it's like—you're always with Lyle."

"It just seems like you're not really into hanging out with us anymore," Carrie said. "I mean, it's just like you pick Joey first and us second. Like if Joey's busy, *then* you'll hang out with us."

"He's my boyfriend! You of all people should be able to understand that. I mean, look at you and Lyle."

Carrie scrunched up her face. "What about me and Lyle?" Her brown eyes widened and for a second I thought she might cry.

I took a drag off my cigarette. "What's going on with you?" I asked.

"Nothing! God! You're the one!"

I waited.

"I had an abortion two weeks ago," Carrie said.

She dropped her cigarette and walked toward the double doors, her long dark hair swishing behind her. I followed her, too shocked to say anything. All I could think about were Carrie's parents, with their rules against miniskirts and eyeliner and black clothing. Carrie was walking with her back straight and her shoulders back. I wanted to hug her, but something told me not to.

When she was almost at the doors I shouted, "Carrie, wait!"

She stopped. Turned around. Her large, silver-hoop earrings swayed. "You want to know why you didn't know? Because you're too busy with Joey!"

"I'm sorry," I said. And I was.

We turned around and walked back in the direction we had come from. Now that I had Carrie's attention I didn't know what to say. I thought of the other girls I knew who had gotten abortions. There was Jenny Randall who I knew from playing soccer, who had an abortion in the tenth grade. She told me about it in French II, mouthing the words I had an abortion like she was telling me important gossip about someone else. And there were rumors about other girls. I pictured the abortion clinic as being kind of like McDonald's, sitting like an island in the middle of a wide parking lot. I wanted to know how long it took and if it hurt. And before that, when she'd been pregnant—did she throw up and get cravings?

"Look, I know I should have told you," Carrie said finally. "I just want to forget the whole thing ever happened, you know?"

"Yeah, I can see that," I said. I wanted another cigarette. I waited for Carrie to say she wanted one. "So who else knows?"

"Lyle, duh. And Theresa went with me. I didn't want Lyle to go."

I felt a small stab of rejection. Theresa hadn't told me.

"How are you feeling now?" I said.

"I don't know. It's weird. Physically I feel fine, I mean I am fine, but everything's different now. I can't get over being pissed at Lyle. Even though I know it's not his fault really. I'm the one who fucked up my pills."

I made myself put a hand on Carrie's forearm. "It's not your fault," I said. Like I knew.

"Polly, it is my fault." Now Carrie really looked like she was going to cry. "I hope you're using birth control." Her high, girlish voice had become stern, like a teacher's. "I swear to God, I hope this at least makes you finally get on the pill. I hope Joey wears a condom, I hope he pulls out, and I hope you use spermicide. Apparently it's best to use more than one method."

"Is that what the doctor said?"

"Yes, as a matter of fact he did."

I touched the heart on my belt again. "How'd you get the money?"

"Lyle. He sold his P.A. Now he's using this shitty one that used to be his brother's."

If Carrie's parents found out about her abortion, they'd make her break up with Lyle, and that would just be the beginning. She'd probably have to transfer to a religious school. I felt sorry for Carrie. Theresa's parents would understand something like this, probably even make the appointment and go to the clinic with her. Mom would be mad if I got pregnant, but I knew she'd be there if I needed her help. Out of nowhere I suddenly missed Mom. I had the frantic, sad feeling I used to get when I was little, when she'd drop me off at day care in the mornings and I didn't want her to go.

I decided to tell Carrie a secret of my own. "I don't have sex with Joey," I said. She didn't answer, and I let the rest spill

out: "The thing is I'm basically a virgin, except for I sort of did
it with Jason but not really. I can't seem to bring myself to do
it. Sometimes I think I just never will have sex at all, ever."

I waited for her to get angry, to say something about how
I'd been lying all this time. But she just shrugged and said in a
flat voice, "Well I guess you don't have to worry about getting
pregnant then."

I hunched my shoulders, suddenly conscious of my skinny,
undeveloped body, my gross lack of curves. Carrie didn't have
big boobs, but they were bigger than mine. They existed. And
she had beautiful, wide hips. Hips I not only didn't have, but
probably never would. She was a year younger than I was, but
we both knew that in all the important ways she was older.

Saturday Carrie came over to dye our hair. We crowded into
the upstairs bathroom, the one I used.

"Wanna do something tonight?" I asked.

I was wearing the tight plastic gloves that came with the box
of dye, and was shaking powder into a bottle of solution while
Carrie slowly separated clumps of my hair and clipped them
away from one another.

"Lyle's brother is home," Carrie said. "He can get beer."

Mom showed up in the bathroom doorway. "What's this
about beer?"

"Oh, nothing," Carrie said in a singsong tone that she
wouldn't have used with her own parents.

I kept quiet, hoping Mom would get the message and leave
us alone. She stayed planted in the doorway, her hands on her
hips. I replaced the cap on the bottle of solution and shook
it vigorously, like the instructions dictated, ignoring Mom's
anxious surveillance of the bathroom. It was littered with dye

boxes, instructions, hair clips, a timer, and a few old towels, and we were just getting started.

"I better not see one stray mark in this bathroom when you two get finished," Mom said.

"Don't worry," I said. Carrie and I had never made a lasting mess before, and we did this every six weeks. I sat down on the toilet seat and Carrie began to slop bleach onto my scalp. The moment the bleach touched my head it started to burn.

"You're getting beer and meeting Joey, is that it?" Mom asked.

"Mom, please," I said. A light sweat began to form on the back of my neck. I couldn't remember if I'd told Carrie that Mom and William were under the impression that Joey was eighteen and went to another high school.

"I'll tell you what I'm tired of," Mom said, as if I had just asked. "I'm tired of you coming and going from this house like this is some kind of hotel we're running."

"I know this isn't a hotel you're running," I said.

Carrie had finished my head, and I changed places with her. She was trying something new, a semipermanent dye in blackberry. I squirted the dye onto Carrie's head and dragged the thick mixture through her hair with as much precision as I could muster.

"You better plan on making some changes around here, Polly," Mom said. "Because there *will* be consequences if you keep this business up."

She marched back down the hallway. I kicked the door shut and turned my attention back to Carrie, who had dye running down her neck.

"Sorry I said that about the beer," Carrie said. "I didn't see her."

I dabbed at her neck with a piece of toilet paper. "That's okay. Except I doubt I can go out tonight."

"Give it a little while. Tell her we're going to the movies."

"I'll have to do better than that. She's not an idiot."

We set the timer and carried it down the hall to my bedroom. Carrie stretched out on my bed with my *Cosmopolitan*. I called Joey.

"I just found out I have to go to Baltimore tonight to sell T-shirts for Dag Nasty," Joey said. "They just called me. I'll be gone for two days."

"Oh, well," I said. I had thought maybe we could drive down to Joey's and surprise him with our own beer for once.

"You should come with me," Joey said. "There's room in the van."

I thought about the conversation I'd just had with my mother. "I'll come over the second you get back," I said.

"I'll be so lonely without my honey," Joey said.

I blushed. "Me, too," I said.

As soon as I hung up, the phone rang. It was Theresa. In a high, strange voice she repeated what she'd just heard from Adam: Mike Franklin's father had been killed the night before in a car accident. He was on his way home from a bar, and he swerved to miss what police assumed was a squirrel. He veered off the road into a tree and died instantly. No one else was in the car.

I handed the phone to Carrie and burst into tears. I felt like someone had just dropped a giant sandbag on top of me. I didn't know anyone who had ever had a parent die, except for my parents, and that was different. Mike was young.

Carrie and I rinsed out our hair in silence. As soon as we'd cleaned up the bathroom Carrie left for Lyle's. With my hair still wet I slunk downstairs to dinner. It felt like my fight with Mom had happened months ago.

As soon as I saw Mom and William at the table my throat got tight. Someday they were going to die. Maybe soon.

"What's the matter?" Mom said.

"Mike's father died."

I put my hands up to my face and sobbed. I heard the squeak of Mom's chair being pushed back and then I felt her arms around me. I was crying harder than I'd expected. After a minute William got up and stood beside me. He placed an awkward hand on the back of my head, which made me cry even harder. I wanted to tell them that I loved them. I wanted to promise that I wouldn't upset them ever again, even if that meant never going out again for the rest of my life.

"I don't know why I feel so bad," I said instead. "I never even met him."

Mom and William sat back down at the table. I told them how it happened. William got up and looked through the paper for an article, but there wasn't anything yet.

"It'll probably be in there tomorrow," he said.

We were having one of William's favorite meals: fried chicken with mashed potatoes and peas. It was one of my favorites too, but tonight I could barely eat. My throat was sore and my muscles were worn out from crying. Finally I gave up on dinner all together, but I stayed at the table while Mom and William ate. I didn't know anyone who had died. Three of my four grandparents were dead before I was born, all from various forms of cancer. My grandmother on my mother's side was alive when I was born, but she died of a heart attack when I was two. My mother must have grieved, but I didn't remember it. It was strange to think of Mom losing her mother. It was the worst thing I could imagine happening to me but here she was, pushing peas onto her fork, a functioning person. Since both my parents were only children I didn't have much family, and I'd never been to a funeral. I felt a fresh set of tears coming on when I thought about Mike and his sister going to their father's funeral. As far as I knew Mike didn't even own a suit.

• • •

Mom didn't try to stop me from going out. I went with Carrie and Lyle and Theresa to the seventh hole of the Reston Golf Club. The seventh green of the course was positioned far enough away from surrounding neighborhoods that you could make a fair amount of noise without the police getting called. It was dark when we got there, and I had to concentrate to make out everyone's faces.

I hadn't counted on seeing Mike but there he was, his feet nestled in a sand trap and the rest of him spread out on the green. There were several empty beer cans beside him. I panicked. What if I said the wrong thing and made him cry? What if I cried and made him uncomfortable? Did he want to talk about it or pretend like nothing happened? I wanted him to tell me.

"That's right, it's your estranged ex," he said as I peered into his face.

"I'm sorry about your dad," I said. Mike looked away from me and everyone went quiet. I wished I'd said something else.

"Yeah, thanks," Mike said.

"Yeah, all of us are sorry, " Theresa said. "We all feel terrible."

Mike took a long drink from his beer while I stood and watched him. People began to murmur again. "It hasn't really hit me yet," he said. He tossed his beer behind him and looked around for another one. I wanted to ask when the funeral was but was afraid to.

We sat down and opened our beers. I wondered when Mike had last seen his father. From what he told me when we were going out, I was willing to bet it had been almost a year.

It had been about a year since I'd seen my own dad. Before I stopped talking to him he came up once or twice a year for brief visits consisting of a few meals spread out over a couple of days. It wasn't bad. Just awkward, mostly. He stayed at a motel, and although I would visit him in his room I didn't stay over with him. He invited me to visit him in North Carolina sometimes, but I didn't want to go and Mom didn't make me. I couldn't imagine what we would talk about if we spent a whole weekend alone together.

But Mike's dad hadn't lived a state away, he'd lived less than twenty minutes away. I thought about the story Mike told me about his dad punching him. I looked over at him. He was sipping his beer and staring glassily into the distance. Maybe he was thinking about the time his dad punched, him too.

I hadn't even finished my second beer when I had to pee. Neither Carrie nor Theresa had to go yet and I couldn't wait, so I went by myself behind a clump of trees at the edge of the golf course. I was sorry I had worn jeans instead of a skirt.

I had just finished buckling my heart belt when Mike loomed up before me.

"Please tell me you didn't see me peeing," I said.

He put an unsteady hand against the nearest tree. "Do you still go out with that guy?"

"Yeah." I wanted to say something real, something that would let Mike know how horrible I felt, how much I wished this hadn't happened to him.

"Let me ask you something," he said.

"What?"

He slumped forward, and I put my arms around him. He kept his arms limp at his sides. I shut my eyes and leaned into him.

"Mike, I'm so sorry about your dad," I said. "I don't know what else to say except I'm sorry. I feel awful. And your sister and God, your mom—"

He pulled me to the ground. We stayed hooked together for a long time, not talking. I waited for Mike to say something about his father. After a while, we stood up and brushed at our grass stains. Then Mike leaned over and kissed me, and I felt the familiar craving I used to feel when he was my boyfriend. I braced a hand against his chest, and we separated.

We jogged back to the green, and Mike pulled out ahead of me. I watched his long legs widen further and further apart until he was sprinting.

"Cop?" Carrie said when I reached her.

"No," I said. "Just getting some exercise." I plopped down on the turf next to Theresa and looked around for my beer. My lungs hurt from running, and I didn't feel like drinking anymore. After he'd finished his beer Mike curled up in the sand trap and passed out. I thought of Joey selling shirts in some club in Baltimore right this minute, his puffy red hair bobbing up and down as he moved back and forth behind the table.

Mike was out of school for a week. When he came back he acted like nothing had happened. Nobody brought up his dad, but we didn't go back to treating him the way we did before, either. For one thing, we didn't make fun of him like we used to. We were nicer to one another when Mike was around, too. Even Adam calmed down. Mike didn't say anything, but I don't think he liked it.

At night before I went to sleep I would inevitably think about Mike's dad. I'd wonder what it was like for him in those seconds before his car went into the tree. Whether he knew what was happening or if it was like a switch being turned off. Sometimes in the middle of class or riding around in Carrie's car it would just hit me, like ice water running over my skin: *Mike's dad is dead*. I waited for the shock of it to wear off for good.

I thought Joey might say something gory or insensitive when I called and told him about Mike's dad, but he didn't. He said he couldn't imagine what he would do if something happened to his dad, even though his dad was a bigoted asshole that he hadn't spoken to in two years. He told me about his cousin, who died in a car accident in California. Joey was in junior high when it happened, and even though he wasn't close to his cousin he went around feeling depressed for months.

It felt good talking to Joey on the phone. But when I went over to his apartment I felt skittish and distracted. I felt my insides caving in under the pressure of his kisses, and I was irritated by the happy way he kept one arm slung over my shoulder. And then there was the inevitability of his mattress.

"Let's sit outside for a bit," I suggested after we'd opened beers.

Joey placidly followed me outside. I felt better as soon as I stepped out of the musty, dark apartment into the warm, light afternoon. We sat with our backs against the house and our feet in the gravel driveway. I snuffed match after match as I tried to light my cigarette.

"Is something wrong, honey?" Joey asked.

"I have a name," I said.

"I know. Holly, right?"

"Very funny." I got my cigarette lit. Joey took my free hand in his and stroked my palm. It tickled, and I drew my hand away.

I had planned on keeping it a secret, but there was something about Joey's desperate, cloying attention that made me want to tell him.

"I kissed Mike Franklin when you were in Baltimore. After I found out his dad died."

I watched Joey's expression go from disbelief to disgust and back again. He set his beer down and pressed both palms against his forehead. "I take it you did this out of some sort of misguided pity," he said.

"It was just a kiss," I said.

Joey kept his head in his hands. His bony arms stuck out of the baggy sleeves of his Ramones T-shirt, his pointy elbows rested on his knees. I was starting to feel bad.

"I don't want us to have secrets," I said.

He kept silent. Then he brought his hands to my waist and unclasped the heart belt. I stared down at the flat, gray gravel of the parking lot as he slid the belt through the loops of my jeans. I didn't know what I had expected would happen when I told him, but this wasn't it.

Joey stood up, and then I heard the door to his apartment click shut. I didn't hear the lock, which I took as a good sign. I sipped my beer, wondering what to do next. I ran my boot across the gravel, and silvery dirt flew up. Neither car was in the parking lot today. I hadn't met or even seen the other people who lived in the house, though I had gotten used to their footsteps upstairs.

I got up and went inside. Joey was sitting at his big metal desk. He was bent over paperwork of some kind, ignoring me. My belt was coiled up beside him. I sat in the gray chair and watched him, but he still refused to look up from his work. This was the first time I had ever seen him at his desk. There was an old, heavy-looking black phone sitting on top of a stack of papers. I realized I had never heard it ring. When my beer was gone I found my backpack and stood by the door.

"Well, I'm going now," I said, my voice stiff.

"I'll walk you out," Joey said without looking up.

As soon as he had shut the door behind us Joey put both hands on my shoulders and turned me around to face him. He looked at me in his now familiar, searching way. I dropped my eyes from his and came to focus on his Adam's apple.

"Just tell me something," he said. "Do you still like him? Is that what this is about?"

"No! God! Is that what you think?"

"And are you sure you still want to be my girlfriend? 'Cause I don't really get why you told me about this."

I threw my arms around his waist and kissed his Adam's apple. "I'm sorry," I said. "I still want to be your girlfriend."

I could tell Mom and William had been fighting when I came in, because they were standing quietly in the kitchen. I rushed upstairs and arranged myself on my bed with a couple of my school notebooks, hoping Mom and William were absorbed with whatever they were arguing about.

There was a quick rap at my door. Before I could answer Mom was standing before me, holding a glass of white wine. She was wearing a light blue floor-length cotton nightgown, and her wavy black hair was loose around her shoulders. Her face was scrubbed clean of makeup and her cheeks were flushed. She looked pretty.

"You're late," she said.

I sat up and looked at the clock radio on my nightstand. It was nine thirty, an hour and a half past when I had said I would be home.

"It's only nine thirty," I said. "It's not like it's the middle of the night or anything."

Mom set her wineglass on top of my turntable and straightened herself back up again.

"I'll tell you something, young lady, you're really pushing it," she said.

"I'm sorry," I said. "It wasn't my fault. Carrie and I got stuck in traffic on the way home from the mall."

"Carrie called here twenty minutes ago."

"She had to stop at Lyle's, so I walked home from there. She probably just forgot to ask me something."

Mom snorted. "The school called me at work today."

I scooted toward the edge of my bed. One of my notebooks spilled to the floor, but neither of us moved to pick it up. I knew what was coming.

"You've been absent from sixth period eight times the last three weeks." Her smooth, easy voice had deepened, like it did when she was really angry. "You want to tell me what's so important you have to leave school early?"

I looked down at the floor. "I'm sorry," I said. "It's just what seniors do at the end of the year. I won't do it again, I promise."

I got up off the bed and gathered up the clothes that were strewn around the room. Mom watched.

"Don't think I don't know what you're doing. Do you think Joey is worth not getting into college for? Do you want to get rejected from college? Is that it?"

I stuffed the clothes in my laundry basket. I could feel my body starting to wilt under her stare. "I already applied," I said. "My transcripts have already been sent. They don't check these grades."

"Well, guess what? You're grounded. You're going to stay right here, in this house, until I say otherwise. You got that?"

The Bad Brains were playing Friday night. They hadn't played live in two years. I'd bought tickets weeks ago. Everybody I knew was going. Even Mike Franklin.

"If you let me go see the Bad Brains Friday I promise I won't go out for the rest of the year," I said.

"Absolutely not!"

Mom turned and went out into the hallway, slamming the door behind her. She stomped into her bedroom and slammed that door, too.

I went to see William. He was in the basement, watching an old episode of *Star Trek*. I settled down on the couch next to him and rested my Converse next to his Hush Puppies on the coffee table.

"I guess you know I'm grounded," I said when the TV went to a commercial.

William sniffed.

"There's this band playing Friday," I said. "Bad Brains. They're probably one of the most important bands I'll ever see. And they haven't played in years—this is probably my only chance to see them."

William didn't answer. On TV a blond woman held up a white T-shirt that was covered with spaghetti sauce. She plunged it into a glass box filled with clear blue liquid.

"Bad Brains are one of the best bands in D.C., if not the best," I continued. "Maybe even the best on the entire East Coast. This show is a really big deal."

William kept staring at the television. The woman on TV held up the same white T-shirt and beamed. The spaghetti stains had disappeared. "If it were up to me, I'd ground you for good," he said. "God only knows what illegal activities you and those hooligans you run around with are up to."

I got to my feet. "I'm trying to talk to you!" I shouted.

William looked at me over his glasses. "You're lucky your mother is in charge," he said. "If it were up to me you'd have been shipped off to boarding school a long time ago."

Mom was in bed, reading. Her door was open. I waited for her to look up.

"William doesn't love me."

"Well, maybe he doesn't," Mom said. "You think he's just supposed to, just like that? You think that's how it works?"

Back in my room I pulled my duffel bag down from the top of my closet. It was a navy blue duffel bag with a soccer ball patch on one side. I'd had it since elementary school. I grabbed a few pairs of underwear and a couple of T-shirts that Joey had given me and stuffed them in the bag. I pulled the green spiral notebook I used for an address book out of my desk and threw it on top of the T-shirts. I went down the hall to the bathroom and got my toothbrush, deodorant, and Noxema. I had $250 in babysitting money I'd been saving for college tucked in my sock drawer. I grabbed the money along with a couple of pairs of socks and shoved it all in the duffel bag. I picked up my backpack and the duffel bag and put on my army jacket. I ran downstairs and went out the front door.

I jogged to the elementary school a few blocks away and called Joey from a pay phone out front.

"I had a fight with my Mom and William," I said. "I'm on a pay phone."

"Oh, sweetie," he said.

"I hate my family," I said. "I can't wait until I'm out of that house for good."

"Where are you?"

"Hiding out in my neighborhood." I was standing near a bunch of parked school buses, away from the streetlight. I didn't think anyone could see me from the road.

"I wish I were there with you," Joey said.

"Actually, I was thinking I'd come over," I said. Tomorrow

was Wednesday. I'd skip school. We'd wake up and make coffee, maybe go out to breakfast at a diner.

Joey cleared his throat. "I don't think that's such a good idea."

"My stepfather doesn't want me living with them," I said.
Tears sprang to my eyes.

"Honey, you're not eighteen. Do you have any idea how
much trouble I could get into?"

I set my backpack on top of the duffel bag at my feet. "They
don't even know your last name. Plus they think you're in high
school."

"Have you called Theresa or Carrie? Why don't you go over
to one of their houses and call me from there?"

I banged the receiver down as hard as I could.

I walked one bus stop farther than my stop, in case Mom and
William were looking for me. I had to wait almost thirty minutes for the bus to show up. I took it to the main bus terminal in Fairfax, which was deserted and smelled like urine and
gasoline. There was a bus leaving for Charlotte at midnight. I
waited near the ticket window, where the clerk could see me.
A large clock over the vending machines buzzed, like the ones
at school. I half expected Mom or William to walk through the
door, but they didn't.

The bus was mostly empty. I could have had my own seat, but
instead I sat next to a heavy, middle-aged black woman. I felt
safer with her next to me, even though she slept the whole
way. I stared out the window at the black highway and marveled at how much trouble I was in. Mom and William had
probably called the police by now. I wasn't sure if I could be
arrested for running away.

The bus made so many stops we didn't get to Charlotte until eight thirty in the morning. It wasn't until we pulled into the terminal that I started to worry about my father. Mom would have told me if he'd moved, but there was a chance he was out of town. Or at work. I decided to call him from the bus station but changed my mind when I saw a cab pull up out front. I ran toward it, waving my free arm.

I had to ask the cab driver to wait while I dug in my duffel bag for my spiral.

"You comin' from a long ways away?" he asked. He was old and unshaven, and he looked like he'd been up at least as long as I had. A cigarette dangled from his mouth, and on a whim I bummed one from him. He gave me one of his Newports and lit a match with one hand. I read off my father's address and we pulled out onto the road. I tapped my cigarette on the ashtray that protruded from the cab's partition. This was my first ride in a taxi.

Dad didn't live very far from the bus station. I had pictured him living in a high-rise, but his apartment complex was made up of several low, redbrick buildings that formed a horseshoe around a drained pool. As we rounded the horseshoe I spotted his white Mustang at the far end of the parking lot, gleaming in the morning sun. I had the cabdriver let me out in front of it.

"You want me to wait until you're safe inside?" the driver asked after I'd paid him.

"No thanks," I said.

I watched the cab pull back out onto the road, and then I sat on the curb next to Dad's Mustang and rummaged in my backpack for my brush. The Newport had given me a head rush, and now I was nauseated.

I thought about the last time I'd seen Dad. He had come up the Christmas before last. We didn't spend the actual day together, but the weekend before it. We passed Saturday at the mall among the hordes of shoppers, looking for a present for me. I let Dad hold my hand while we walked, even though it embarrassed me. Finally I picked out a few albums at the record store and we went out into the cold, dull parking lot, both of us unable to figure out what to do next.

His doorbell was broken. There were wires poking out from the brick where the button had been. I knocked. A copy of *USA Today* leaned against the door and I bent down and picked it up.

Dad opened the door and stared at me. "I thought this'd be the last place you'd show up," he said. "Your mother is worried sick."

He was wearing navy blue work pants and a white undershirt. His feet were bare. I handed him the newspaper. He tossed it on the floor behind him and pulled me into a hug. His cheek scratched against my temple.

"I have to make a couple of phone calls," he said.

I stepped inside and he disappeared down a short hallway. His apartment smelled like cigarettes and coffee. I set my backpack and my duffel bag down next to a small table stacked with mail. I could hear his muffled voice from the next room. The rust-colored couch was strewn with newspapers. I moved them around until there was room for me to sit down. There were rabbit ears on top of the TV instead of a cable box. Next to the rabbit ears were an empty pack of cigarettes and a coffee mug that said KISS ME I'M IRISH. I wanted to open a window, air things out a little, but I stayed where I was. I tried to make out what Dad was saying, but he was speaking too softly.

He came out and stood next to the TV. "Your mother's on her way," he said.

I forced myself to breathe. "Oh," I said.

"You mind telling me what's going on?"

I picked up one of the newspapers next to me and set it down again. "I wanted to see you," I said.

Dad chuckled. "That's it? You wanted to see me, so you boarded a bus in the middle of the night and came on down?"

"Something like that."

"Your mother says you've been skipping school and staying out late."

"Did she tell you how good my GPA is? How well I did on my SATs?"

"Polly, your mother and I are both concerned. That's all I'm getting at."

"Everything's fine."

"What about William?"

I looked up at him. He'd put a gray sweatshirt on. It was tight in front where his gut was.

"What about William?" I said.

"He treats you okay?"

"He's fine."

Dad came over to the couch and sat down, right on top of the newspapers. He put an arm around me and the newspapers crinkled underneath him. I had to pee, but I didn't move.

"I didn't want to give you up," he said. "Not ever." He tightened his arm around me.

I started to cry. "I know," I said. I sobbed harder. Dad put his other arm around me and I buried my face in his sweatshirt. His skin had the bitter smell of alcohol.

"I still go by Polly Clark," I said.

He took me to Friendly's for breakfast. When we got settled at our table, Dad peeled a photograph out of his wallet and showed it to me. It was a picture of the two of us. I was about three years old in the picture, and we were sitting on the front porch of our old house. The house was tan, but the porch was painted dark green. We sat with our backs resting against the screen door. It was summer, and I had on peach-colored shorts and a royal blue T-shirt with a rainbow on it. Dad had puffy seventies hair and big sideburns. His face was tan but his legs were stark white sticking out of his shorts. We were both laughing, probably at something Mom was saying as she took the picture.

I didn't really remember the house we lived in then, but I told Dad I did. After we were finished eating he pulled a camera out of his jacket pocket and asked the waitress to take a picture of us standing up by our table.

"It's about time I updated my wallet," he said when the waitress was gone. He touched one of the curled-up edges of the old picture. "You keep this one," he said. "You probably don't have too many photos of us."

"I've got a few."

"I just can't believe you're graduating from high school soon and going off to college," he said.

"I know," I said. "Me neither."

"You're still my baby, you know. You'll always be my baby."

I took a sip of my coffee.

"I still remember the night you were born as clear as if it happened yesterday," he said.

"Well, it was almost eighteen years ago."

Dad coughed. It went on for almost a minute. "I hate to say what I'm gonna say. I really do," he said when he was finished coughing. I waited for him to say he had cancer. Or a heart condition. Instead he said, "It doesn't look like I can come up for your graduation."

I laughed. "It's just a dumb ceremony," I said. "I don't even know if I'm going."

"Your mother told me the date. I'm just heartbroken about it. Try as I might, I just can't make it happen, workwise. What with the sick day today, and my vacation time gone—you'd think they'd do it on a weekend."

"Seriously. It's not important," I said. I wondered what he had done for a vacation. "We'll see each other after that."

"It *is* important! I wanted to watch my little girl walk across that stage!"

"Well, there's always my college graduation. I'm not making any promises after that, though."

"I'll come up over the summer. Take you out big. Someplace fit for a young lady with a high school diploma under her belt."

I forced a smile. "Deal."

Mom showed up around five, and we were on the road by six. In the parking lot Dad squeezed my shoulders and told me to stay out of trouble, and I felt the tears rise in my throat again. Mom and Dad shook hands and then hugged. The diamond studs William had given her for her birthday glittered in Mom's ears. She was wearing jeans and sneakers, and the earrings didn't fit in with the rest of her outfit. I turned away, pressed my tears back down to my belly.

I slept most of the way home. I expected Mom to yell at me as soon as we were alone in the car, but she didn't. She didn't say anything at all. It was late when we got home, and William was already in bed. There was a sheet of yellow notebook paper on the kitchen counter. *Call Joey* was written in William's small, loopy handwriting. I picked up the message and threw it in the trash can under the sink.

Everybody knew I'd run away. Mom had called Carrie and Theresa almost as soon as I left. Since I had my spiral notebook with me Mom hadn't been able to find Joey's number with its 202 area code. And somehow Carrie had convinced Mom that it would be better if one of my friends called him. They'd all been sure that Joey was hiding me, until Dad called.

Carrie and Theresa followed me around at school, offering me cigarettes and asking if I needed to talk. Joey pleaded with me to forgive him for not letting me come over, and promised he'd make it up to me when he saw me next. I told him I wouldn't be seeing him anytime soon, since I was grounded. Lyle told me that I was always welcome to come over to his house, day or night. He reminded me that I could have tapped on his basement door, slept on the scratchy couch next to the band equipment without his mother finding out. Adam called me Huck Finn and asked me if any pimps had come up to me in the bus station. I told them all the same thing. I'd gone to visit my dad and that was all. I felt Mike Franklin's eyes on me at the lunch table, but I pretended not to notice.

The rest of the week I came straight home after school and spent my evenings locked in my room. I stayed off the telephone and avoided the TV. I did my homework. William and Mom ate their dinner in front of the TV and I ate my dinner in my room. Friday night came and went. Nobody mentioned the Bad Brains show, even though everybody was going.

Saturday Mom woke me up early. There was a final winter clearance sale at Hecht's. Normally I slept in, but I was glad to get out of the house. We got there just as it was opening, and Hecht's was nearly empty. We started in outerwear, and then moved on to sweaters.

Mom held a pink wool cardigan under my chin to see how it looked with my complexion. She was a *Color Me Beautiful* addict. Mom was a winter, and I was a summer.

"Did your father seem all right when you saw him?" Mom

asked, moving her eyes from the sweater to my face and back to the sweater.

"I guess so," I said. "Why? Did he seem weird to you?" I pushed the sweater away. Pink was supposed to be my color, but I hated it.

"There was a time when—well, he's usually okay during the day."

We wandered over to Shoes. The sale shoes were crammed together in tight rows. I was starting to wish I'd stayed in bed.

"Dad was fine," I said. "He wasn't drunk, if that's what you're asking."

Mom picked up a maroon loafer and turned it over.

"At least he was nice to me," I said. "At least he didn't tell me he didn't want me living with him. Or refer to my friends as hooligans."

Mom put the loafer down. "Do you want William and me to get a divorce?"

I felt my breath go out of me. I didn't have an answer. I turned and walked over to a stack of jeans by the dressing rooms. Mom followed me.

"I could get a second job to pay for your college and go back to living in a crummy apartment. Would that make you happy?"

I thumbed through the jeans to find my size. I was still waiting to breathe.

"You know, life isn't always how you want it to be. We don't always have control over things. That's something you're going to have to learn."

I exhaled. "Believe me, I know," I said.

We walked in silence toward the mall entrance, through the makeup counters with their heavy perfumes struggling to stand out against one another. Mom walked slightly ahead of me. Her shoulder slumped under the weight of her oversized brown zippered purse.

We made our way around an overweight, middle-aged couple in matching sweat suits to the glossy floor of the mall's main
thoroughfare. It was our habit to stroll the mall after a Hecht's
sale and have lunch in the food court. But today it felt forced.
Mom's mouth was tight and small. I could tell she didn't want
to be here any more than I did.

We paused in front of Linens 'n Things to let a woman with
five or six little boys in birthday hats get by us. "You don't
know how lucky you've got it," Mom said.

"No, I guess I don't." The boys raced off in the direction of
the multiplex, all shouting at once.

"William does a lot of things for you. You should be more
grateful," Mom said when we started walking again.

"Just because Dad was a jerk doesn't mean that William is
some perfect father figure," I said.

"William is not an alcoholic. William cares for you in ways
your father is not capable of."

I didn't answer her. We came up on the main fountain. The
fountain was rectangular and spanned the length of four stores.
The rushing water drowned out the piped-in Muzak. At the far
end of the fountain were a couple of benches and next to them,
an assortment of giant, fake potted plants. An old man sat next
to the plants, tapping the ash from his cigarette into fake plant
dirt. I sucked in his leftover smoke as we passed.

Mom wasn't finished with me. "I wish you'd try to be a little
more respectful of the rules," she said. "I spend more time than
I'd like defending you to William."

"I'm seventeen," I said. "I hate to tell you, but you guys are
basically through raising me."

"Can't you just try to get along with him?"

"What if I don't want to?"

"I want you to. Doesn't that mean anything?"

I fell silent again. I hated this. In front of us a group of
skinny, heavily made-up middle-school girls breezed into the

Photomat. Three short skater boys hovered next door at the entrance to the record store, staring after them. Mom and I were people watchers. Sometimes we'd sit down on one of the benches at the mall just to look. She liked me to name all the different kinds of teenagers.

"What's that one?"

"A bop."

"How about that one?"

"In the leather jacket with the denim vest over it? That's a metalhead."

"And is that one a metalhead?"

"That's a grit. See the beard? Definitely a grit."

"What about her?"

"She's a deadhead. You can tell by her skirt and her bracelets. And over there, those girls are new wavers. You can tell they're vegetarians because they're all wearing those cloth Chinese shoes."

Mom laughed at the names, praised the cleverness as though it were mine.

"What are you?" Mom asked me once. I told her I didn't know.

We stepped onto the down escalator. Sweet, greasy food-court smells floated up to us. We looked down at the brown plastic tables with yellow umbrellas.

"You're not the only one who can run away," Mom said in a small voice. "I could run away tomorrow."

I gripped the sides of the escalator.

"I have a car and money. I could run away, and neither one of you'd ever see me again," she said.

I shut my eyes and waited for the escalator to run out.

• • •

When we got home there was a message from Theresa. There
was an afternoon party going on. Bands were playing in someone's garage, and supposedly the neighbors weren't calling the
police. Everything had been arranged ahead of time, and Theresa was calling on the off chance I could go.

"You can go this afternoon, but you're still grounded," Mom
said. I guessed she felt bad about the things she'd said at the
mall.

Carrie picked me up. Theresa was in the car with her.

"Hey, how was it?" I almost hated to ask. "I'm still so pissed
I couldn't go," I said.

Carrie put the car into gear and pulled away from the curb.
"We have to tell her," Theresa said.

"Tell me what?" I felt a dull dread begin to wash through
me. Maybe someone else had died. Or maybe Mike was going
out with someone.

Theresa turned around in her seat. "We were gonna call you
last night but we decided to wait until we saw you in person."
She tossed her box of Camel Lights onto my lap. "We saw Joey
kissing a girl."

"Are you sure it was him?" I said. "Maybe it wasn't him."
We turned out of my street and onto the main road.

"God, Polly, he was like, totally making out with this chick
in front of everybody," Carrie said. "We walked right by him
and totally fucking stared at him and everything, and he didn't
even act like he knew us or anything."

I dug my nails into my palms and waited for the shock I was
feeling to fade.

"Totally ignored us, the fucking snake," Theresa said. "He's probably been skeezing all over D.C. this whole time like some gross, cheesy asshole."

"I told Lyle I had a bad feeling about him," Carrie said. "I mean, after he told me he liked my miniskirt that one time in that *tone* of his, I said to Lyle, I was like, 'I don't know if Polly should trust that fucking guy, because—' "

"He's a blight on the entire D.C. scene!" Theresa shouted.

Mike Franklin had seen Joey, too. Probably at this very second he was feeling sorry for me. Or laughing about it with Adam and Todd Wilson. I couldn't decide which was worse, being pitied by Mike or being laughed at.

Theresa and Carrie moved on to the girl Joey was with. They said she looked like the kind of girl who would be more comfortable in a cheerleader uniform than at a punk-rock show ("She didn't even look like she knew one Bad Brains song, it was, like, so obvious," Theresa said). And she was definitely still in high school, they were sure of that. Probably not even a senior.

Finally they were quiet. I lit one of Theresa's Camel Lights. I wondered if Joey had met this girl at a show, too. Maybe he had given her a note. I balled my hands up and sat on them. My cigarette was still in my mouth, and my eyes stung from the smoke.

"Okay, so there's something else I have to tell you guys," Theresa said as we pulled into the cul-de-sac where the party was. The street was packed with people, and one of the bands was already playing.

"Okay, let's have it," Carrie said.

Theresa laughed. "This is stupid, but. I totally made out with Todd Wilson last night. I don't know what the fuck came over me."

I let out a moan. I wanted to switch places with Theresa. She knew the difference between a guy you just made out with and a guy you could actually call your boyfriend.

"Are you okay?" Carrie asked. She was pulling over behind an old, wood-paneled station wagon.

A few warm tears rushed down my face, disappearing as quickly as they had come. "I don't know," I said. "I guess. I mean, I feel like shit and all."

"Do you want me to take you home?" Carrie asked. Theresa had already opened her door and had one foot on the ground.

"It's not that big a deal," I said. "I can go to a stupid garage party."

Fred Paige was the first person to stop me. Fred went to the other high school in Reston, and I knew him only in passing. His long hair was permanently tangled, and he was at all the hard-core shows.

"Dude, I saw that guy you go out with at the Bad Brains show last night," he said. "Is he your boyfriend still?"

Carrie made a clucking sound.

"I'll be right back," I said.

I found a phone in a kitchen that was decorated in varying shades of yellow. Even the appliances were yellow. I picked up the yellow phone that was mounted on the wall and dialed Joey's number. As it rang I crouched down on the floor and lowered my head into my chest. I didn't want anyone to overhear me.

"It's my honey!" Joey crowed when I got through. "I just tried to call you!"

I couldn't help smiling. I had gotten used to his joyous, nasal voice.

"So Joey, I have to talk to you about something," I said. Now that I had him on the line I wasn't sure what to say.

"I miss you! When are you coming over? It's been forever!"

"I'm calling you from a party," I said. "A party full of people who saw you making out with someone else last night."

"Oh, they must mean Dawn," Joey said, and for a second

I thought there might be a reasonable explanation. "That's no big deal. That was just because I was upset over what happened with you and Mike. I guess you could say I staged the whole thing."

I lifted my head from my chest. He sounded like a sports announcer, not like someone who had just been caught cheating on his girlfriend.

"So we're even now," he said.

I forgot about not wanting to be overheard. "We're not fucking even! So don't turn this around on me! Something happened with Mike by accident, and I told you about it! I didn't go to some show and make out with a random guy for no reason! And if you were so affected by it, why didn't you just break up with me?"

"Because I didn't want to break up with you. You're my honey."

"Don't call me that. I hate it when you call me that."

"Wow. This is like our worst fight ever," Joey said.

"This isn't a fight, Joey. I'm breaking up with you." I felt a small, unexpected sense of relief as soon as I said it.

"Oh, come on," Joey said. "Don't be like this. Come over and we'll talk."

"No." I twisted the yellow phone cord around my finger. "I don't want to be your girlfriend anymore."

"Well then, if you're going to be like that, I should tell you that Dawn isn't the only one I was with while we were going out." He finally sounded how he was supposed to sound. "You know, that first night at Verbal Assault I asked you if you had a boyfriend, but you never asked me if I had a girlfriend."

"Are you telling me you have a whole other girlfriend?"

"I wouldn't go that far. But there was Tiffany. You met Tiffany when she watched the table for me, remember? She was upset when she saw us holding hands that first night, but I told her you were my old girlfriend and I was consoling you because you'd just been dumped and she bought it. And then Robin—you never met her. She came over and gave me a blow job one night after you had gone home. She still calls me, but she's even younger than you, so I really shouldn't—"

"Is that all, because I'm in the middle of a party here," I said. My stomach was queasy. He had been waiting to tell me. To let me in on the joke.

"Come on, Polly," he said. "I'm twenty-two. You're seventeen. We weren't even sleeping together."

I found Carrie and Theresa standing at the foot of the driveway, watching the band. We chose a place on the lawn to sit and drink from a bottle of tequila Theresa had brought. Fred and a couple other guys that I was used to seeing him with came over to our spot. Everyone but me started talking about how great the Bad Brains show had been. They had played for two hours. H.R. had done a standing front flip onstage.

The band that had been playing in the garage stopped, and Massive Hemorrhage started setting up. Lyle and the Chrises were putting the drum set together. Mike was moving back and forth between his amp and his guitar, turning knobs, making adjustments. I took a sip of tequila and passed the bottle to Fred. The liquor burned its way down my throat, settling warmly in my stomach. More people sat down around us on the lawn. I was starting to have a pretty good time.

five IAN

Virginia Tech was in rural southwestern Virginia, built in a valley of the Blue Ridge Mountains. Blacksburg was in the middle of nowhere, but there were people everywhere—more than twenty-five thousand students, all of them roughly my age. I felt like I had joined a large cult or the armed forces—albeit one marked by backpacks and textbooks and parties instead of weapons or religion or Kool-Aid. The boys wore baseball hats and T-shirts with slogans like WHY DON'T WE GET DRUNK AND SCREW or listing ten ways beer was better than women. The girls had large, unmoving hair and sorority allegiances.

The locals hated the students. They were outnumbered, and mostly employed by the school. In town they stared menacingly over their steering wheels as they rolled by in their pickups, waiting for a reason to shout obscenities at us.

I had no family or friends for 250 miles, and I was scared.

Theresa had insisted on leaving the state for a small liberal-arts school in Ohio, and Carrie had another year to go before college. I had wanted to apply to the same schools as Theresa, but Mom and William could only afford to send me instate. Besides, they reasoned, Virginia Tech had a terrific math department.

I wasn't the sort of person who made friends easily. "Shy at first," my elementary school teachers wrote in the Comments section of my report cards, "but opens up just fine once she has time to adjust." I wasn't adjusting. There was something about college that kept me in a permanent state of embarrassment. I felt flattened by the sheer effort it took to act normal as I traveled from one awkward situation to the next, and I hated the conspicuousness of not knowing anybody. My dormitory had the barren, impermanent air of high turnover, and it was impossible to think of the skeletal bunk beds flanked by two desks and two dressers as home. I kept my headphones on constantly and waited for someone to befriend me.

Mom sent me large padded envelopes filled with things she picked up at Kmart: undershirts and socks and long underwear and Bic ballpoint pens. She didn't include a letter or even a note; there were just the envelopes showing up every so often, addressed in her handwriting with our return address.

Every night on the way to the dining hall I wondered what Mom and William were having for dinner at home. I missed Mom's fried chicken. I missed William's meatballs and biscuits. All I could bring myself to eat at the dining hall was soggy noodles with a sugary marinara sauce, and maybe a wilted salad drenched in oil and vinegar. For breakfast and lunch I ate cereal. I'd heard jokes about the "freshman fifteen," the extra weight that girls tended to put on in college, but I was in danger of getting even skinnier than I already was.

At least I didn't have to eat dinner alone. To "foster friendship," the dorm resident advisers required us to eat with our hallmates for the first two weeks of school. There were eight rooms and sixteen girls on my hall. Most of these girls were of the big-hair, sorority-rush variety, with a few notable exceptions. I ate with the notable exceptions.

Notable Exception Number One: Laura was my roommate. Laura was from Burke, a suburb near Reston. Laura played clarinet in the Virginia Tech marching band, but had elected not to live in the band dorm so she could make "regular friends," as she put it. Laura was one of those people who looked normal from the waist up, but from the waist down she was larger than you'd expect. She wasn't huge, exactly, just out of proportion, with a wide butt and thick thighs. Laura was way ahead of me on the friend-making front, as the marching band got to school three weeks early to practice for football season. When she wasn't with her band friends, Laura was usually talking on the phone with one of them. When I came in she would put whoever it was on hold to say hi and to remind me to just let her know if I needed the phone. I had nothing against Laura, but it was clear that we weren't going to be spending a lot of time together.

Notable Exception Number Two: Sharon lived across the hall from Laura and me. She was from Virginia Beach. If you couldn't guess that Sharon was a deadhead from her printed peasant skirts and her tie-dyed shirts, she was ready to remind you at every lull in conversation that she had seen the Dead eleven times in the last two years. A long shelf in Sharon's room was filled with bootleg tapes, and Sharon could identify the date and location of a particular Dead show with her eyes closed. "That's 1986, Madison Square Garden," she'd report as I passed by her room on the way to the bathroom. Sharon liked to keep her door open so we could see her swaying back and forth to the music, her eyes closed and her arms upraised. There was something evangelical about the way Sharon danced. It gave me the creeps.

Sharon was quickly adopted by the other deadheads on campus, and after the second week of school I rarely saw her. When I did see her she greeted me with an enthusiastic "What's up, *sister*," that I found off-putting.

Notable Exception Number Three: Marissa was from Norfolk. She was the dorm slut. At first I pegged Marissa as a sorority girl, but then the stories started to circulate: Marissa had snuck a guy into the dorm and fucked him in the shower. Marissa gave a guy she met in the laundry room a blow job. Marissa didn't come home all night. All this in the first two weeks of school.

Marissa wore tight jeans and had big boobs. She had long bangs that she parted on the far right so they covered her left eye. Marissa had pouty lips and a menacing grin that she flashed around in the hallway. Instead of eating a regular meal in the dining hall, Marissa drank Coke after Coke. You could tell she wasn't interested in making friends with any of us. I envied her steady gaze and her unflinching attitude in the face of all that gossip. When I passed Marissa in the hallway she looked right through me, smiling that vague grin of hers. She reminded me of the girls in my high school who got into fistfights. Only the girls in my high school who were like Marissa didn't go to college.

Notable Exception Number Four: Julie was from Richmond, and had the room diagonal from mine. She smoked Marlboros and had hung a Clash poster over her bed. Julie was definitely not in the "shy at first" category. She said hi whenever she saw me like we were already close friends. She complimented me for being the only girl on the hall besides her without a floral print bedspread. Sometimes after dinner Julie would invite me over to her room for a cigarette.

Julie's roommate, Debbie, had come to college with her boyfriend. Debbie spent most of her time in her boyfriend's dorm room, which was just fine with Julie. Julie had gone to boarding school, so she had a blasé attitude about living away from home that I found comforting.

"Just avoid anyone wearing white sneakers and you'll be fine," Julie said over cigarettes in her room after dinner. She was balancing a cup of coffee and a plastic ashtray on her stomach as she lay in the hammock she had hung up under her loft bed. Though I hadn't known her long, I knew that footwear was one of the markers Julie used to measure who could be trusted. Also brands of cigarettes and, especially when it came to boys, haircuts. She reminded me of Theresa.

Now and then in the dining hall or traveling back and forth to class I would recognize a bop from high school. There were five or six of them that I'd noticed so far, and every one of them went out of their way to say hello, as if there hadn't been an unbridgeable chasm between us for years. It was no surprise to me that these warm greetings were discontinued as soon as they began rushing various sororities and fraternities. Greek letters appeared on their clothes much in the way their varsity letters had figured on their clothing before, and with the new letters came their familiar blindness to those who were not a part of their scene. But I didn't care. Even if they'd wanted to look me up in the student directory, they wouldn't have been able to. I was no longer known as Polly Elaine Clark. I was Polly Elaine Hessler.

I decided that Polly Hessler wouldn't take any math classes first semester. The only problem was, no other subjects leaped out at me. None of my classes had fewer than two hundred students, and my teachers were openly disinterested. Geology was the most boring. We looked at slides of rocks while the professor droned away in the shadows. My English professor read aloud to us in Olde English, without bothering with the translations. My Introduction to the History of Art professor mumbled and cleared his throat every fifteen seconds. Sociology was interesting, but I didn't get the this-is-it feeling I felt I needed to declare a major.

Five weeks into college, I had racked up a couple of bad grades, an advanced smoking habit, some seriously dark roots, and a startlingly large phone bill. I liked the way my roots looked, but I was determined to raise the grades and lower the phone bill. I needed something besides studying to replace the hours I spent on the phone with Theresa and Carrie. But I was in Blacksburg. There was nothing to do in Blacksburg.

One afternoon on the way home from class I noticed a flyer in the lobby of my dorm announcing a meeting for the campus radio station. I tore off one of the takeaway parts of the flyer that had the date and location on it. When I was a kid I liked to watch *WKRP in Cincinnati*. I had fantasized about being a DJ like Johnny Fever or Venus Flytrap.

That night over a cigarette in her room I asked Julie if she wanted to come with me to the meeting.

"I don't know," she said, without a glimmer of interest.

"Don't make me go by myself," I said. "It could be weird."

The meeting was held in a classroom on campus instead of at the radio station. Most of the seats were filled with people wearing band T-shirts. A couple of aloof, unfriendly-looking guys from the station stood off to the side, waiting their turn to speak. Once everyone was settled in their seats, one of the unfriendly-looking guys walked over to the chalkboard. He picked up a stub of yellow chalk and scribbled *Ian Cross, Music Director*.

"First off, I'd like to thank you all for showing up tonight."

Ian Cross's English accent wasn't pronounced, but I noticed it right away. His face was pudgy and boyish, even though he had a lot of stubble. And he was wearing a beat-up old army jacket that was a lot like the one I owned. I was sorry I hadn't worn it.

"You won't get anywhere at the station if you aren't willing to work," Ian admonished us. "And even if you do work, it will still be a long time between your first day as a volunteer and becoming a DJ."

"Jesus, it's not like there's any money involved," Julie whispered. She kicked her shoe against the carpeted floor.

A girl with long stringy hair and cat-eye glasses raised her hand. "How much of a time investment are you talking about? I mean, most of us are full-time students."

"The time investment depends on you," Ian said. "I think you'll find that it's entirely possible that you can do schoolwork and the radio station, too." The girl nodded and wrote something down in her notebook.

"I suggest that you think about how much you really care about music, in addition to how much time you're realistically able to put in, before you commit yourself to WUVT," Ian continued. Instead of saying the call letters, he pronounced them like a word, *woovit*.

"I definitely don't have what it takes," Julie said in a stage whisper.

I gave Julie my best Be Quiet stare, the one I used when I was a babysitter. Julie had the kind of face that was so perfectly in proportion, it made me realize that most people's faces were actually lopsided in one way or another. (For example, Ian's chin jutted to the left slightly.)

"I don't mean to scare you off, but you musn't think that the radio station is a place for hanging out, or listening to music with your friends," Ian said with renewed fervor, as if we hadn't really been listening until now. "You can do that in your dormitories. What I need is real, honest, unglamorous help."

He produced a clipboard from on top of a file cabinet and placed it in front of a pasty kid with frizzy hair, who set upon it as if he were being timed. The next unfriendly radio station guy stepped forward, and Ian leaned back against the desk, focusing his eyes somewhere over our heads. When the clipboard reached Julie she made a show of not signing it, letting the pen that dangled from a string drag noisily across her desk as she handed it to me. As I wrote down my name I wondered what a cute boy with an English accent was doing in rural Virginia.

The radio station was housed in a run-down, three-story building a few blocks from campus. Even though the new volunteers had been told to report there Thursday at three, climbing the dingy stairs to the station I felt like I was showing up at a party I hadn't been invited to. I pushed open the door and inhaled stale, smoky air, which gradually gave way to another smell, what I later identified as the oily scent of records.

Sitting on a battered couch was a guy in Creepers with reddish hair that stuck straight up. I couldn't tell if the color was natural or a dye job. Next to him was a voluptuous girl dressed all in black, smoking a cigarette.

"I can't make up my mind about Peter Murphy and Love and Rockets," the voluptuous girl was saying. "I mean, are these just side projects until Bauhaus gets back together? And what about the Bubblemen? What the fuck was that all about?"

The guy with red hair shrugged.

Ian appeared beside me in the doorway. "Bauhaus is over," he said, like he'd heard it straight from Peter Murphy himself.

I moved farther into the office to let Ian by. He was wearing an olive green T-shirt with the words WOLFGANG PRESS printed across the front in black. I guessed Wolfgang Press must be a band.

"We were wondering when you were going to get here," the voluptuous girl said, even though it was only five after three. She was wearing red lipstick that left a bright smear on her cigarette, and she had perfect white skin and straight blunt bangs. She was the most beautiful girl I had ever seen.

"Is it just the three of you then?" Ian sighed. "Fucking freshmen. It was like this last year, too. A big crowd shows up at the first meeting, all of them anxious to become DJs, and as soon as I use the word *work,* they disappear."

The most beautiful girl I had ever seen gave Ian a pointed look. "I'm not intimidated."

"All right. Let's get started, then."

Without bothering to make introductions, Ian showed us how to unpack the records that came in from the record companies and write the station's call letters in permanent marker on both sides of the record and on the jacket. There were records everywhere. They were stacked up on the couple of desks and the few chairs that were the only additional furniture in the room, and piles of records were lining the walls. There were more records still in their shrink-wrap in the front hallway, waiting to be opened.

Once he was satisfied we were equal to the task of cataloging records, Ian pointed at a turntable that rested on top of an upside-down wooden crate. Two oversized speakers sat nearby.

"You're welcome to play anything you're curious about," he said. "I just don't want to hear any REM or U2. This is a college radio station, not a commercial conglomerate."

He disappeared down a hallway to what I presumed must be the DJ booth. I helped the redheaded boy, who identified himself as Andrew, lug a box of records upstairs from the lobby. The girl, who was named Cynthia, seated herself behind one of the desks and began examining a stack of records.

"Jesus Christ. This band's called 'Assume the Position,'" Cynthia said, holding up a record and throwing it down again. "Can't we just toss some of these straight in the garbage?"

"We should stage a record-burning bonfire out back later," I said.

Cynthia smirked and shook a cigarette out of her pack. "Anyone want one?"

I jogged over to her. "Thanks. I didn't think you'd be able to smoke here, so I left mine at home." My words came out in a nervous jumble, and I noted that I had referred to my dorm room as home.

"Oh, I keep mine with me at all times," Cynthia said. "I'm at two packs a day."

"Wow."

Cynthia waved at Andrew. "Want one?"

"No thank you. All four of my grandparents died of lung cancer."

"I've got cancer all over my family," Cynthia said. "I figure I might as well smoke, you know? I mean, I'm gonna get it anyway, so."

"So, do you guys want to listen to something?" Andrew asked. "We have to be careful. I don't want to offend Mr. Pretentious."

"He might be pretentious, but he's hot," Cynthia said.

I pulled a record out of its jacket without pausing to examine it and scrawled the station's call letters across it. I'd been hoping Cynthia wouldn't notice that Ian was hot, though I admired her for saying it out loud, like she didn't care who might overhear. She struck me as the sort of girl who hadn't experienced a lot of rejection in her life.

After about an hour, Ian came back and led us down the hall to the library. We each carried an armful of records that we had labeled. As we passed the DJ booth I peered through a glass partition. A chubby girl with horn-rim glasses and blue-black hair was placing a record on one of two turntables. A pair of headphones rested around her neck.

"That's Sarah," Ian said. She raised a hand in greeting without looking up.

Ian led us further down the hall into a large room that held nothing but shelves of records. The shelves were so jammed I couldn't imagine how we were going to squeeze in any new records. They were separated into classical, country, bluegrass, blues, and jazz, but the majority of the shelves were devoted to rock.

"As you might imagine, when you become a DJ you'll want to pull your play list before you start your show," Ian said. "You want to minimize the running back and forth."

Andrew cleared his throat. "Um, exactly how long will it be before we can, you know, go on the air?"

"Ask me again in a month."

When I saw *Polly Hessler* on the address label in William's handwriting I sat down and opened the package on the floor of the mailroom. He'd sent me a brochure about registering to vote and a schedule book for keeping track of my assignments. Unlike Mom, he included a note on an index card. *I thought these things might come in handy,* he wrote. I turned over the index card to see if he'd written anything on the back. It was blank. Tucked inside the schedule book was a check for fifty dollars. I couldn't stop smiling the whole way back to my room.

I went to the radio station most days after class. I'd spend a couple of hours logging and filing records before meeting Julie at the dining hall for dinner. It was just Julie and me eating together now; the rest of the Notable Exceptions had moved on.

Andrew and Cynthia were at the station most afternoons, too. Instead of listening to records we tuned the stereo to WUVT. The three of us became acquainted with the various DJs who had afternoon shows. Mostly the DJs kept to themselves, pausing only to check if a particular record had come in or to ask for a cigarette. But I felt like I knew them from listening to their shows.

Marcus had shoulder-length hair and played punk from the late seventies and early eighties. I loved Marcus's show. Sarah played bands like the Church and Joy Division, and sometimes she read her friends' poetry over the air. Andrew groaned whenever she did this.

Karen played everything from speed metal to classic rock, depending on her mood. "People want to know what fucking genre they're fucking listening to," Ian would shout at her when she arrived at the station. As music director Ian's job was to oversee the play lists, so part of his job was to yell at the DJs.

Gary had a crew cut and was a few years older. He played hardcore. I wanted to talk about bands with Gary, but I couldn't get up the nerve. Gary usually didn't talk on the air, and when he did speak his voice was a monotone.

Cynthia stayed in the front office with Ian, writing down the names of the records that came in on a master list. Andrew and I were stuck lugging stacks of records down the hall to the library for filing. I found out—mostly through eavesdropping on Cynthia's constant questioning—that Ian's family was from a suburb of London, that he had moved to Blacksburg when he was twelve, and that his father was a professor in the architecture department. He was supposed to be a junior, but he was taking the semester off to concentrate more on the radio station and think about what he really wanted to do.

My conversations with Ian were limited to perfunctory comments about which bands I had and hadn't heard of, and whether I liked them. Hanging out with him made me feel like a game-show contestant. He would name band after band, and we would shout out whether we'd heard of the band and, if so, whether we'd seen them live.

"You're one of those DC hardcore girls," he said once, winking at me.

"Not really. I mean sort of," I said. "I mean, that's where I grew up and all." I went back to marking up the record I was cataloging, letting my hair fall into my face.

"Ian's amazing," I told Julie at dinner. *Amazing* was a word that Ian used a lot. He thought the Pixies were amazing. Dead Can Dance were amazing. Sonic Youth were amazing. London and New York City were amazing.

"Shoes?" Julie asked.

"Black."

"Well, be careful," Julie said. "He might just seem cooler because of the accent."

I considered this.

"No. He's different from other guys I've known. He's smart."

"Smart how? Like he has a big vocabulary?"

"I don't know. Not like that. Like mature smart."

Julie twirled spaghetti around her fork. "So what are you going to do?"

"What do you mean?"

"Aren't you going to *do* something? We should make a plan."

I liked that Julie said *we,* like the two of us were in on it together. She made it sound like all it would take to get Ian's attention was the right strategy. Like if we put our heads together we could trick him into going out with me. I wasn't ready to plan, though.

"I guess I need to hang out with him more first," I said.

Julie came by the radio station to see Ian. When I introduced her to him she pretended not to know who he was. She lit a cigarette and picked up an INXS record that was lying on top of a stack by the door.

"I kind of love this band," she said. "I have to admit it."

Ian gave her a sharp look. "That's in the trash pile for a reason," he said.

"So can I have it then?" Julie asked.

Ian shrugged and walked out of the room. Andrew made a face at his back.

When Cynthia invited Andrew and me to a keg party, I accepted without giving it much thought. Julie and I had been to a few keg parties already. We spent our time in out-of-the-way corners, getting drunk and making fun of people's outfits. Sometimes Julie threatened to pick up a guy, but every time anyone approached us (especially if he was wearing white tennis shoes and a baseball hat, which he usually was), we gave out fake names and made sarcastic comments until the guy got the hint and moved on. Julie liked to go by Beverly. I was Chloe.

This party was different. We didn't have to be Beverly and Chloe here. Nobody was wearing a baseball hat or a Greek sweatshirt, and a punk band was playing in the living room. And it was crowded. Until now I had assumed that the only cool people in Blacksburg were the twenty people who worked at the radio station.

As we wound our way through the house in search of the keg, I caught sight of Ian in the bathroom line talking to Cynthia. He had his arms crossed in front of his chest and he was smiling at something Cynthia was saying. He had little teeth. Or maybe he just had big gums.

I kept my head down and went around a corner into what turned out to be the kitchen. A crowd was slowly moving toward the keg in the center of the room. We grabbed two blue plastic cups from a stack on the kitchen counter.

"Ian's here," I said.

"For someone who supposedly likes Ian, you sure have a funny way of showing it," Julie said in a low voice. "I mean, it's not like you don't know him. Just go up and say hi."

We moved closer to the keg. The soles of our shoes stuck to the beer-sodden wooden floorboards as we walked. "I don't know. I think he's here with Cynthia," I said.

Once we had our beers we went back out to the living room to check out the band. When we passed by the bathroom line Ian and Cynthia were gone.

The living room was packed. We drank quickly from our beers so they wouldn't spill when people knocked into us. There wasn't a stage, and it was too crowded to see what the band was doing. We crossed over to the far side of the living room, near the front door, where there was slightly more space. I looked out the one window and spotted Andrew's stuck-up red hair.

I brought Julie outside to say hi. Andrew was on the front porch with a couple of other boys. They were all holding blue plastic cups. A tall guy with a mop of wavy hair was talking.

"So I covered my hand with the chocolate sauce, went into the stall next to somebody, and after a minute said, 'Hey man, you got any toilet paper?' Then I stuck my hand under, and the guy totally screamed."

Everybody laughed.

"Hey, Andrew," I said.

"Hey." He pointed at the guy who'd been talking. "This is Mark. And this is Sam."

"I've seen you two in the dining hall," said Sam. He was wearing a patterned, button-up shirt and round wire-rimmed glasses.

Julie pointed at the window. "How come you guys aren't in there moshing?"

"We don't have to mosh in there," Mark said. "You can mosh anywhere, really." He swung a hip into her, and beer sailed out of her cup. "Like, if you're in a crowded elevator, why not get a pit going?"

"Or you can mosh in line at the dining hall," I said.

"Andrew likes to mosh in the dorm showers," Sam said. We laughed.

"Shut up," Andrew said.

"Seriously, that band in there kinda sucks," Mark said. "I mean, they're okay, but I've seen way better."

"Hey, what's the first band you guys ever saw?" Sam asked, "Like I saw REO Speedwagon with my older sister when I was in elementary school."

"That's a good one," Julie said. "My first concert was Shawn Cassidy. I was eight, and I wallpapered my entire bedroom with posters of him.

"I saw Cheap Trick when I was ten," Andrew said.

"I saw the Go-Go's with A Flock of Seagulls," I said. "I was thirteen, and I wore a red miniskirt and black-and-white striped tights. I wanted to be Gina Schock."

Ian's voice floated up behind me. "A Flock of Seagulls were nothing but a creation of a corporation," he said.

I swallowed. "Yeah, well, I was more of a Go-Go's fan anyway," I said.

"'I Ran' is a great song," Sam said.

Andrew introduced Ian around. Mark told another story. This one was about pulling leftover pizza out of the trash and giving it to a frat guy on his hall. "When I offered it to him, he was like, 'Sweet!' " Mark said. Julie laughed so hard she spit her beer out.

Ian turned to look at me. "You need another beer?" he said.

I forced my face into a noncommittal expression and followed him into the house. I wondered if he was thinking about how dumb I was for going to see A Flock of Seagulls and the Go-Go's. I was never going to be a DJ.

• • •

"I thought you might be here," Ian said when we got inside. The band had stopped, and three boys were in front of a stereo picking out records from a red plastic crate. I guessed it was their party.

"Yeah. Cynthia told me about it." We were strolling toward the kitchen. I took a long drink of the remainder of my beer.

"I figured you'd be here, what with the punk rock band playing and all," he said.

"Are you making fun of me, Ian?" I said this in my best imitation of an English accent.

He smiled. "Of course not. I'm not the sort that makes fun of people."

"'I'm not the sort.' That's an English thing."

"What?"

"Your accent makes you sound English, but not just that. The way you say everything makes you sound English."

"Well, I don't know what to tell you," he said. "I'm English."

We had reached the kitchen. The party had emptied out somewhat since the band had finished so we were able to walk right up to the keg. I wondered where Cynthia was.

Ian filled up my cup and then his own. Then he fished his cigarette pack out of the pocket of his windbreaker and pointed it at me. Even though I had my own pack I took two out and put the pack back in his pocket.

Ian looked down at his pocket where my hand had been. "When's the last time you ate anything homemade?" he asked. "My mother dropped off some soup for me this morning."

● ● ●

Ian's apartment was on the first floor of a drab brick building
a few blocks from the radio station. It smelled like stale coffee
and cigarettes and faintly of something else—something like
oranges and vinegar that was the smell of Ian himself. There
wasn't much in the way of furniture, but records were everywhere, stuffed into bookshelves and filling up milk crates that
lined the perimeter of his living room.

"Shit," I said, following him into the kitchen. "Why do you
even bother with the radio station when you have this much
music in your apartment?"

Ian laughed. I sat at a large wooden table with mismatched
chairs while he peeled off the top of a Tupperware container
and dumped soup into two bowls. I couldn't see what kind
of soup it was. He shoved the bowls into the microwave and
pushed the door shut. Together, we watched the bowls ro-
tate.

"Seriously," I said. "How did you manage to get so many
records?" There were even a few in the kitchen, in a stack on
the counter.

"It's what I do," Ian said, a note of pride creeping into his
voice. "I don't know if you've heard my radio show, but a lot
of what I play I bring from home."

"I've heard you a few times." In fact I had recorded every
one of Ian's radio shows since the first radio station meeting. I
listened to him over and over on my Walkman.

The microwave beeped. Ian took a paper towel in each hand
and popped open the door.

"It's not too hot," he said. He handed me a bowl.

It wasn't because it was hot that I dropped the bowl. It just
slipped from my hands somehow, and before I could get a grip

on it again the bowl was spinning and ringing on the floor, unbroken. I let out a shriek as the soup, which appeared to be vegetable beef, seeped through my shirt to my skin. The shriek was more out of embarrassment than pain.

"Are you okay?" Ian picked up a roll of paper towels from the counter and began to unroll it.

"I'm fine, but I think my shirt is dead," I said. I slouched forward in my seat. My shirt was dark green and buttoned up in the center, and I was grateful that Ian couldn't see through it.

Ian retrieved the bowl from the floor and put it in the sink. Then he crossed the room to examine my blouse. I laughed, my voice booming in the still kitchen. His hands were full of paper towels. I stood up so he could wipe off the chair.

"I'm really sorry about this," I said. "I guess I'm a little drunk."

Ian straightened up before me. "It's not your fault. It was an accident."

That's when he kissed me. At first he was sort of formal about it, but then he reached both hands around my shoulders and pulled me toward him. The soup on my shirt oozed onto his.

He backed me out of the kitchen. As we moved down a short hallway there was the light and breathy sound of our kissing over our footsteps. When we reached his bedroom I grabbed both sides of the doorway and braced myself. We tilted backward, like unsteady dance partners.

"I'm not going to sleep with you," I said.

"Okay."

I let go of the doorjamb and we backed our way over to the bed and dropped down on top of it, our bodies bouncing against the mattress. He had made his bed. I could see the shapes of records everywhere.

Ian unbuttoned my shirt. Soup had soaked through to my chest and stained my bra. He took his shirt off and tossed them both over his shoulder. For the first time I wasn't nervous in his presence. This was something I knew how to do.

Ian climbed on top of me. "It would be so easy," he whispered.

"I know," I said. I wriggled away from him. He pulled me back and we kissed.

"Don't you want to?" he whispered a few minutes later. A condom in an orange wrapper had materialized beside us on the mattress. I left my eyes open when he kissed me again so I could look at it. One side of the wrapper was folded over, so the condom sat at an angle. He must have carried it around in his jeans all night.

I was still. I let him take off my underwear. I watched him put on the condom. I waited. Everybody lost their virginity at some point.

It didn't hurt like it had when Jason had tried. And although it wasn't pleasure I felt exactly, it wasn't painful, either. It was mildly uncomfortable, just like my tenth-grade health teacher had promised. Up until now I hadn't been sure whether Jason had taken my virginity. Now I knew he hadn't. What Ian was doing was something new. I studied the shape of his shoulder in the dark, listened to his quick breath moving in and out of him. I wanted to remember everything.

Afterward we propped ourselves up against the pillows and shared a cigarette. I hugged my knees to my chest and smiled. I was capable of having sexual intercourse. I told myself that even if Ian never spoke to me again, I would always be happy about tonight. When he got up to go to the bathroom I checked the sheets for blood, but there wasn't any.

I still went to the radio station after class, but things were different now. For one thing, as soon as Cynthia realized Ian and

I were together she stopped showing up. Andrew was still nice to me, but he didn't joke around with me like he used to, and he kept quiet when Ian came by to talk to me.

"I guess we know who's getting the first DJ slot that opens up," Andrew said once while we were filing records.

"That's not funny," I said.

"I'm just kidding," he said. But I knew he wasn't.

Ian's radio show was on Sundays, Tuesdays, and Thursdays from ten P.M. to two A.M. Usually I hung out with him in the DJ booth. I drank beer and watched Ian choose records, put the headphones on and take them off, make announcements every fifteen minutes, check levels, and line up the needle in the right place on the record. There wasn't much more than that to being a DJ. After his show we would go back to his apartment. We stayed away from my dorm room.

I put asterisks in my schedule book for the times we had sex. If we slept together more than once in a day I would put more than one asterisk down in the space where I should have been writing the dates papers were due and quizzes were held. When I showed Julie my schedule book, she insisted on going with me to Planned Parenthood to get on the pill. Ian and I had been using condoms, but I didn't think the pill was such a bad idea.

Planned Parenthood's waiting room was as calm and plant-laden as every other doctor's office I had been in. I beamed at Julie after I signed in, and she shrugged back at me over her *People*.

When the nurse said my name I sang out "Here!" as if roll were being called. I followed her down a carpeted hallway to an examining room. The nurse had oversized glasses and a no-nonsense tone. She instructed me to put on a paper gown and rest my feet in a set of stirrups at the bottom of the examining table. Julie had complained about the stirrups on the way over. She said they made her feel like she was being experimented on.

The nurse disappeared, and a few minutes later the doctor showed up. I was relieved to see that she was female; I had been too shy to ask when I called to make the appointment. She had a round, kind face and a bobbed haircut that made it impossible to guess her age. She picked my chart off the counter and studied it. Her placid face reminded me of a nun's.

"Are you and your partner monogamous?" she said by way of introduction.

"Yes."

The doctor sat down on a stool with wheels on it and rolled over to me. I leaned back on the table.

"Scoot down a little," she said. A few seconds later I felt pressure against what I guessed was my cervix. The instrument she was using was cold.

"Are you satisfied with your sex life?" the doctor asked. "Do you have any questions you'd like to ask me?"

"I think I'm okay."

I hadn't thought about whether I was satisfied with my sex life. It wasn't so much the physical aspects of sex that I enjoyed. What I liked was the fact that it was taking place at all. It reminded me of how it felt when I learned to drive—I knew it was inevitable, but until I was actually behind the wheel, piloting the car myself, I hadn't fully believed it was something I could do.

I loved waking Ian up in the middle of the night to do it again half asleep. My mother was bedtime conscious: the rule had been off the phone by nine thirty, in bed at ten. She made a big deal out of the health reasons for a good night's sleep, but now I suspected she just wanted me out of the way so she and William could have sex.

When Ian and I did it, I thrashed around on the bed under him for a spell and then came with giant thrusts and moans. I wasn't *really* coming, at least I didn't think so. I knew there was something more to orgasms than what was happening to me. I opened my mouth to ask the doctor about orgasms but then shut it again.

"I want you to consider using a backup method of birth control in addition to the pill if you're not completely sure that you can remember to take it every day," said the doctor when she was finished examining me. "We don't want to see you back here with a pregnancy scare."

"Okay, " I said. I thought about Carrie. "And if I take my pill at the same exact time every day I definitely won't get pregnant, right?"

"Right. If you have any questions just call the office."

"How many people have you slept with?" I asked Ian. He was standing in front of his bathroom sink, shaving. I was perched on the toilet seat with my knees folded in front of me. Watching Ian shave made me feel like I was ten years younger than him instead of two.

"Seven," he said, tapping his razor against the edge of the sink. He hadn't had to think about it. "What about you?"

"Oh, like three." I moved my gaze away from Ian to the orange and black can of shaving cream that sat next to the toothbrush holder.

"How come you shave every day?" I asked. "It's not like anyone minds if you have stubble." Although Ian's hair was medium brown, his beard grew in darker.

"My face gets itchy," he said, screwing his mouth to the left as he brought the razor down his right cheek. He turned on the faucet. "You're not going to tell me about the other people you slept with?"

I felt my cheeks redden. "Is that something you want to know?"

He lifted his razor off his cheek and smiled at me. "Well, yeah, sure."

"Well, you know. They were old boyfriends. From high school."

"Tell me about them."

I stretched my legs out and rested my feet on the edge of the bathtub.

"Jason, Mike, and Joey," I said.

"Jason, Mike, and Joey. Was this all on one occasion?"

I laughed. "No."

"Which one did you go out with the longest?"

"Mike, for like half a year. It was sort of off and on."

Ian was almost finished shaving. He leaned forward and splashed water on his face. I pulled his towel down from the rack and handed it to him.

"There were other guys, too," I said as he patted his face dry. "I just didn't, you know, *do* them." I wasn't sure why I was telling him this. Maybe because I was Ian's seventh.

"*Do* them? Is that how you refer to it?"

"Yeah, I guess," I said. "What do you say, *make love?*"

"Sometimes. Not always. I always make love to you."

"Oh, well, me, too, monsieur."

Since my birthday fell on a Thursday, Ian found a sub for his radio show. Laura had gone home for the weekend a day early, so we celebrated in my dorm room. Julie gave me a bottle of spiced rum she'd bought from a senior who'd been a friend of her brother's in high school. Ian gave me a cactus and a mix tape. He gave me the song list separately, with descriptions like "representative of their raw, earlier work" and "a nice blend of new wave and plain old rock" next to the song entries.

That night Ian spent the night in my dorm room for the first time. We huddled together in my narrow top bunk under my comforter, which still smelled new. When we did it Ian's head came precariously close to the ceiling, and I put a hand in between to protect him.

"I'm glad you're my girlfriend," Ian said when we were finished.

"Me, too."

We hadn't said *I love you* yet, and since it was my birthday I wanted to. Except I wanted him to be the one to say it first.

Julie and I were trying to study on the floor in her room, but I couldn't concentrate.

"What's an orgasm feel like, exactly?" I said.

Julie marked her place in her Intro to Psych textbook and shut it. "What do you mean?"

"I mean, I don't know if I've had one yet."

I stared over her head, at the plastic fishbowl on her dresser that was full of bottle caps.

"You know when it happens," she said. "It's kind of like fishing."

I'd never been fishing. "Well. I guess I haven't had one then," I said.

"Haven't you masturbated?"

I shook my head no. Every time I reached a hand down there a silly feeling came over me, killing any arousal that had built up.

"Does an orgasm from masturbating and an orgasm from sex feel the same?" I asked.

"Basically, yeah. There's just somebody there for the one." Julie ran a hand through her hair, spread her fingers to release the tangles. "I'll tell you this, though. It's way easier to give yourself an orgasm, once you figure out how to do it. Most guys I've been with didn't know what was up in that department at all."

I picked at Julie's royal blue rug. Ian knew what he was doing. He'd been with seven girls.

"So what's it feel like?"

Julie put a cigarette in between her lips and lit it with my
yellow plastic lighter. She was wearing white boxer shorts
with red chili peppers all over them. "It's like, a big release.
And it feels really good all the way through your body, like
this big, huge, full sensation. But it's not like being stoned
or drunk or anything like that. You can't even compare it to
being high."

"It's better than being high," I said. Like I understood.

Julie opened her psych book back up. "You just need to
relax, and it'll happen," she said. "The first time I came with a
guy I was totally surprised."

I was waiting in Ian's car while he went into 7-Eleven to buy
cigarettes. The 7-Eleven in Blacksburg was different from the
ones in Reston: Reston 7-Elevens had trees planted in front of
them and were built with the same wood as the houses so they
would blend into the neighborhood. The Blacksburg 7-Eleven
stood alone in a parking lot and had a neon sign. Neon wasn't
allowed in Reston.

Mark, Andrew, and Sam crossed in front of the car without
noticing me. Mark was carrying a guitar case with stickers all
over it. I tapped the horn and they looked over and waved. I
wondered if they were starting a band.

Ian came out and nodded at Andrew without stopping. When
Ian opened the car door I could hear them laughing. I rolled
down the window.

"Need a ride?" I asked as Ian started the car. Mark and Sam
were already halfway inside, and Andrew smiled and shook his
head no.

Ian tossed one pack of Camel Lights into my lap and put another pack on the dashboard.

"Freshman idiots," he said as we pulled away.

I pushed my pack of cigarettes into the backpack at my feet. "Why don't you like them?" I asked.

Ian shrugged. "I barely know them."

"You just said they were idiots. Freshman idiots."

"You're not like them," Ian said. "I wouldn't be going out with you if you were."

"I think they're funny," I said.

Ian told his parents that he was spending Thanksgiving with my family, and I told Mom and William I was going to Ian's. Mom didn't agree to it until I said that I could really use the quiet time in the dorms to catch up on studying. We spent the long weekend in Ian's apartment, ordering in Chinese food and pizza. It was fun not having turkey on Thanksgiving; I felt like I was getting away with something.

Ian played me record after record that he thought I should hear. "You really need to check out this band," he'd say, or "This is the only album you need to know by this band." When I wondered aloud if he was going to test me at some point he wrinkled his nose and said, "Don't you want to know about cool music?"

Saturday night we took a walk. The whole town was shut down. Even the doughnut shop, which was popular with the locals, was closed. We stared into the windows of closed-up stores. I couldn't understand it. It was two full days after Thanksgiving, and it looked like there'd been a power outage. Suddenly I missed Reston. I wanted to be home with Mom and William and my friends.

We walked to the edge of town and over to the side of campus where most of the academic buildings were. It was strange to be here, too, especially at night. The buildings loomed larger, and our footsteps echoed on the sidewalks as we walked. My geology professor called the stone of the buildings Hokie stone. The football team was called the Hokies, and so were Tech students.

"What's a Hokie?" I asked.

"Who cares?"

"I was just wondering."

"That's where all my math classes have been," Ian said, pointing up at a large, modern-looking building that stood in contrast to all of the other buildings with their stone exteriors.

"I guess I'll take classes there next semester," I said. I shivered against the cold. I was doing so poorly in the rest of my classes, I wasn't even sure whether I'd do well in math.

Ian pulled me against him and kissed my neck above my scarf. The top of my head fit just under his chin.

"Next semester we might run into each other on campus," he said into my hair.

I thought of Ian coming toward me through the daytime crowds, a backpack tossed over his shoulder. I stepped away from him and he extended an arm. I took his hand and he spun me in toward him, catching me in his other arm and holding me there. I wondered what song he was thinking of.

In the dining hall the following week, Sam dumped half the salt-shaker into Mark's drink while Mark was telling a story about his roommate, and Mark drank it all in one swig before spitting it across the table onto Andrew. When I told Ian about it later at his apartment, I had to stop twice to laugh.

Ian gave me a tight smile before turning back to the TV. He was sitting on the floor, watching *The Young Ones,* cracking up every four seconds. I was on the couch behind him, catching only every third or fourth joke.

"It's because you're not English that you don't get it," he said.

"Maybe it's just not that good," I mumbled, peeling a slice of black polish from my toenail and letting it fall between Ian's couch cushions. I slid to the floor and picked up Ian's course catalog for next semester.

"Maybe I'll take life drawing," I said. "I like to draw. Sam says people who are good at geometry are usually good at drawing."

Ian turned away from the TV. "Sam doesn't know what he's talking about."

"It makes sense when you think about shapes and proportions and stuff," I said.

"Since when are you interested in art?"

I thought about my Introduction to the History of Art class. I usually fell asleep when my professor turned off the lights to show us slides. "I like art."

"Like what?"

I stretched my legs out behind me. My toes touched a crate of records. "Well, I like Impressionist painting," I said.

Ian shook his head back and forth as he turned back to the TV. "Everybody likes the Impressionists," he said. "That's not really liking art. Give me something else. Something modern."

I shut the catalog. "What about you? Aren't you supposed to be figuring out what to do next semester?"

"In the scheme of things, formal education means very little," he said. "You should know that."

I got to my feet. "I have to go home," I said. "I have a test tomorrow."

I took the bus home for Christmas break. I hadn't been on a bus since I had gone to North Carolina. It was pretty much the same as that time, except there were people my age on the bus and my mother and William knew where I was. I stared out the window at the dense rock that lined the highway like the walls of a fortress and let myself think about what it would be like to be at college without Ian. I hadn't really been on my own since the first few weeks of school. I had friends now. It might be fun.

William picked me up at the bus station. We shared an awkward hug and then he helped me lug my laundry to the car.

"Don't throw your back out," I told him. "I've been saving this laundry for over a month."

"My parents didn't let me bring my laundry home from college. They made it clear from the day I left that they expected me to act like a grown-up and take care of myself."

"Well, sorry to disappoint you. Again."

I spent the evening following Mom from room to room. I told her about Ian and Julie and Andrew and the radio station. I told her about my dorm room. She had heard it all on the phone, but I told her again. I had pictures of campus and the radio station. I had one of Ian doing his radio show. He was wearing headphones and staring at the console, pretending not to pose. When I showed the picture to Mom she nodded with approval.

"Well, he seems nice at least," she said.

I wondered what she meant by "at least."

"He's really serious about music," I said.

I went Christmas shopping at the mall with Carrie and Lyle.

"You missed like, six good shows," Lyle said over lunch in the food court.

"Whatever. I can't wait to go to school and get the hell out of here," Carrie said.

Lyle put down his Coke. "And leave me all alone?"

"What's Ian like?" Carrie asked.

"I already told you."

"Are you in love?"

"What kind of question is that? He's my boyfriend. We sleep next to each other practically every night."

At night I pretended Ian was in bed with me. If I thought about it long enough I could almost feel him there beside me, could almost smell his orange-vinegary smell. He was coming to visit for a few days after New Year's, but he would be in the guest room down the hall.

Theresa and I went to the new movie theater complex. While we waited for the movie to start, Theresa told me about why she was wearing glasses now instead of contacts.

"I'm not going through all that shit for vanity's sake anymore," Theresa said. "I want to be the real me."

Her glasses were horn-rimmed. I thought they looked cool.

For Christmas I got a boom box, three sweaters, a black wool winter coat (it actually fit, unlike the sweaters), an instant camera, a stack of blank tapes, and three rolls of quarters for laundry. My father sent me flannel pajamas that were two sizes too big. I gave my mother a John Irving novel and a pair of silver hoop earrings. I got William a brown leather wallet and a Beethoven piano CD Mom said he wanted. I sent my dad a gray sweater that Mom helped me pick out and some pictures of my dorm and the rest of the campus. He had promised to visit me in the spring, but I wasn't expecting him. I hadn't seen him since North Carolina.

• • •

On the phone I told Ian about the trouble I was having picking out a Christmas present for him.

"I take that as a compliment," Ian said. "You can't just get me any old thing at the mall."

I laughed. "Then I can't get you anything. Reston is one big mall."

My report card arrived in the mail two days after Christmas. I was hoping it would take longer. It was mostly made up of D's, with a couple of C's thrown in. Even though I knew it was going to be bad, I still felt shocked to see those grades next to my name.

"It's your life," Mom said at dinner. We were still eating turkey leftovers from Christmas. "If you want to squander your education and wind up scraping to get by the rest of your life, I guess there's nothing much I can do about that."

I set my fork down. "You think I wanted this to happen?"

"We're not going to just keep paying, you know."

Her voice had a hard, dramatic edge to it that I couldn't stand. The only sounds coming from William were the noises his knife and fork made against his plate—he hadn't so much as looked at me since my report card had come.

"What are you going to do, pull me out of school and make me live here?" I asked. My voice shook.

"We can't make you do anything," Mom said. "But we're not paying all this money for you to hang around and go to parties."

I fought back tears. "I said I'll do better, and I will."

"I don't know where you're getting all this confidence."

"Not from you guys, that's for sure."

William bent his head further over his plate. I stared at the stark white line of his part, slashing through his dark brown hair like he'd measured it with a ruler. He probably hadn't gotten a bad grade in his life.

The next day I met Andrew at the mall for lunch. He lived nearby in Woodbridge, and I was excited to see him. He was exchanging everything he had gotten for Christmas. We sat in the food court, eating Philly cheese steaks and fries, and I told him about my bad grades.

"Yeah, it's hard to study when you're going out with someone," he said. He smiled.

I squirted more ketchup onto my fries. "What, are you seeing someone?" I asked.

He nodded.

"How come I don't know this already?" I asked.

Andrew stared at me before he answered. "Because I go out with Sam."

I tried to make a blasé expression as I took a bite out of my cheese steak. I thought about Sam, pouring salt into Mark's drink in the dining hall. A crowd of teenagers pushed their way by our table, knocking over a plastic chair.

I lowered my voice. "What about Mark?" I asked.

Andrew raised his eyebrows. "What about him?"

"Gay or straight?"

"Straight." He tilted his head. "Yeah, definitely straight."

"So, how long have you guys been together?" I asked.

"Pretty much all semester," Andrew said. "But we just started telling people."

I shrugged. "Well, that's cool," I said. "I mean, I don't care either way."

Andrew rolled his eyes. "Polly, you're doing fine. You should have seen my parents when I told them."

When I got home from the mall I called Julie.

"What's the matter with you?" she asked. "I thought it was totally obvious."

I spent New Year's Eve in the city with Carrie and Lyle. We didn't have anywhere to go and it was too cold to get out of the car, so we drove around to the memorials on the mall, watching crowds of drunken revelers run around under the streetlights. At midnight I looked out the window while Carrie and Lyle kissed.

"Why couldn't there have been a party?" I asked.

"I'm sick of having parties," Lyle said.

When I got home I took the phone into the downstairs bathroom so Mom and William wouldn't hear me and called Ian. He answered on the first ring.

"I knew it was you," he said.

"I miss you."

"I'll be there the day after tomorrow."

I leaned into the sink and peered into the mirror. My skin looked even pastier than usual. "Things are tense around here with Mom and William," I said. "They're really pissed about my grades."

Ian sighed. "It's such a freshman thing to do," he said.

"I'm glad you find me so predictable."

"Well, Polly, what do you want them to say? Of course you should have done better."

I straightened up. "What kind of thing is that to say?"

"It's not like I think you can't do better," Ian said. "You're certainly smart enough."

"I'll see you in two days," I said.

•   •   •

Ian arrived an hour and a half later than I expected. I watched
with irritation from the dining-room window as he got out of
his car and ran to the door. He stood on the front steps, shiver-
ing in his thin army jacket. When he handed me his jacket to
hang up I noticed his sweater. It was royal blue with a wavy
yellow stripe across the front. It reminded me of the paint job
in my high school lunchroom.

"Christmas present?" I said, pulling away from his embrace
and staring at the sweater.

"Yeah, isn't it funny? It's like, so ugly it's cool."

"I wouldn't go that far."

Mom was just around the corner, in the kitchen. William
was skulking around in the basement, protesting the visit because of my grades.

I brought Ian into the kitchen. Mom stood at the sink beam-
ing, her hands clasped together. She was wearing the yellow
rubber gloves she wore when she washed the pots and pans.
Her half empty glass of white wine sat on the counter next to
the sink.

"This is my mom," I said.

"Hi Eye-an, are you hungry from your trip?" Mom asked.

"Mom, It's Ee-an. Not Eye-an."

"Actually, either pronunciation is technically correct," Ian
said. A fresh wave of contempt washed over me.

"Can I fix you something?" Mom asked.

"I could eat."

I stole a sip from Mom's glass of wine while she pulled Tupperware out of the refrigerator and put it in the microwave. I hadn't
noticed until now that Ian wasn't one to say please or thank you.

I watched Ian in his ugly sweater gobble down the rest of

the Christmas leftovers. The turkey and stuffing were mashed together on a small plate, the gravy congealing in places that hadn't heated all the way. It was weird to have him here, in this world, seeing where I came from. I didn't like it.

But this was Ian. After he finished eating we would put his bag upstairs in the guest room and then we'd go for a ride in his car and smoke cigarettes, and everything would be back to normal. I was looking forward to smoking. Mom and William still didn't know, and I'd had to make do on only a couple a day. And Lyle was having people over. I was anxious to show Ian off, ugly sweater and all.

Carrie was the first one to greet us. She rushed forward with her arms outstretched, like she hadn't seen me in years. When we hugged I could smell her Finesse shampoo.

"Mike's here," she whispered into my ear, and then louder, "Is this the new boyfriend?"

Ian squeezed my hand. "He's not new," I said. She was worse than my mother.

"He's new to us," Carrie said. Mike was hunched over the stereo, examining a record. His hair had grown out some since I had last seen him.

Ian accepted a Milwaukee's Best from Lyle and took a seat on the couch. Then he hooked his fingers through my belt loops and pulled me onto his lap. I opened my beer and slid off Ian's lap into the space beside him. People were scattered here and there throughout Lyle's basement, drinking beer and stepping outside every few minutes to smoke. There were a couple of younger guys there I didn't recognize, but other than that Lyle's basement was the same as ever.

"How's the band?" I asked Lyle. Mike looked over at me and then back down at the record he was holding. I had gotten a postcard from him the second week of school. The front of the postcard was a picture of the Washington Monument. On the back he had written, *I hope we stay friends, even though you're in college now. I won't say that I miss you 'cause I don't want you to get the wrong idea but I don't want there to be anything bad between us either.* Next to his words was a doodle of a guitar.

I was impressed by the gesture, even though he'd managed to find a way to reject me at the same time. It was the most Mike had said to me about our relationship since we had broken up. I sent him back a postcard of an aerial view of campus. On the back I wrote, *I hope we can stay friends, too. I'll never forget you or think anything negative about you.* I pondered whether the last sentence was too dramatic, but ended up mailing it anyway. I didn't hear back from him, and we hadn't spoken since. I had taken his drawings to school. Instead of hanging them up I kept them hidden in my desk drawer, as if he might surprise me in my dorm room one day. Once in a while I took them out of their hiding place and thought about what Mike might be doing. If there was a girl he liked.

Lyle nodded toward the drum set that was set up in the corner. "I'm thinking I'm going to officially switch from singing to drums," he said.

The Minor Threat album that had been playing ended and Mike put on the record he was holding, which turned out to be Dag Nasty. I hadn't listened to Dag Nasty in months.

"Wow. So Reston really is all hardcore all the time," Ian said. He said it like it was something I had told him. Mike looked over at Ian with interest, and I felt myself blush.

"Sit tight," Lyle said. "We're gonna break out the disco as soon as we get drunk enough." He thrust his hip out to the side and pointed one finger into the air. Carrie rolled her eyes.

"Hi, Mike," I called out.

Mike waved but didn't come over. If Ian guessed that Mike was my ex-boyfriend, he wasn't saying.

Theresa arrived just as we were leaving.

"Hi and bye," she said.

"Cool glasses," Ian said.

The next day while Mom and William were out at the grocery store Ian and I had sex in my bedroom. My room was exactly as I had left it, from the hardcore flyers to the gray bedspread to the faded gray rug. I couldn't get over the feeling that Ian didn't belong here.

"Is something wrong?" he asked afterward. I was already out of bed, pulling my jeans back on.

"No, it's just, you know, it's just weird being in my parents' house. In my room and everything with you here. I mean, what if they come back?"

Ian propped himself up on the bed on one arm. "Haven't you had sex in here before?"

"No," I said. I shoved my hair into a ponytail and hurried downstairs to the kitchen.

I turned on the TV and plopped into one of the kitchen chairs. *General Hospital* was on. A woman I didn't recognize was lying in a hospital bed, crying to a nurse.

"I can't lose my baby," the woman moaned. Her mascara was running.

Ian came downstairs and opened the refrigerator. I watched him get a glass down from the cabinet and fill it with orange juice. He was barefoot.

"Want anything from the fridge?" he asked.

"No thanks." I could hear the garage door going up. Mom and William were home.

Ian came over and stood by me. "I don't know how you can watch that crap," he said. "It's absolutely soul-killing."

William came through the doorway, holding two bags of groceries in his arms. Mom was right behind him.

"I couldn't have put it better myself," William said. He set his bags down on the counter and straightened back up. He and Ian were looking at me with identical expressions of contempt. I turned back to the TV, feeling sick to my stomach.

That night I stayed awake long after everyone else was in bed, listening to Dag Nasty in the dark on my Walkman. Tomorrow we were going back to school. I moved my pillow out of the way and lay flat on my back. My breath felt tight in my throat.

I took off my Walkman and crept down the hall to Ian's room. I could hear William snoring. I pushed open Ian's door and sat on the edge of the bed. Ian had rolled himself up in the blankets like he was in a cocoon. It was the way he liked to sleep. This was the room where Mom sewed. I could make out the shape of the sewing machine in the corner and the wicker picnic basket under the window, where she kept spools of thread and needles and scissors.

Ian stirred and sat up, tilted forward to kiss me.

I leaned away from him. "That's not why I came in here," I whispered.

"Are you all right? What's the matter?"

It didn't seem possible that he wouldn't know what was coming. But as I said the words, "I don't want to go out with you anymore," his face crumpled and I understood he hadn't known. I was tempted, watching his face slip into sadness, to take it back, to say something that would make him feel like this was a fight instead of a breakup.

"I just don't feel the way I'm supposed to feel," I said.

Ian clenched the blankets in both hands, but kept silent.

"It's like we don't get each other," I said. I stood up.

At first I slept lightly, awakening with every sound, worrying that it was Ian coming to confront me. Finally I fell into a heavy, dreamless sleep, only to be awakened a few hours later by sounds from the kitchen. I threw back the covers and slunk downstairs.

Ian was fully dressed and sitting on a stool at the counter, eating toast with jam and drinking coffee. Mom was unloading the dishwasher. "I visited England when I was your age," she was saying. "I didn't get to spend nearly enough time there, but I loved it. I keep meaning to go back one of these days."

"Mmm," Ian said. His mouth was full of toast. I poured a glass of orange juice and walked around him to sit at the table. Mom opened the silverware drawer and dropped a stack of clean forks inside. I had no idea that she'd ever been to England. I thought of the way she looked in her wedding album. Her long, wavy black hair. I wondered if Dad was with her in England, or if she'd gone with someone else. Maybe she'd had a British boyfriend, too. I wanted to ask her about it but it didn't seem right, in front of Ian.

After my orange juice I took a long shower. I took my time packing my things while Ian waited downstairs. When I was ready, Ian helped me carry my bags outside and load them into his trunk.

"Do you think you have enough shit here?" Ian slammed the trunk closed, and his car swayed back and forth.

"It's just my laundry plus some stuff I got for Christmas," I said. I turned back toward the house, where my mother was waiting to say good-bye. It was then that I remembered that Ian and I hadn't exchanged Christmas presents. I hadn't gotten him anything at all.

Ian waited in the car, gunning his engine, while I hugged Mom.

"I'm sorry William isn't here to say good-bye," she said. I nodded. William had gotten up earlier than usual and gone into the office.

"Bye, Eye-an!" Mom yelled. Ian jerked the car away from the curb.

Once we were on the highway he finally spoke.

"Your mother told me this morning that you were really disappointed in your report card, and that you were going to be making a lot of changes when you got back to school."

"Yeah, well." I took a cigarette out of his pack and lit it. I caught sight of myself in the side mirror; there were dark circles under my eyes and my hair was even flatter than usual.

Ian shifted in his seat. "So I was trying to figure out who you're going to go out with now," he said. He had sped up and was tailgating a station wagon. "I'm guessing Andrew. I assumed he was a fag or something, but you're always talking about how funny he is."

I opened my mouth and then shut it again. "If you're going to act like this the whole way home, you can just drop me off at the bus station," I said.

We drove in silence for two hours. When I got hungry I asked if we could stop somewhere for lunch. Ian acted as if he hadn't heard me, and then made a show of speeding up to pass the next exit that had a sign for food. I turned off the radio and sulked in my seat until he finally found a McDonald's. We ate our Big Macs in the parking lot, and then Ian sped back out to the highway, screeching the wheels as he made turns. When he wasn't cutting people off, he was tailgating. I locked my knees and waited for us to crash.

It wasn't until we passed the first sign for Virginia Tech that Ian spoke again.

"I hope you know what you're doing," he said, "because you don't just break up with someone for no reason."

"I know."

"When I met you I thought you were mature for your age," he said. "But you're not. You're a child. A freshman."

"I can't help how old I am," I said.

"You'll probably be like this your whole life."

It was only a few minutes past five, but it was getting dark.

I thought about the first trip I made to Virginia Tech the August before. It seemed unbelievable that only five months had
gone by.

"You have no concept of what it means to love someone."
Ian was yelling now, and his accent was almost gone.

I reached for a cigarette. "We never said we loved each
other," I said. "We never talked about that."

"You want me to tell you I love you? Is that what you want?"

My hands were shaking. "I just know I don't want to go out
anymore. That's all."

"That's all? You just don't want to?"

"I'm sorry," I said.

We were heading into town, past the Ford dealership and
the Photomat and Kroger Foods. I stubbed my cigarette out and
pushed the ashtray in. We passed the turnoff to Ian's apartment
and continued on toward campus and my dorm. I hoped Julie
was back. Maybe the dining hall was open. I wanted to see Andrew and Sam and Mark. Even Cynthia.

Ian pulled over in front of my building and turned the engine off. Students were herding themselves inside, dragging
large suitcases and plastic bags. I had that long-car-trip feeling: I
wanted to eat and sleep and shower all at the same time.

He surprised me by carrying most of my bags to my room,
leaving only a duffel bag and my new boom box for me to
carry. Even though he carried more weight than I did, he
walked quickly and I lagged behind. I watched the way his hair
curled over his jacket collar. When I'd met him, his hair had
been shorter. I concentrated on how this was the last time I
would see him here, climbing the stairs of my dorm.

It took me a minute to find my keys. Ian let out a dramatic
sigh. When I got the door open he stepped past me and dumped
my stuff in the center of the room. There was a crash, like
something had broken. Laura wasn't home, but her clarinet case
was on her bed.

I sat on the edge of my desk. "I think it would be better if we didn't talk for a week or so," I said. "And then maybe we can—"

Ian had lurched out into the hallway, slamming the door behind him. His footsteps were drowned out by the sound of my phone ringing.

six BRENDAN

Other people went to Florida for spring break, or volunteered for Habitat for Humanity. I went home to Reston.

Mike's mom and sister were out of town visiting his grandparents, and according to Carrie he was having people over Friday night. I cut my last couple of classes and got home late Friday afternoon.

I hadn't seen anyone since Christmas, and I wanted to look good for the party. My roots had grown past what I thought of as my Debbie Harry stage into something I was just going to have to wait out. I was growing my bangs out, too, and had taken to wearing a wide, black headband every day. I thought the headband made me look mod.

It was spring break, but it was still cold out. I put on the gray crewneck sweater I wore practically every day at school, and my baggy blue-and-gray-satin pajama pants. I'd bought the pajama pants the summer before at Classic Clothing, a used-clothing store in D.C. Classic Clothing was dark and dusty and jammed with racks of old clothes. Up front under a glass counter they kept vintage pocket books and white gloves and plastic cigarette holders and sunglasses with rhinestones on them. I felt artistic and cool when I shopped there. I bought the pants, which weren't something I would ordinarily wear, because the cute, older salesclerk said they looked good on me.

"That's what I like to call an exact fit," he said, circling behind me when I came out of the dressing room. The pants had an elastic waistband and were baggy all the way to my ankles. The salesclerk was wearing a turquoise and black bowling shirt with the name RICKY stitched onto the left pocket, and his dark hair was gelled up into a perfect pompadour. He had a tattoo of a pinup girl on his forearm, and he was smoking right inside the store. The pants were more than I could afford, but I bought them anyway. Whenever I wore them I thought of cute Ricky with his tattoo and his cigarette.

"Don't be surprised if Mike gets all flirty with you," Carrie said on the ride over. "He hasn't gotten any action in forever, and today he came by my locker to ask me if you were getting back in time to come over. Then at lunch he asked me if you were going out with anyone."

"I'll try not to take it personally," I said. I pulled my cigarettes out of my coat pocket and lit one, cracking the car window as I did so. I understood how Mike felt. In the three months since breaking up with Ian I hadn't kissed a single boy. Neither had Julie. We told ourselves it was because we spent all our time with Andrew and Sam. But my grades had gotten better. That was something.

It wasn't much of a party. The same Minor Threat blared

out of the stereo while the same bored people stared blankly around the living room. Adam Schreiber was being his usual self, sneering over his beer. I wondered why I had been looking forward to this so much. I was sorry that Theresa's spring break was a week later than mine.

Mike rushed in from the kitchen and hugged me. I waited to feel attracted, but nothing happened. Brendan Davis wandered in behind him. I didn't know Brendan very well because he had spent most of high school completing various rehab programs. He had a world-weary air about him, like an old man. He was carrying two beers, one stacked up on the other. I caught a whiff of patchouli as he passed me.

"Hey," Brendan muttered in my direction.

"Hi."

I watched him arrange himself on the couch next to Adam. There was a large, yellowing bruise on his forearm.

"You need a beer. I'll be right back," Mike said.

I went over to a brown, fake-leather La-Z-Boy and sat down. I pulled the handle and flipped the leg rest out and then back in again. Mike reappeared with my beer.

"Hey, Polly, want a bong hit?" he said. "I think you remember where everything is." He pointed up at the ceiling.

"That's okay. I don't really smoke pot anymore."

"Does it make you paranoid? That's what happened to Adam for a while, but then he got over it."

I held up my can of Budweiser. "I don't like to combine."

Lyle came up behind Mike. "Do you have pot for everyone, or just for people with high school diplomas?"

The two of them went upstairs. After a minute, Carrie followed. I watched her body vanish as she climbed the stairs. Black thermal shirt, red and green kilt, black tights, black boots. Red and green kilt, black tights, black boots. Black tights, black boots. Black boots.

I swiveled the La-Z-Boy. Todd Wilson was standing at the

entrance to the kitchen, drinking by himself. He hadn't changed a bit since I'd last seen him: skinny, pasty, noticeably drunk already—he reminded me of a blond Sid Vicious. And there was something of his brother there, too, around the mouth. Even the way he raised his beer to his lips seemed mean. I swiveled again before he could catch me staring.

Brendan cleared his throat. "So things have really changed around here, huh Polly?"

"If you say so."

I got up from my chair and went to the kitchen to get another beer, finishing the one I already had on the way. Todd nodded when I passed by him, and my stomach tensed up. I wanted him to follow me into the kitchen, to look at me like I was something he wanted.

The next few hours slipped by without incident. We drank beer and talked about bands and drugs. We figured out what was going on in other people's love lives. We smoked cigarettes in the backyard.

I was hanging out in the kitchen when Carrie asked if I was ready to go.

"Since I have a car now, I can drive you home if you want," Mike said before I could answer. He had told me about the car earlier. It was an old brown Datsun stick shift with 150,000 miles on it that he had talked his mother into buying from their neighbor. I was impressed that Mike had learned to drive a stick shift.

Peering around Lyle and Carrie, I glanced into the living room. I hadn't exchanged a single word with Todd all night. I didn't see him, but his leather jacket was lying across the back of the couch.

"How are we doing on beer?" I asked.

"We can always break into the liquor cabinet." Brendan was sitting on the counter, his baggy work pants fluffed out around him on the Formica. I looked into his hooded, bloodshot eyes.

"Liquor after beer will make you sick," I said.

"Polly, do you think you can make a decision on this?" Carrie said. "Some of us still have curfews."

"Okay," I said. "I'll stay."

Mike clapped his hands together and hooted, and I felt a wave of embarrassment come over me. He walked over to the fridge and opened it with the bravado of a magician's assistant.

"Uh-oh, I think there's only one left," he said, still rooting around in the refrigerator as Carrie and Lyle shut the door behind them. He straightened up. "Are you sure you don't want to get stoned?"

"Let's just split it," I said.

Since the beer was gone the rest of the party emptied out within fifteen minutes. Todd took off without so much as a backward glance at me. I was alone with Mike, Adam, and Brendan.

"I guess I'm ready to go," I said.

But Mike was driving Adam and Brendan home, too, and they wanted to get stoned again before we left. As I looked for my coat, I tried not to think about whether Mike was okay to drive.

I was coming out of the downstairs bathroom when Brendan loomed up before me, close enough to make me stumble backward. I could smell his patchouli.

"Jeeze, look out," I said, stepping around him.

He kissed me, grabbing me in his arms as if we had been waiting to be alone together. For a second I kissed him back. A part of me was flattered. Even when the biggest loser I knew kissed me, there it was.

I pulled away from him. "I don't really, you know, I don't really like you like that," I said. I edged toward the front door.

Brendan's face was uncomprehending. He gestured toward the staircase that led to the basement. "Can we at least talk?" He looked up at the ceiling. "Will you come downstairs?"

I folded my arms in front of me. "Talk about what?" I asked.

"About this."

I followed him down the basement stairwell, which was wallpapered with the same garish floral pattern that covered the basement walls. Brendan sat down in the middle of the couch, so he was on both cushions. I sat on the arm. There was dim light from the stairwell, but other than that the room was dark. I knew Brendan was probably going to try to kiss me again, but now I was prepared. I would tell him that we could be friends. I would remind him that Mike was my ex-boyfriend, and Brendan was Mike's friend.

I was reaching for the lamp that sat on the side table when I felt him on me. He pulled me down onto the couch and pushed his face into mine. He was half kissing me, and half holding my head in place. I struggled to move out from under him.

"Jesus Christ," I said. "Get off me."

Brendan gathered my wrists together and brought them up over my head while I wriggled and grunted. When I tried to yank my wrists free, he tightened his grip.

The reality of what was happening dawned on me, and I shut my eyes. Then I opened them. It was worse with my eyes closed.

Brendan put his mouth back on mine. He was holding my wrists with one hand. With his other hand, he yanked the elastic waist of my pajama pants until it was halfway down my thighs. He tugged my underwear down after them. Beer swirled around in my stomach and traveled partway into my chest. I broke my face free of Brendan's face.

"You have to stop," I said. My voice sounded strange. Matter of fact.

He shifted his weight on top of me. I heard the slow, quiet sound of his pants unzipping. I thought about Mike and Adam two floors above us.

I cried out when he got inside me, and Brendan forced his tongue further into my mouth. He brought his hips down against mine. The smell of patchouli and pot only faintly covered the sharp smell of his body odor, and our muffled breathing was the only sound in the quiet. Again I tried to yank my wrists free, but his grip was still too tight. I let myself go limp.

He took his tongue out of my mouth, gasped for air.

I turned my head to the side, away from his face. "You'll get me pregnant," I said. He didn't answer me.

"I'll get pregnant," I said again. And then more times. "I'll get pregnant you'll get me pregnant I don't want to get pregnant just please stop just stop."

Then he did stop, tearing out of me like he had only just now heard what I was saying. I had not felt him come. He lifted up and released my arms, and I felt the blood begin to circulate back into my wrists.

Brendan stood and pulled his pants up. My eyes had adjusted to the dark, and I could see a flash of white skin beside me. He wasn't wearing any underwear. My pants and underwear were still bunched up around my knees, exposing my dark, full pubic hair that stretched from thigh to thigh. I hadn't shaved in more than two months.

I jerked my pants up, scrambled to my feet. Brendan stepped out of my way and I ran up the basement stairs and into the living room. I could hear Mike strumming his guitar upstairs. I opened the front door and ran down the porch steps and across the yard and to the sidewalk. The cold hit me all at once.

It was too far to walk home. Slowly I crossed the front yard and sat down on the porch steps. It wasn't even a real porch, just a tiny structure tacked on to the front of the house, supported by two pillars scarcely five feet apart. The porch matched all the others on the street. The whole neighborhood looked like it was made out of plastic. There wasn't a single tree to block out the hideous, man-made landscape. I wanted to burn it all down and start over. Let Mike's house burn with Brendan still in it.

I wrapped my arms around myself and breathed in. Then I closed my eyes and opened them again. I didn't feel drunk anymore.

I heard the door open behind me. Brendan was holding my coat in one hand and a cigarette in the other. I stood up. On the porch steps I was much shorter than Brendan, though in fact he was the same height as me. He was one of those guys who was big through the shoulders and had thick arms and legs, which made him formidable despite his height.

He held my coat out. I grabbed it by the hem so I wouldn't have to touch him. One of my gloves slipped out of the pocket, and we both leaned over to pick it up. The glove was one of my mother's old black leather gloves. Mom called them her driving gloves, though she didn't wear them just for driving. She teased me when I pulled them down from the top of the coat closet and asked if I could have them. They were nearly worn through in places, but I loved them. They were broken in just right, and they reminded me of my mother at her most glamorous, when she had worn dark sunglasses and shift dresses and high heels every day. This was how she looked when she met William.

I reached the glove before Brendan did. I was conscious of his stare as I straightened up, stuffed the glove in my pocket, and then pulled on my coat. Smoke from his cigarette wafted over to me. My zipper stuck, and I struggled with it.

"I'm sorry," he said. For a second I thought he was referring to the trouble I was having with my zipper.

"I guess we're both pretty drunk tonight, huh," he said.

I gave up on the zipper. "Give me a cigarette," I said. I wanted to sound tough.

Brendan took a pack of Camel Filters from the front pocket of his pants and tossed them at me. I caught them easily. If this had happened an hour ago I might have remarked on my good hand–eye coordination. I pushed the matchbook out from between the pack and the plastic wrapping. There was an advertisement for a phone sex number printed across the matchbook in red. "We'll make your fantasies come true," the matchbook promised. I lit my cigarette and threw the pack back, aiming for Brendan's chest. It fell short and landed at his feet. I watched him bend over to pick it up as smoke traveled into my throat and chest. Instead of a coat he was wearing a thin pullover with a hood, the kind surfers and hippies wore. I stifled a cough. I wasn't used to the harshness of his cigarettes. I smoked only lights.

"I'm really sorry," he said.

I dropped my cigarette and stepped on it. I could smell his patchouli everywhere. It was on me, on him, hanging in the air between us. I made a break for the front door, cutting as wide a circle around him as I could manage on the tiny porch. Brendan stayed perfectly still, staring at the spot I had just been in. When I got inside I slammed the door behind me. The carpet slowed the door down, and it bounced softly against its frame.

When I got home I sat at the kitchen table, listening to the ticking of the antique grandfather clock in the foyer. I looked at the digital clock on the microwave. It was 1:37. Not early, but not late either. Nothing in the kitchen looked real. Not the beige cloth toaster and blender covers. Not the dark brown floor tiles. Not the rust-colored countertops. Not Mom's pink and orange carnival glass that she kept on display in a glass cabinet. Not yesterday's newspaper stacked in the corner. All of it seemed like props, like plastic imitations you'd see in a model home kitchen.

Already I was starting to feel like it had happened to someone else. I felt like someone trying to recall what it was like to be hypnotized or have an out-of-body experience.

I hadn't screamed. If I'd screamed, Mike and Adam would have heard, and Brendan would have stopped. Or maybe Mike and Adam would have come downstairs and seen us. I hated the idea of them seeing me like that. Would they have understood what was happening?

I let go of the screaming scenario. Instead I pictured myself somehow pulling the lamp off the side table and crashing it over Brendan's head. I doubted the lamp would have knocked him out, so maybe I would have just gotten a black eye for my trouble. Still, I could have tried.

I didn't want to think about it anymore. I got up from the table and crept upstairs to my room. Mom was a light sleeper, so I was careful to take it slow on the stairs. If I woke her she'd turn the light on in the hallway before going to the bathroom to pee. Depending on her mood, she might cross the hall to my room and tell me to get to sleep.

I changed into a T-shirt and got into bed. I was exhausted, but I still couldn't sleep. There was something else that was bothering me, something important. I wasn't convinced Brendan knew what he had done to me. The way he'd said he was sorry made it sound like he'd spilled beer on me or something. Maybe he didn't think he had really raped me. Maybe he thought he'd done something short of that, something that meant saying he was sorry was enough.

And I'd told him I was scared of getting pregnant. I was mad at myself for that. It was true, of course, but that wasn't the main reason I wanted him off me. I wanted him to know I hadn't wanted him.

And he hadn't come. If he didn't have an orgasm, what was the point?

• • •

The phone woke me up in the morning. I wasn't about to answer it. I felt as if I hadn't slept at all. I dragged myself out of
bed, pulled on a pair of sweatpants, and staggered down the hall
to the bathroom. I sat down on the toilet, barely remembering
to kick the door shut behind me. My urine felt like it was pouring from an open wound, and I pressed my forehead into my
knees to keep from crying out. When I was finished I checked
for blood on the toilet paper and in my underwear, but there
wasn't any. It felt like there should have been blood.

I went down to the kitchen. Mom and William were sitting
at the kitchen table. A jar of mayonnaise, a loaf of bread, cold
cuts, and a bag of chips were spread out before them.

"There's cereal in the cabinet, if you'd rather have breakfast
than lunch," Mom said. I grunted and opened the refrigerator
door. I wasn't ready to hold a conversation yet, much less eat
solid food.

"Or there's bread and cold cuts here, if you'd rather have
that."

"Jesus, Fran, she has eyes in her head," William said. His
mouth was full of sandwich.

I poured a glass of orange juice and eased into a chair, ignoring the pain in my crotch as I sat down. I blinked into a
sunbeam that bored through a space in the window blinds like
a searchlight.

"Honey, you don't have socks on. You're going to catch a
cold."

I slowly turned my head in Mom's direction, holding back
the tears. I studied her turquoise sweatshirt. I wasn't ready to
look into her face yet. "I'll put something on in a minute," I
said. "I'm not quite awake yet."

"If you ask me, I think someone needs to cut back on her alcohol intake," William said. "You look like you've been beat up." He shoved a handful of chips into his mouth.

"Well, nobody's asking you," I said.

Mom pushed her chair back and carried her plate over to the sink. "That was Mike who called just now," she said as she turned on the faucet.

I spent the afternoon on the couch in front of the television. When the balm of the TV wore off I went upstairs to shower. The heat of the water was soothing, but I couldn't keep my mind off Brendan Davis. Maybe I'd moved my hips when he'd gotten inside me. Maybe just at first, from the memory of being with Ian. Maybe I had. I couldn't be sure. As I dried myself off I thought about how on TV rape victims scrubbed themselves raw under scalding water as soon as they got home. These women also tended to do things like call the police and get forensic reports. Hardly anybody believed them, but at least they tried.

Instead of packing for spring break I had brought my laundry home. While I'd been watching television, Mom had washed and stacked a month's worth of clean clothes on my bed. When I came in from the shower and saw what Mom had done I wanted to curl up on her lap and bawl, like I had when I was little. I wanted Mom to run her hands up and down my back and tell me I was going to be okay. I waited for the tears to come, but they didn't.

For the first time that day I thought about food. I would brush my teeth, get dressed, eat a decent meal. I was still me. I could do these things. I draped my towel over my desk chair and dressed myself with random items from Mom's piles. A pair of gray cotton underwear. A black bra. My favorite Ramones T-shirt.

I was pulling my jeans from the middle of one of the stacks

when I saw them. My blue and gray pajama pants, resting between my long-sleeved thermal undershirt and my black hooded sweatshirt. My clothes from last night had been in a pile beside my bed. Mom must have scooped them up with the rest of my laundry.

I grabbed the pants, knocking the pile over. I turned them around in my hands, examining them for evidence, stroking the dull, worn satin. I wasn't sure what I was looking for exactly, but my pants had survived Brendan Davis intact. There wasn't so much as a frayed seam to indicate what they'd been through. I refolded the pants and set them back down on the bed, away from the rest of my clothes. I couldn't imagine wearing them again, but I didn't want to throw them away either. Finally I decided to hide them at the top of my closet, between my parents' wedding pictures and my old yearbooks.

I put my jeans on and combed out my hair. I looked around for my headband. It wasn't anywhere. I moved my clothes to the top of my dresser and pulled my bedding apart. It wasn't there either. Finally I gave up and shoved my hair into a ponytail.

Hiding out during the week wasn't hard, but I had the problem of the weekend to sort out. There were bands playing at the high school Saturday night for some sort of benefit. Since I wasn't going back to school until Sunday, I had told everyone at Mike's party that I was going. Massive Hemorrhage was playing, along with just about every other Reston hardcore band. It was safe to assume that everyone I knew would be there. It was safe to assume that Brendan Davis would be there.

I could tell Carrie I was sick. But a small, crazy part of me wanted to see Brendan again. I was sure that something in his face would confirm what I needed confirming. I needed to know that I had a real reason to feel the way I did.

• • •

Saturday Mom woke me up early to go shopping. I was too tired to think of a good reason why I couldn't go. Besides, it was time. I hadn't left the house in a week.

Mom kept one hand on top of the steering wheel and rested the other on the gearshift while she drove, like always. The sight of it made me mad. I was mad at everything familiar, especially the way Mom kept up with her domestic habits and rituals. Running the dishwasher when it was full, laundry twice a week, keeping the bathroom clean. Her daughter had been raped, but there were things around the house that needed to get done.

I tore my attention away from Mom's hands and stared out the window, listening to the dull hum of the car's engine. Reston was ill-suited to the depressed, with its neat rows of houses and manicured lawns. We passed the golf course and the man-made lake. Freshly painted rowboats were thoughtfully secured to well-built docks. If I wasn't an outsider before, now it was official.

In Hecht's I sifted through a pile of T-shirts while Debbie Gibson's sexy, childish balloon voice blasted from a speaker directly above me. I could see Mom over in Shoes, examining the size-nine sale rack. Her tan raincoat was slung over one arm. I drifted over to a row of junior dresses that were 30 percent off. I scraped one hanger after another across the rack. I didn't wear dresses. Maybe I would start.

I watched Mom slip off her loafers and try on a pair of brown pumps. I could walk over to the shoe department and say it. *Mom, I got raped over at Mike's house last Saturday.* It would be that easy.

Mom walked to the end of the size-nine sale rack and examined her feet in the shoe mirror. What would she say when
I told her? Would she comfort me? Would she stop what she
was doing and wrap herself around me, like she had when I told
her that Mike's dad was dead? Would she get angry? Would she
blame me? Would she tell William? Would she call the police?
Would she call my father? Would she cry? I didn't want her
to cry.

"See anything?" Mom was holding a shoe box that had an
orange sticker on the side. The orange sticker meant the shoes
were 25 percent off. Yellow was 50 percent off.

"Not really. It's hard when you don't have anything in
mind."

"Isn't there anything you need for school?"

I studied her wide, dark eyes. Ask, I thought. Just ask.

"I don't see anything," I said.

I called Carrie when I got home.

"Where the fuck have you been?" she said. "I was starting to
think you had some kind of family tragedy or something."

"I was sick," I said. "But now I'm better."

"You don't have anything contagious, do you? I just got over
strep two weeks ago, and if I get sick again I'll kill myself."

"I don't think so. I feel fine now."

"Do you still want to go out tonight?"

I stayed in the shower a long time, deep conditioning my hair
and shaving everything that needed shaving. I blew my hair dry
and brushed it until it was glossy. At the mall I had found a

black headband identical to the one I had lost, and I fitted it carefully behind my ears. I wore jeans (button fly—Brendan would have had trouble with these), boots, a black sweater, and my army jacket. I put on red lipstick. I looked normal. Happy. Adjusted.

I went downstairs to wait. Mom was in the kitchen, chopping onions at the counter. There was olive oil heating up in a frying pan on the stove. I sat on a stool on the other side of the counter.

"I've been meaning to talk to you," Mom said. She kept her eyes on her chopping.

"What about?"

"You don't know this, but your father had some trouble with depression when he was your age. That was when he started drinking."

I checked out the window for Carrie's headlights. "I guess that makes sense," I said.

Mom stopped chopping and brought the cutting board over to the stove. There was the hiss of the onions hitting the pan.

"You remind me of him," she said. She wiped away onion tears with one sleeve as she carried the cutting board over to the sink.

"Like how?"

"Your sense of humor, for one. And he has a head for numbers." She was at the refrigerator, rooting around in the crisper.

"I didn't know Dad was good at math."

"Where do you think you got it? Not from me."

"I never thought about it."

Mom shut the refrigerator door without getting anything out.

"Polly, I want you to talk to me about this depression of yours."

"I'm not depressed."

"Honey, I know depressed when I see it."

"Where's William?" I asked.

"He ran over to the hardware store."

I shifted on my stool. The room smelled like onions. "I got raped," I said.

Mom went over to the stove and turned off the burner.

"Someone you know?"

I looked down at the countertop. "Sort of. Not really."

Mom exhaled, and my eyes filled with tears.

"Don't tell William," I said.

"I won't." She came over to my side of the counter and stood beside me. After a minute I leaned into her, and she put an arm around me. I had stopped crying.

"This happens to a lot of women," Mom said. "It's not your fault."

"I feel like shit," I said into her shirt.

"I know."

Outside, Carrie honked her horn. I hadn't heard her pull up. I straightened up and looked out the kitchen window. I could see Lyle's elbow poking out the car window. He was wearing his leather jacket. His elbow went up and then down again. Lyle used his hands when he spoke.

"I have to go," I said.

"I was supposed to be there to help set up," Lyle was saying as I got in the car.

"You're not even playing first," Carrie said, louder than she needed to. She looked like she wanted to kick him out of the car.

"Howdy, folks," I said.

"You know, Lyle, if you had to be there so early you could

have found someone else to drive you," Carrie said. "I'm not the only person in Reston with a car."

"But you're my girlfriend," Lyle said.

I saw Mike as soon as we turned into the parking lot. He was sitting on the curb near the lane that was for school buses during the week. He stood up as soon as he caught sight of us and jogged the short distance to where we were parking. Carrie beeped her horn and waved, but Mike kept his arms at his sides. His expression reminded me of the one he wore when he couldn't figure something out on the guitar.

"He's pissed that I'm late," Lyle said. "Shit."

"You're a slut," Mike said as soon as I got out of the car.

I looked around to see if anyone had heard him. We were late by Lyle's standards but early by audience standards. Except for Carrie and Lyle, everyone was out of earshot.

"I know you fucked Brendan Davis," he said.

I stepped around him, and Mike grabbed my arm. Carrie and Lyle stood off to the side, watching.

"That's not what happened," I said.

Mike held up my missing headband. "I've been trying to call you all week," he said. "Look what I found on the couch in my basement."

I felt the blood rush to my face. "That's not what happened," I said again. I was dimly aware of a group of people getting out of a car across the parking lot, turning off the radio, laughing, slamming doors.

Mike let go of my arm. "You're a slut," he said. "You were with Brendan in my house."

"He raped me," I said. I turned around and pulled on the passenger door handle of the car. It was locked. Carrie hurried forward, her keys in her hand.

"He raped you?"

I could tell he didn't believe me. Carrie got the door open and I sat down. Mike grabbed the door before I could shut it.

"Brendan raped you?"

Lyle put his hand on Mike's shoulder. "Mike man, leave her alone."

Mike shook Lyle off and kept staring at me. I'd never seen him this angry. I thought he might actually hit me, but then all at once his face sagged and his expression turned desperate. He let go of the door and I slammed it shut.

"Both of you just get out of here." Carrie's words were muffled through the door. Mike and Lyle started off toward the school and Carrie went around to the driver's side of the car and got in. I pushed the car lighter in.

"Why didn't you tell me?" she asked.

"I don't know. It's not exactly something I was dying to talk about."

"You should have told me, though."

"I know."

"So what happened?"

The car lighter popped out and I pressed it to my cigarette. "Down in Mike's basement. After you guys left."

"So he just jumped you? Jesus. You must have been so freaked. Did you just start screaming or what?"

I exhaled and watched the smoke melt into the windshield. Mike had thrown my headband, and now it rested on the right wiper.

"I think I forgot to scream," I said. "It's complicated."

"I can't believe you didn't tell me. This is totally huge."

"I'm sorry," I said.

"Oh, God!" Carrie's cigarette froze in midair. "Brendan's probably here."

I shrugged. "I know."

"If I were you, I wouldn't go in there."

• • •

As we entered the school I was struck by the leaden, oppressive school smell of mildew and, as we neared the gymnasium, the hot, stale odor of old sweat. The dull paint job and low ceilings were so familiar, I felt as if it had been nine days instead of nine months since I had been in the building.

Lyle was waiting for us by the door to the gym. He took Carrie's hand without looking at me. Carrie and I paid the five-dollar admission and got our hands stamped, and then I pushed the heavy doors open and we stepped inside. Guns N' Roses blasted out of the P.A. system. People moved around the gym in clumps. Some of them were lugging band equipment. Todd Wilson passed us, his guitar case dangling from one muscled arm. He curled his lip up as our eyes met, and I looked away.

"Lyle, come talk to me for a second," Carrie said.

Lyle looked toward the stage. "I need to set up."

"I'll come with you," she said. "We need to talk." They hurried away from me. "We'll be right back," Carrie said over her shoulder.

I nodded. Mike was at the foot of the stage, talking to Adam. Adam was holding up his hands and shaking his head. Then Brendan Davis came around the corner and was standing beside them, and I felt the floor drop out from under me. I looked around for Carrie, or anyone I might know. There were scarcely thirty yards separating me from Brendan.

I looked back over in time to see Mike give Brendan a shove. Brendan took a step backward, his brown flannel shirt swinging out behind him. Then Brendan put both his hands on Mike's shoulders. He was saying something. Mike shook his head and looked down at the floor.

Adam was staring at me. I edged along the wall until I got to the water fountain. I needed to find someone to stand beside.

Adam tapped Brendan and pointed, and Brendan fixed his eyes on me and started walking.

I ran. I dodged legs and backpacks and amps and various-sized drums that were moving through the growing crowd. I plunged out the gymnasium doors and down an empty hallway until I reached the girl's bathroom. I ran all the way to the far wall of the bathroom and sank down on the tile, gasping for breath.

One of the sink faucets was dripping as steady as a metronome. I lit a cigarette and blew smoke up at the fluorescent lights. There was nothing to do now but wait. At least I could smoke in the school bathrooms now, without worrying about getting suspended. I lowered my head to my knees and wrapped my arms around my legs. This was all Mike's fault. I should have begged him not to tell Brendan what I'd said.

I made a plan. I'd stay in the bathroom until the first band came on and then sneak out to Carrie's car. I wasn't sure I'd be safe waiting there by myself, though. On the other hand, it was a big school. There were plenty of places to hide. Carrie was bound to come looking for me eventually, and when I found her I'd make her drive me home. She'd understand. And tomorrow I'd be leaving. Tomorrow I'd be back at college, away from all this.

The door creaked open and I lifted my head. A frizzy-haired girl came in and went into a stall. I put my cigarette in my mouth and left it there, letting the smoke trail up to sting my eyes. I watched the frizzy-haired girl's black Doc Martens move under the stall as I listened to the sound of her peeing. When she'd flushed and gone (without bothering to wash her hands, I noticed), I stood up. I went into the nearest stall and flushed my cigarette into the toilet. Then I walked over to the sinks.

"Polly."

He was leaning against the first stall, not four feet from me.

"You're not supposed to be in here," I said. There was no way I could get around him and out the door.

Brendan hooked his thumb through one of the belt loops of his corduroys.

"Why are you saying I raped you?" He sounded as if he were just curious.

"I don't want to talk about this. Please just go."

Brendan blinked a few times, and I wondered if he was stoned. "Listen," he said. "If you still lived here I would go out with you."

I took a step sideways. "Please. Just leave me alone, okay?"

He shook his head, narrowed his eyes. "Why are you being like this?"

The door swung open and three girls filed in. "He so totally makes me want to smack someone," one of the girls was saying. She was wearing a leather motorcycle jacket that was much too big for her. Brendan turned around to look at them. His thumb was still hooked through his belt loop. All three girls started giggling.

"I can't pee if you're in here," one of them said through her laughter. She was wearing dark pink lipstick and blue eyeliner. She looked about twelve.

"Well, I don't even care if he is here, 'cause that's how bad I have to go," another girl said. She ran into a stall and latched it. The other two burst into new fits of giggles. I stared down at my shoes.

Brendan disappeared out the bathroom door as quietly as he had come in. As soon as the door swung shut behind him the two remaining girls rushed into adjoining stalls.

I listened to their chorus of peeing. My legs shook when I tried to walk and my breath was shallow. I washed my hands in cold water.

As I left the bathroom I heard applause and a few howls coming from the gym. There was the hiss of feedback and then the high wail of a guitar. Then came the drums, echoing through the empty hallway.

seven TODD

I went back to school. I did math. I stopped goofing off around the dorm and in town and went to the library between classes instead. My favorite class was Introduction to Fine Arts. At first I wasn't good at drawing, but then I learned how to do the proportions. I liked painting better than drawing, and I liked sculpture even more. Sam was in my class, and he showed me how to stretch a canvas. We sat together in the studio, our easels before us. Sam wore his glasses to see far away but took them off when he painted. He looked older without his glasses. He liked to paint outdoor scenes, and he brought in photographs to help him remember.

When we did collages I painted the word *traitor* across a canvas in big black letters. Over that I glued all of Mike's drawings that I had saved. Then I splashed red and black paint over everything until there wasn't any more white space. You could see only parts of Mike's drawings, and parts of the letters. I got a B-, but the teacher complimented me on my layering.

When we did sculpture I made a plain-looking suburban house that was about half a foot tall. While it was still wet I broke a highball glass that I bought at the Salvation Army over the roof. The top of the glass shattered, and I spread the pieces of glass around until they jutted out all over the house. I left the bottom of the glass intact, embedded in the roof. Everyone in class thought I was trying to say something about glass houses. I didn't tell them it was about my dad.

I spent the most time on my painting of Brendan Davis's face. I painted him even uglier than he already was. I exaggerated his heavy eyelids, made them so droopy he looked inhuman. I put dark circles under his eyes and gave him a thin, cruel mouth. I painted his nose stubby and wide, like a boxer's. By the time I got to his straggly, matted hair, I realized I was having trouble remembering what he actually looked like.

"Who the hell is that?" Sam asked when he saw it.

"Nobody," I said. "I'm not a good enough painter to do anyone real."

"You got that face out of your mind? Scary."

On the phone I told Mom and William that I was thinking of majoring in art and minoring in math.

"You'd be better off reversing that," William said.

"Let her do what she wants," Mom said.

I wrote Theresa a letter about the rape because everyone else in Reston knew. I wrote about how stupid and embarrassed and angry I felt. She wrote me back a long letter about the oppressive origins of rape, how it was a violent act and not a sexual one. She wrote that she understood why I hadn't called the police, but that I needed to take control of what had happened to me in my own way, or at least go see a therapist. After I read her letter I was sorry I'd told her.

Julie was the only one I told at school. We were drunk, on our way home from a party. I thought maybe she wouldn't remember it, but the next day she told me it had happened to her, too, in high school. She'd lost her virginity that way.

"Don't you just hate all boys?" she asked. And then, "It'll pass."

I did hate all boys, except for Sam and Andrew.

"The thing you have to remember is that one day you'll be fine, just like I am," Julie said. I was glad to hear it. I felt different now. More serious.

I saw Ian in the math building. He didn't want to be friends, but he stopped whenever he saw me and asked how I was. I told him I was fine, everything was the same, nothing to tell, and did he have a cigarette. I expected him to sense that something had happened, maybe ask if I really was okay or tell me I seemed different, but he didn't. Nobody did.

The weather got warm and then warmer—the temperature went into the eighties for three days straight before returning to a normal spring. We spread bedsheets out on the grass in front of our dorms and lounged in our bathing suits. Summer was almost here. I didn't want to go back to Reston, but I had nowhere else to go.

I was home only a week when Mom nagged me to apply for a job at The Disney Store. She got the idea because a girl in our neighborhood, Missy Marshall, applied there and put Mom down as a reference. Missy was three years younger than me, and spent most of her free time parading around our street with her friends, giggling at the skaters' wipeouts and feigning an interest in their ollies and rail slides. Mom was friendly with the Marshalls from neighborhood cleanup days and garage sales. When the manager of The Disney Store called, Mom gave Missy a stellar reference, told him about me, and set up an interview.

"Don't forget to tell them about your theater experience," Mom said as I left for my interview. She was referring to the two summers I had spent at a drama day camp when I was eleven and twelve.

The manager of The Disney Store was named Jeffrey. He was an effeminate, balding gay man who I guessed was about ten years older than me. He interviewed me in front of the store, on a bench surrounded by a forest of fake potted plants. One of the mall's many fountains roared behind us. Jeffrey scribbled things on a clipboard while I sat up straight, pointed my head toward his, and pasted a smile across my face. I didn't mention drama camp. Instead I talked about my years of babysitting and my uncanny ability to communicate with kids.

Jeffrey pushed a wisp of blond hair back from his forehead and drew his face into an expression that let me know we'd come to the most important part of the interview. "When you think of the Disney characters, the films, the songs, the multimedia experience of Disney, how do you feel?" he asked.

I pretended that Jeffrey had asked me my feelings on winning the lottery, and broke into a wide grin. "Who doesn't love Disney?" I said.

Jeffrey flashed me a quick smile and scribbled something on his clipboard. The next morning he called to tell me that I was hired.

I told myself it wouldn't be that bad. It was only for the summer, and it paid a dollar an hour more than most of the other mall jobs. And Missy Marshall had taken a job at The Limited, so at least I wouldn't be expected to forge a friendship with her.

Before I could actually begin working, I had to go through Disney's orientation. This is where I was given my uniform (*costume* was the official word Jeffrey insisted we use). The Disney costume consisted of white Keds, white bobby socks, flesh-colored panty hose, a gray polyester skirt, a pink oxford shirt, and an oversized turquoise button-up sweater adorned with a bright pink *M*, for Mickey.

No jewelry was permitted, but I *was* allowed—even encouraged—to wear Mickey Mouse earrings. The earrings were miniature flat gold studs in the shape of Mickey's head. I told Jeffrey I was allergic to gold.

Then there were the ears. We all had to wear them, even in the bathroom. I hated the ears most of all.

Mom and William decided that since I'd be required to work some evenings I needed my own car. They surprised me with it at the end of Disney orientation. It was a 1983 maroon Subaru stick shift with no power steering and more than 100,000 miles on it that William had taken off the hands of one of his coworkers for next to nothing.

"William won't say it, but he's proud of you," Mom said when he drove up in it.

I gave Mom a hard look. "You didn't tell him, did you?" I asked. We hadn't talked about Brendan since it happened.

Mom put an arm around me. "I wouldn't do that," she said. And then, "Look how much better you did this semester. Can't he be proud?"

My new car stank of air freshener and the tape deck didn't work, but I loved it. I had wanted a car for as long as I could remember. The scratchy costume, the infernal forty-five-minute Disney medley that piped into the store on a loop, the screaming children and demanding parents—my car made it all worth it.

Sometimes, especially when I was alone in the car, I would imagine Brendan Davis crossing the street in front of me. There was one intersection I saved for him in particular, a four-way stop close to my house where there was rarely any traffic. I'd slam my foot on the gas and picture Brendan Davis crumpling under my tires. I'd imagine the bump his body would make under the Subaru's frame, picture his lifeless form in my rear-view mirror.

There were two reasons why I didn't have to worry about running into Brendan Davis. The first reason was that Brendan had taken off to follow the Grateful Dead. The second reason was even better than the first. I had Todd Wilson.

"That's not very punk rock," Todd said when I told him where I was working. We were sitting together on his single mattress, chain-smoking and drinking Milwaukee's Best.

"Yeah, well, not all of us are punk rock enough to get a job at Circuit City," I said, a blush rising on my cheeks. Todd was probably used to dating strippers and cocktail waitresses, not Disney cast members. And at least Circuit City wasn't in the mall.

"What do you know about being punk rock?" Todd asked. "Did you take a class on it at school?" He said *school* like I should be more embarrassed about going to college than working at The Disney Store. Like college was a secret he knew about me.

"Yeah, the class is called Hanging Out with Loser Rock Assholes," I said. "I'm doing the summer seminar part right now."

"You think you can impress me with a big vocabulary? Is that it?"

"What'd I say?"

Instead of answering me, Todd pulled a new beer out of the case he was using to prop up his feet. He opened the beer, then pulled another one out and handed it to me. Besides the mattress we were sitting on, Todd's room was unfurnished, unless you counted the boom box that sat on top of an amplifier in the corner. The guitar that went with the amplifier was strangely absent. The rest of Todd's room was strewn with empty beer cans and cigarette packs, dirty clothes, tapes, and old copies of *Playboy* and *Hustler*. The magazines were right there on the floor, like he didn't care who saw them.

I took a drink of my beer. "This is the worst job I've ever had," I said. "The costume is unbelievable."

I leaned my head against the wall and shut my eyes. I was drunk. Todd lifted my T-shirt up and felt for the clasp of my bra. There was no shade on his window, and I was grateful that his mattress was too low to be seen from outside. Todd wasn't one for foreplay, unless you counted the frantic way he tore our clothes off. I didn't mind. He still made my stomach drop when he so much as looked at me. That was all that mattered.

Things started up between Todd and me a couple of days after I got home from school. I was at a party in a newly built section of Reston. Reston had a way of staying unfamiliar. You could make a wrong turn a mile from your own home and get hopelessly lost in the web of a new neighborhood that wasn't there the last time you drove by. It wasn't uncommon to spot a homeless deer bounding across someone's front yard, searching for the vanishing woods.

Todd came up next to Carrie and Theresa and me while Carrie was telling us about prom. Lyle had worn a purple tuxedo shirt and gelled up his hair for the occasion, and Carrie's mother still hadn't gotten over it. Instead of joining the conversation Todd leaned against the wall and stared at us as we talked. When Todd finally opened his mouth it was only to ask for a cigarette. He caught my eye for a second when I offered him my pack, and I didn't look away.

An hour later he came up behind me and put his arms around my waist as I climbed the stairs to the bathroom.

"Is there somewhere we can go?" I could feel his breath on my neck.

I leaned into him, and he rubbed his hand back and forth across my stomach. I arched my back so that the top of my head pressed into his chest. Todd Wilson's hand on my stomach was the most exhilarating thing I could remember happening to me in a long time.

We found a bedroom that obviously belonged to the younger sister of the guy who was having the party. The walls were painted pink, and there was a queen-size canopy bed in the center of the room. A bulletin board was covered with horseback riding ribbons. Todd pulled a beat-up-looking switchblade out of his jeans and tossed it aside before pressing me against the pink carpet, which was littered with stuffed animals.

"I think I've pretty much wanted to have sex with you for, like, years," I said when Todd was finished with me.

"I would've had sex with you before," he said. He was still hovering over me. He smiled, and his right eye squinted shut. Light from the hallway seeped in under the bedroom door, making his pale skin look stony and unreal. He leaned down to kiss me again and I got that cold feeling I liked.

• • •

I ran into him at a Dag Nasty show two weeks later. We did it
in the back of my Subaru after watching the band from opposite
sides of the club. We'd been hanging out almost every night
ever since, mostly at Todd's apartment. I didn't tell Mom and
William I was at Todd's, and they didn't ask.

Todd was roommates with Fred Paige. I hadn't seen Fred
since I'd broken up with Joey. Fred worked the night shift at
the video store, so Todd and I usually had the apartment to
ourselves.

"That's an interesting choice," Theresa said when I told her
about Todd and me. Theresa had a summer internship at an
abortion rights organization and a part-time night job at a record
store in D.C. I saw her only once every couple of weeks.

"I mean, I can see doing it once obviously, but—" she said.

"It's just for the summer," I said.

"I can see why you like him," Theresa said. "But be careful.
He's crazy."

It was the same with Carrie. "He's hot and all, but Lyle says
he's a psycho," she said. "I hope you don't want to double-date
or anything."

"Don't worry about it," I said. The last thing I wanted was
a bunch of public outings with Todd. Lyle was right about him.
In high school he'd punched a kid on the bus for a dollar. I'd

heard another story about a skinhead punching him straight in the mouth at a hardcore show, knocking him on his back. Blood pouring from his mouth, Todd got up and kicked the skinhead in the stomach before the bouncers got to them.

And it wasn't just the violent stories that made me think Todd was crazy. It was everything. His squinty blue eyes were creepy and vacant. He hadn't finished high school. He was twenty-one, and already his driver's license had been taken away. He was given to loud, drunken rants that didn't make sense. He'd spent more nights than he could count in jail. I wanted everyone in Reston to know I was his girlfriend.

At first, my primary role at The Disney Store was as a greeter. I stood at the store entrance for six hours at a stretch, startling customers as they entered.

"Hi! Welcome to The Disney Store!"

I greeted for a month straight before I got promoted to the cash register. I still had to greet two shifts a week, but I didn't complain. I had aspirations of being full-time on the register, so I wanted Jeffrey to like me. Running the cash register was the best job in the store because time passed the fastest there.

I wondered if Jeffrey had ever met anyone like Todd Wilson, or if Todd had ever known anyone like Jeffrey. I couldn't imagine many places more immune to the magic of Disney than Todd's apartment.

The night Todd got fired from Circuit City he was even drunker and madder than usual. He hadn't shown up for work in two days, and they'd fired him on his answering machine.

"They said I should have called in," Todd said. "What if I was too fucking sick to call in? Did anybody ever stop to think about that? Did anybody so much as ask me?"

"I guess if you're that sick you're supposed to have someone call in for you," I said.

"Oh, so it's my fault now," Todd said. He stood up from his mattress and walked across the hall to the bathroom. After a minute I got up and followed him. He was peeing with the door open.

"It's not like you can't find another job," I said. "There's a lot of jobs you can get."

Todd zipped up his pants, flushed the toilet.

"I guess you can't use anyone at Circuit City as a reference, though," I said. "Maybe you could make something up. You could say that your boss got fired right after you quit, and you're not sure where he is."

"Why don't you just shut up?" Todd shouted.

I set my can of beer on the towel rack. I wanted to ask Todd why he didn't show up for work for two days, if he took his job so seriously.

He wasn't finished. "You don't get it," he shouted. "You can just go ask your fucking parents if you don't have any fucking money."

"For your information, I happen to have a job," I said.

He pushed me so hard I fell over the side of the tub and hit my head against the tile.

"Fuck you," he said, and stalked out of the bathroom.

I struggled to untangle myself from the dirty shower curtain, which was wrapped around my calves. My legs were half in the tub and half out, and the back of my shirt was wet.

I pulled myself out of the tub, picked my beer off the towel rack, and walked to the doorway of Todd's room. Todd was kneeling in front of his boom box, rewinding a tape. The back of my head throbbed, just above my neck.

"I never want to see you again!" I screamed. I threw my beer, and it landed with a dull thud on the carpet beside him. Beer spilled out onto the rug.

I turned and ran for the door. Fred was sitting on the couch in the living room with his feet up on the coffee table. It was his night off, and he was watching television. He didn't take his eyes off the TV as I went past him. I thought I heard Todd's footsteps behind me as I slammed the door shut, but I couldn't be sure.

Two weeks passed. Now that I didn't have Todd to look forward to, The Disney Store became unbearable. There was the woman who paid for a stuffed Winnie the Pooh bear with sweaty dollar bills she pulled out of her bra. The kid who took a dump behind a closed register. The man who screamed at me because I thought he was purchasing something he wanted to return. I tried to think of it as inspirational. Maybe I'd make a sculpture of dismembered Disney characters.

Lyle's mother went to Ocean City with her boyfriend, so Lyle had a party. It wasn't one of the small basement parties he had when his mother went to her boyfriend's for the night. This was a real party that took up the whole house.

Todd was already there when I arrived. He was hanging out in the kitchen, talking to Fred and a couple of other guys. I was careful not to look in his direction.

Mike Franklin was getting stoned in Lyle's room.

"Hi, Polly," he said when I walked by. I ignored him.

After I'd walked by the kitchen door a few times, I settled on the couch in the living room with Carrie and Theresa.

Theresa was wearing contacts again and had cut her hair really short. It made her look sophisticated, like a French girl.

"I don't know, I'm still getting used to it," she said, touching her head.

"I like it," I said.

"You don't think it looks sort of masculine?"

I looked at Theresa's C-cup boobs in her V-neck shirt. "You could never look masculine," I said.

Carrie looked down at her beer. "I'm thinking about breaking up with Lyle."

"Why?" I asked.

"I'm just gonna try it on for size," Carrie said. "If it's too weird we can always get back together."

I stood up, spilling some of my beer on the couch.

"You can't just break up with someone you love," I said.

In the bathroom, I decided I would talk to Todd. I couldn't decide whether it was better to demand an apology for the shoving, or focus on how he was ignoring me. I brushed my hair. I needed a trim. Then I put on more lipstick. Most of it settled onto a crack on my lower lip, and I grabbed a wad of toilet paper and blotted.

When I got to the kitchen, Todd and Fred were gone. "He took off," Lyle said.

I called Todd from Lyle's mother's room, which smelled of baby powder and the same Charlie perfume my own mother wore.

"Don't you even feel bad?" I said when he answered.

"Last I heard you never wanted to see me again."

"You could at least say you're sorry," I said.

"What do you care? I saw you. You're fine."

"I'm not fine," I said.

Todd was quiet. Somebody put the Clash on downstairs. It was my favorite Clash song, "Police on My Back."

"Come over," he said.

"No way." I danced in place.

"Come over. Me and Fred have beer."

"How come you didn't try to talk to me tonight?"

"I'm talking to you now," Todd said. "Get over here."

I left without saying good-bye to Carrie and Theresa.

Lyle came to visit me at The Disney Store. It was a weekday afternoon, not too busy.

"There's something going on with Carrie," he said. "I thought you might know what it is."

I widened my eyes in what I hoped was an approximation of dumb surprise. "What do you mean?" I asked.

"She's strange lately. Distant. And mad at me all the time."

I rang up a customer while he waited.

"Maybe it's hormones," I said. "Has it just been the last couple days?"

Lyle forced a smile. "She hasn't talked to you about anything?"

"No. At least not anything strange, distant, or mad."

Lyle looked down at his shoes. "Is she cheating on me?"

Now I really was surprised. "No! Do you think so?"

He didn't look up. "I guess not," he said.

A customer came up to us with a *Little Mermaid* video. I ran it over the scanner.

"I'll see you later," Lyle said.

I watched Lyle walk out of the store and down the mall corridor. He was tall, over six feet, but you couldn't tell at first because he didn't have good posture. He slumped when he walked.

• • •

I was driving home after work when my right rear tire blew
out. There was a high-pitched hiss that I could hear over the radio, and then I felt the car heave and tilt. I turned off the radio,
put the car into neutral, and gripped the steering wheel with
both hands. I forced myself not to slam on the brakes; I knew
you weren't supposed to do that when you hit ice, and I figured
this might be similar. I coasted to the highway shoulder.

Once I'd come to a complete stop I pulled up the emergency brake and dropped my head to the steering wheel. My
forehead was slick with sweat, and the vinyl of the wheel stuck
to it. I raised my head back up and reached for my cigarettes.

I got out of the car. The tire was gone, and I stared at the
silver skeleton in its place. Pieces of rubber trailed out behind
the car and onto the highway. It was five thirty, and traffic was
heavy. Cars whipped by without stopping. I was only about a
mile away from the mall. I turned on the hazards, locked the
car, and started walking.

William picked me up in front of Hecht's.

"Did you see it?" I asked.

William nodded. "You're lucky you weren't stranded."

"Tell me about it."

"You might have considered putting out flares."

I patted my cigarettes that I'd hidden inside the waist band
of my skirt. "Why do you do that?" I asked.

"What?"

"Criticize me. Tell me how I could do everything better."

William pulled off the highway and stopped behind my car.
"I just want you to be safe," he said. "It's what anyone who
loves a child wants."

I tried not to cry. "I'm not a child anymore," I said.

"I know."

I wasn't sure if I even had a spare, but there it was, under the floor of the hatchback. We pulled it out and I sat on it while William jacked up the car and loosened the lug nuts. They spun around but stayed tight.

"I think you're supposed to loosen them before you jack the car up," I said.

William took off his glasses and pinched the bridge of his nose, and I noticed the deep creases at the corners of his eyes. "You're right," he said. "It's been a long time since I've done this."

Once the car was jacked up again, we each grabbed a side of the spare. I shifted my weight and William grunted beside me. There was the sound of the gravel underneath our feet and then William slipped, causing me to lose my grip on the tire. I turned my head in time to see William fall backward into the gravel.

"William!"

"Shit," he said. He wasn't getting up.

"Are you okay?"

"Yes."

"I'm sorry," I said. There was grease on my pleated skirt and my pink oxford.

Still flat on his back, he started to laugh. His T-shirt was riding up, and the skin on his stomach was lighter than the skin on his arms. "It's not your fault," he said. "I'm just a klutz."

I held out my hand. "Yes, but you're a lifesaving klutz," I said.

Todd called me at work the next day.

"Can you buy orange juice on your way over here?" he asked. "I have vodka."

It was eerie to hear his voice in The Disney Store.

"I can't," I said. I was using my customer service voice. "My dad's here. We're having dinner."

My dad had called me the week before to tell me he was going to be in town. I'd only remembered at the last minute to bring a change of clothes to work that morning.

I met Dad for dinner at a Mexican restaurant adjacent to the mall. He was waiting at the bar when I got there. The restaurant was bright and heavily decorated with Mexican streamers and sombreros and lights shaped like chili peppers, but the bar was dark and nondescript.

"Sorry I'm late," I said after we hugged. "I had to change out of my Disney costume."

He turned to the woman sitting next to him at the bar. "This is Gwen," he said.

"Hi," I said. Gwen beamed at me like I was her own daughter.

I assumed Dad had met Gwen at the bar, but I started to wonder when she followed us over to our table and squeezed in on his side. It wasn't until I heard her accent that I realized he had brought Gwen with him from North Carolina.

"Polly, I can't tell you how nice it is to meet you," she said as the waiter passed out our menus. "Bob's told me so many wonderful things about you."

"I wish I could say the same thing," I said. I couldn't figure out how old Gwen was. She had short gray hair, but her face was unlined.

"I wanted it to be a surprise," Dad said.

The waiter asked if we wanted anything to drink. Dad ordered a beer, and Gwen and I ordered Diet Cokes.

"So how did you guys meet?" I asked when the waiter was gone.

"Bob rear-ended me in a parking lot," Gwen said.

"She was so nice about it, I called her up and asked if I

could take her out to dinner," Dad said. Gwen looked at him and smiled.

"Wow. That is nice," I said. "When was this?"

"Three months ago," Dad said. "But it feels like longer."

"It really does," Gwen said.

The waiter came back with our drinks and asked what we wanted for dinner. After we'd ordered we sat in silence, eating the complimentary chips that the waiter had brought with our drinks. A Mexican love song played from a speaker above us.

Dad asked me about school, and I told him I was looking forward to going back. I asked Gwen what she did for a living, and she told me about her job at a bank. She dealt in home owner loans, among other things. Dad mentioned that he and Gwen were going to visit the Vietnam Memorial before they drove back to North Carolina the next day. I said I was sorry but I had to work and couldn't go with them. It wasn't until we were almost finished with dinner that Dad said he and Gwen were getting married.

I stopped chewing. "Congratulations," I said. "When's the big day?"

"We're not sure," Gwen said. "Sometime this fall."

"We'd like you to come down," Dad said.

"Sure," I said. "Now that I have a car I can drive down from school anytime."

"It's not going to be anything fancy," Dad said. "Just something small at the house."

"What house?" I asked.

"Gwen's," Dad said.

"Ours," Gwen said.

I thought about how I wouldn't know anyone at the wedding, besides Dad and Gwen. Dad got up to go to the bathroom, and Gwen beamed at me again. I smiled back at her.

"I feel so lucky to have met your father," she said. She

looked down at her plate. "I never had any children of my own or anything."

"Well, that's good," I said. "I mean that you met my dad."

The waiter came by and dropped off the check. When he was gone I said, "I'm glad Dad met you, too."

I didn't realize until the words were out of my mouth how true it was. Gwen looked like she was going to cry. I excused myself to go to the bathroom.

After dinner I took them out to the parking lot to see my car. "It's pretty crappy, but I love it," I said.

Dad clamped an arm around my shoulder. "You really are all grown up," he said.

My cigarettes were on the dashboard, but neither of them said anything. After we said good-bye I watched them walk across the parking lot to Gwen's Toyota. There was a dent in the trunk where Dad had hit her. Just as they reached the car Dad grabbed Gwen's hand and squeezed it, and she looked over at him and smiled again. They were both wearing oversized T-shirts and baggie jeans. They looked like they'd been together for years.

I bought orange juice on my way over to Todd's. When he saw me at the door he picked me up and ran to his room, accidentally bumping me against the wall in the hallway. He threw me down on his mattress harder than I knew he meant to. I shut my eyes and waited for the rest.

Afterward it dawned on me that this was the first time I had slept with Todd sober. I put my underwear and my T-shirt back on, and went to the kitchen for a beer. A bottle of vodka sat on the counter, half empty. When I got back Todd was moving around the bedroom with nervous energy, gathering beer cans, scooping up cigarette butts, and dumping them all in the trash can. He was still naked. I sat down on the mattress, lit a cigarette, and watched. He was energetic sometimes when he was drunk. It was hard to predict.

"I got a flat tire yesterday," I said. "It just totally blew. It was scary."

Todd grunted and kept moving.

"William had to come and help me."

Todd rifled through his tapes, looking for the one he wanted.

"My dad's getting married," I said. "I have to go to the wedding."

Todd didn't answer me.

"I thought maybe you could come with me," I said.

He came over and sat down on the mattress beside me.

"You don't want me to meet your dad," he said. His voice was flat.

"Yes, I do," I said, realizing he was right.

I put my cigarette butt into a beer can Todd had neglected to pick up. Smoke wafted out of the hole. I shook it to make sure the cigarette was out. Todd stretched out on the mattress and closed his eyes. He was even drunker than I'd thought. I looked at his small, sturdy mouth and his Roman nose, his strong jaw. Since he was asleep I let myself swoon. Todd was actor handsome. Alcoholic handsome. Rock-star handsome.

He started to snore. I located my cutoffs on the other side of the mattress and pulled them on. I remembered at the beginning of the summer, when we ran into each other at the Dag Nasty show. Todd had held my hand on the way to the car. And after, when I drove him home, he had kissed me good night like he meant it. His voice had scratched when he said my name.

I leaned over and kissed his neck just above the collarbone.

"You're not real," I said.

He snored into my hair.

I was getting ready for work the next day when Sam called. "Did you get the letter?" he asked.

I balanced the phone on my shoulder as I rolled on my panty hose. I was glad to hear his voice. "What letter?"

"There's a two-week art intensive, but you have to get back to school early," he said. "I think they sent it to all the people who signed up for second-year art."

"I didn't get it," I said. "It sounds cool, though."

"I'm going," he said. "It would be fun if we did it together."

After work I went with Mom to the grocery store. I liked the bulk food section, where everything was labeled and sat in giant wooden bins. When I was a kid I would stick my arms into the bins as far as they would go, until my mother noticed and stopped me.

On the way there we stopped at the gas station. Mom let me pump the gas; I loved the smell. After I'd filled the tank I waited in the car while Mom went inside to pay. Her car was nicer than mine. It ran smoother, and the interior was immaculate. Even though she'd had it for more than two years, her car still had a faint new-car smell.

A beat-up light blue Volkswagen bug pulled into the station and stopped in front of where we were parked. The muffler was so loud I thought it might drop out onto the street. I peered through the windshield. In the driver's seat was Brendan Davis. I hunched down in my seat as the air went out of me. He was grinning.

Brendan got out of his car and came over to where I was.

"Hey, Polly," he said. "Long time no see."

"Leave me alone." My voice came out louder than I'd meant it to.

Brendan rolled his eyes. "I see you're still hung up on that whole thing." He said it like I was mad at him for teasing me at school.

I lowered my voice. "Get out of here. I mean it."

"Polly. Come on."

I folded my arms in front of my chest. I hated the way he was looking at me. Like he had seen me naked.

Mom came up behind him. "Get away from my daughter," she said. She had pulled herself up to her full height—she was taller than Brendan—and she was holding her purse in front of her with both hands.

Brendan turned to face her. He looked bored.

"What are you going to do about it?" he asked her.

"I'm going to call the police is what I'm going to do," Mom answered. "If you ever come near my daughter again, I can guarantee you'll regret it for a very long time."

"Whatever," Brendan said. His face had gone pale under his tan.

"You're lucky I don't call the police right now," Mom said. She gave the Volkswagen a long look.

Without looking at either of us, Brendan got back into his car and started it. He was backing out of the station by the time Mom had come around to her side and sat down. She slammed the door behind her, hard.

"I assume that was who I think it was," she said. She still sounded angry.

I straightened up in my seat and let out the breath I'd been holding. "Yes."

Mom shook her head and started the car. "What an asshole."

"I can't believe you did that."

"I mean it. You tell me if he ever bothers you again."

We drove in silence while I waited for my heartbeat to slow back to normal. By the time we got to the grocery store, I was smiling.

The next day the letter came. The course was painting, sculpture, drawing, graphic design, screen printing, and photography. There would be a day and a half of each, and the goal was to figure out if you wanted to major in art, and also to help pick a focus. It cost five hundred dollars on top of regular tuition. I put the letter on Mom's nightstand with a note that said *Please*.

Carrie's family went to the West Virginia mountains for a long weekend. Carrie stayed behind so she could break up with Lyle. She was also having people over.

"I don't want him over here," Carrie said when I told her I was bringing Todd. "He's such a weirdo alcoholic freak."

"I already invited him," I said. "I didn't think you'd care."

I told Todd about the breakup as soon as I picked him up.

"I thought they were gonna get married or something," he said.

"Please. Nobody our age gets married."

I pulled into the 7-Eleven on the edge of Carrie's development and parked between two pickup trucks. As a consolation prize for bringing Todd, I'd promised Carrie we'd bring beer. Carrie didn't live too far down the block, and in the distance I could see people standing out on her deck.

I pulled a twenty out of the front pocket of my cutoffs.

"Get a case, you know, for everybody," I said.

Todd got out of the car. I leaned my head out the window. "Todd! Get cigarettes."

He held his hand up as he walked through the double doors of the 7-Eleven.

I got my brush out of the glove compartment and got rid of the tangles that had formed on the window side of my hair. It was dusk, my favorite time of the day. I watched the top of Todd's head move down the fluorescent-lit aisle, toward the beer. I could see his stick-up hair.

A fortyish, bowlegged man wearing a baseball hat that sat up high on his head came out of the 7-Eleven and got into the pickup truck on my left. His radio blasted to life when he started his truck, and the parking lot was treated to the loud, false voice of the DJ.

"IT'S ALL HAPPENING THIS SUNDAY AT RFK STA-DIUM," the DJ screamed. The man backed his car out of the space, pausing to give me a quick leer. I pretended not to see him.

Then Todd was running out of 7-Eleven with two cases of Milwaukee's Best. He jumped in the car and slammed the door behind him.

"Let's go!" He flung one case of beer in the backseat and held the other on his lap.

"Did you get cigarettes?"

"Polly, go! Drive!"

I dropped my brush into the space between my seat and the door and started the engine. Todd slammed his hand down on the dashboard as I released the emergency brake.

"Jesus, Polly, will you please move this fucking car!"

A policeman was running alongside the front of the 7-Eleven. He was headed straight for us. I put the car into reverse and stepped on the gas.

The policeman reached my window as I pulled out of our space.

"Stop the vehicle!" he shouted.

I stepped on the brake. The policeman ran around to Todd's side of the car and yanked open the door.

"Step out of the vehicle!" he shouted again.

Todd set down the case of beer he was holding and got out of the car. The policeman threw him against the side of the Subaru and handcuffed him. The Subaru and I rocked back and forth with the weight of it. Before the policeman could shout at me to do so, I turned off the ignition, pulled up the emergency brake, and returned my hands to the steering wheel.

Two police cars squealed into the parking lot. Doors slammed. Big, square flashlights beamed around the inside of my car. I sat frozen.

"I'm gonna need your license and registration, and then I'm gonna need you to step out of the vehicle," a policeman said in a policeman voice. I realized he was talking to me. He had a rectangular face, and looked to be only a few years older than me. Another policeman leaned into the car window and picked up the two cases of beer. He ambled over to the entrance to the 7-Eleven.

I got out of the car just in time to see Todd being pushed into the back of one of the police cruisers. It was just like TV. I watched him lean forward and say something to the two policemen in the front seat.

"I take it he stole that beer," I said to the rectangular-faced policeman.

Instead of answering me, he walked back to his car with my license and registration. Todd was in the other police car. I kept an eye on his profile. I was waiting for him to look at me. Maybe send me some kind of a message. An "I'm sorry" mouthed through the window. Something like that.

"Count yourself lucky you don't have an open container

situation on your hands, little lady," the policeman said when he got back with my paperwork. "Are you aware that drinking underage is against the law?"

"I thought he was buying cigarettes," I said.

"I suggest you find yourself another boyfriend, little lady," he said. "A boyfriend who's law abiding."

I wanted to ask him to stop calling me little lady. Instead I said, "He's not my boyfriend."

There were a few cars parked out front of Carrie's, including Theresa's. I hadn't seen either one of them in weeks. I crossed the front yard and pushed open the front door. The foyer was empty.

"Hi honey, I'm home," I called out.

Nobody answered. I heard music and talking outside.

I cut through the kitchen on my way to the deck. Carrie's mother was a *Southern Living* fan, and the kitchen was decorated with things like salt and pepper shakers disguised as cows and baskets of fake fruit wrapped in checked, lace-trimmed cloth.

Mike Franklin was sitting at the picnic table next to Carrie.

"Hi," I said. Carrie smiled and Mike nodded.

Theresa came up beside me. "Did you see what happened at the 7-Eleven just now?" I asked.

Nobody had. I told them about Todd's arrest.

"I guess I should call the police station or something," I said when I got finished.

"What for?" Theresa said. "That's what he gets."

"Yeah," Carrie said. She ashed her cigarette into a coffee can filled with sand. "Let him rot."

Mike's hand was resting on Carrie's knee.

• • •

When I got home from work the next afternoon I found a check made out to Virginia Tech for $500 on the kitchen counter. William had signed it. I screamed. Then I called Sam.

I drove over to Todd's apartment without bothering to change out of my costume.

"I'm going back to school early," I said when he opened the door. "I'm doing this art program."

Todd shrugged. "That's nice," he said.

I followed him through the living room and into the kitchen.

"You owe me twenty bucks," I said.

Todd opened the refrigerator and pulled out a can of Budweiser.

"Do you still have my twenty?"

Todd slammed the refrigerator door shut. "Can you shut up about your goddamn twenty? I'm the one who got arrested."

I made a grab for the back pocket of Todd's jeans, where I could see the outline of his wallet. He twisted away from me and pushed me against the counter so hard it dug into my back.

"Ow, Todd, fuck!" I yelled.

He took a step toward me. I put my hands in front of my face.

"I didn't mean to," Todd said. His voice was soft.

He kissed me. His face felt hot. He unbuttoned my Mickey sweater and threw it on the floor. I grabbed his hand when he started in on my oxford.

"Let's go to your room," I said.

We stripped off our clothes and got on the mattress. I climbed on top of him and pinned my hands against his shoulders. I lifted my hips up while he positioned himself. I had done it this way with Ian a few times, but never with Todd.

When I leaned over to kiss him, I felt a hiccup in my vagina. The hiccup felt good. I moved further up his torso. There was another hiccup. I kept going. The hiccups moved closer together.

I checked Todd's face. Sweat had appeared on his forehead, and his eyes were half-closed. The sides of his nose were slick with oil. I turned my head to the side and kept moving.

Finally it happened, rushing all the way through my body and evaporating much too soon.

Afterward, we smoked our cigarettes in silence.

"I have to go," I said after I'd stubbed out my cigarette. "I promised my mother I'd be home early."

Todd rolled over and faced me. He smiled his squinty smile. "I don't want you to go back to school," he said.

I kissed him. "I have to go," I said.

I got up and began gathering my clothes, which were strewn all over Todd's floor. I found everything but my pantyhose. I stepped over Todd's boom box and tipped back his amplifier. Something thumped against the inside of the amp. I leaned over and looked closer.

It was some sort of handgun. At first I didn't think it was real, but then I knew.

I looked over at Todd. He was lighting a new cigarette with his last one. I reached down and picked the gun up. It was heavy.

I turned around to face Todd. "Where did you get this?" I asked. My voice shook.

"It's not loaded," Todd said. "In case you get any ideas."

My ears were ringing. "Why do you have this?" I asked.

Todd rested his cigarette in the ashtray and pulled on his T-shirt. "None of your business," he said. He reached for his jeans.

I stood frozen. I was holding the gun like they did on TV, with my finger on the trigger.

"Have you always had this?" I asked. "Like, all summer?"

Todd snickered. "You think it's sexy?"

"No."

Todd stepped toward me. "Here. I'll show you how to use it."

"No thanks." I leaned over and put the gun back behind the amplifier. Todd shrugged and went into the bathroom.

I picked up my tennis shoes and tucked them under my arm. My pantyhose were balled up at the end of Todd's mattress. I decided I didn't need them.

It was still hot out even though it was dark, and I kept the windows rolled down as I drove. There was a Jane's Addiction song on the radio, and I turned it up. The traffic light up ahead turned yellow. I shifted the car into neutral and eased the brake down with my bare foot. A station wagon with a bumper sticker that read MY KID IS ON THE HONOR ROLL cut in front of me. There was a black lab standing up in the back. The light turned red. "Hi, doggie," I said. I was having trouble breathing. The lab sat down, reached a hind leg up, and tucked his head under it. I grabbed my pack of cigarettes off the passenger seat. The light turned green just as I pushed the car lighter in.

"Coming down the mountain," I sang with Perry Farrell's high, raspy voice.

I wanted to see Mom and William, to thank them for letting

me do the art program. It was going to be a brand-new year, with new people to meet and new things to do. I would be a new person.

The car lighter popped back out, and I pressed it to my cigarette. My lungs tightened as the smoke entered them, and I felt a calmness come over me. I was safe now. My life in Reston was ending.

I lifted the turn signal, changed lanes. I was almost home.

epilogue POLLY

It was a three-bedroom apartment with a big, sunny kitchen, just off campus in town. The living room was wood paneled and had dark brown wall-to-wall carpeting. Andrew called it the Brady room. Julie's parents donated their old brown couch, and Andrew added a tan beanbag chair. It was all too ugly to spend much time in, so we centered the ironing board in front of the couch, leaned our bikes against the wall, and went in only when we had to.

Julie hung her hammock up in one corner of her bedroom, near the window. Andrew and I were sure the hooks she'd put in the wall would cost us our deposit, but we loved lying in it after class. Andrew's room was so crowded with band equipment he hardly had space for his desk. His closet stood empty, as he preferred to keep his clothes strewn all over the floor. Julie and I ordered him to keep his door shut at all times.

We spent most of our time in the kitchen. Sam was over

nearly every night. We sat on green plastic chairs from Kmart, at the round wooden table we bought at the Salvation Army, eating macaroni and cheese and complaining about frat boys and rednecks. Andrew's radio show was on Thursday nights, so that was the night every week that Sam and Julie and I sat at the kitchen table with the radio turned up, playing cards and drinking beer.

Early in the semester Mom and William drove down with my dresser and my desk from home. They took me to Sears in Roanoke and bought me a bed frame and a rug for my bedroom. Up until then I'd been sleeping on a mattress on the floor, which I didn't mind. Mom wanted to buy me a new bedspread, but I still liked my old down comforter, even though it was worn through in places. We went out to dinner at a Mexican restaurant in town I'd never been to, and afterward I showed them the art studio on campus, where some of my work was.

"This is impressive," William said when he saw my painting of Mom. I had painted her from one of her wedding pictures with Dad, but I placed her alone in a Laundromat, clothes rotating in the washing machine beside her and a neon sign flickering out the window. She was dressed in the peasant dress she wore in the picture, and looked as young as I did now. It was how I imagined her when she was just starting out. "You're going to be a real artist someday," Mom said. "I'd like to keep this, so I can say I knew you when."

"I'm still minoring in math, just in case," I said.

I couldn't go down to North Carolina for Dad's wedding because it was the weekend before midterms, but I promised him I'd be down for Thanksgiving. Two weeks after the wedding I got pictures in the mail. They'd gotten married in the living room of Gwen's house, surrounded by a few friends and what looked like Gwen's parents. In his letter Dad said that afterward they grilled filet mignons and ate wedding cake that Gwen's mother made. There was a picture of Dad and Gwen, holding up champagne glasses, their new gold wedding bands twinkling on their fingers. This time Dad had worn a suit and tie to get married, and Gwen had worn a long peach dress that looked good on her. On the back of the picture Dad had written, "I'm the one drinking sparkling apple cider." I wondered how long he'd gone without drinking, and if it would last.

When I wanted to be by myself I went to the third floor of the library, where the agriculture books were. There were a couple of tables behind the shelves against the far wall, and there was rarely anybody there. This was where I went with my sketch pad, to work out what my next art project would be. I would think about what I really wanted to make, and how I could make it fit into my next assignment.

Sometimes there was a boy there. He was tall, with long, thick, dark hair. He almost looked Native American, except his skin was pale and his eyes were dark blue. He had a big nose and curled his small mouth into a slight smile while he studied. I sketched him and shaded over it before he could walk by and see.

He wore jeans and Doc Martens and T-shirts with the names of bands I liked. As it got colder he added a flannel shirt and then a black bomber jacket. There was something serene about his face when he concentrated. I found myself waiting for him when he wasn't there.

I followed him out of the library one evening, over to the dorms. That meant he was a freshman. As he turned into the dining hall I thought he caught sight of me, so I looked at my watch and then back toward the library, pretending to be exasperated that whoever it was who was supposed to be meeting me was late.

It took me another month to get up the nerve to speak to him. I'd been at the library for two hours, and he'd just arrived. I gathered up my things in my backpack and put on my coat. I decided I would just say hi, on my way out.

I almost let myself walk past him without saying anything, but as I drew near he looked up and smiled, filling me with hope.

I pulled the sleeve of my coat over my watch.

"Do you know what time it is?" I asked.

He pointed over my shoulder, at the oversized school clock that hung by the elevator. "It's seven thirty," he said.

"Oh, yeah," I said, glancing behind me. "Thanks."

It was Thursday night, the night of Andrew's radio show. Sam would already be at the apartment, starting the macaroni and cheese with Julie.

"I'm Victor," he said. He was still smiling, which I took as a good sign.

"Polly," I said, and then, "I have to go."

I took the stairs instead of the elevator, giving him one last look before I opened the door to the stairwell.

"Maybe I'll see you tomorrow," I said.

Victor looked up from his Introduction to Psychology textbook and pushed his hair behind his ears.

"Yeah, cool," he said.

Out on the street I turned my walk into a jog. I didn't want to be late for Andrew's show.

About the author

About the book

Read (and listen) on

Insights,
Interviews
& More . . .

A Conversation with Amy Bryant

Where were you born and raised? How would you describe your childhood?

I was born in Washington, D.C. I lived in Arlington, Virginia, until I was nine, and then I lived in Reston, Virginia, until college.

What did your parents do?

My father worked as a bluegrass banjo player before I was born. He was a Washington, D.C., policeman for twenty years, and then he worked for the Department of Defense. My mother was a housewife, and then she worked for IBM.

Where were you educated? Have you any unusual or otherwise compelling anecdotes about your college experience?

Like Polly, I went to Herndon High School and Virginia Tech. Unlike Polly, I am not a strong math student or a gifted artist. I majored in communications.

Name some jobs you've had.

I've toiled in retail, food service, and various office environments. For the last eight years I've worked in the pro-choice community.

Much of Polly *is centered around Polly's confusion about sex. She has lots of questions, but no one to turn to with her concerns. How does her lack of education affect her*

" My father worked as a bluegrass banjo player before I was born. He was a Washington, D.C., policeman for twenty years. "

relationships? Is this something you saw a lot of as a teen?

This is something I feel strongly about. When I was a teenager my friends and I gathered most of our information about sex from our peers, and much of it was inaccurate. Research shows that this is still going on. Of the developed countries, the United States has the highest teen pregnancy rates, the highest sexually transmitted infection rates, and the highest abortion rates. Obviously, we're doing something wrong in this country. We need to look at what other developed countries are doing on these issues and copy them. And that starts with accurate, comprehensive, culturally competent sexuality education.

The Bush administration has mandated abstinence-only education, which means kids are pressured in school not to have sex, but they aren't given any facts about birth control, how to use it, or how to confront the emotional difficulties of a sexual relationship once they do have one. Of course it's appropriate to encourage teenagers to be abstinent to a certain extent, but I can't imagine there are any parents out there who don't want their children ever to have sex in their lifetimes. So when are kids supposed to learn about it? Before or after they become sexually active? What the Bush administration is doing is backward, punitive, and destructive.

Polly talks about all the different cliques at her school such as the jocks, the bops, and the bamas. What, if any, group did you fall in with?

I was that girl who didn't talk to anyone in class. I sat by myself in the back and wrote in my journal. I did have a group of friends ▶

A Conversation with Amy Bryant *(continued)*

outside of class, but we weren't big enough to have a clique name. Everybody thinks they weren't part of a clique, though, so I probably was. We liked music and wore a lot of black.

What is your earliest memory of reading and being influenced by a book?

My sister taught me to read when I was four, and I've always been a big reader. Nowadays I read mostly fiction—short stories and novels. I remember reading the short story "Goodbye My Brother" by John Cheever when I was a freshman in college, and it completely knocked me down. I always wanted to be a writer in some form, but that was the first time I ever thought about actually writing fiction.

Do you have any writerly quirks?

I write an hour a day when I have an idea. I'm a big reviser, so I'll work an hour a day on a pass of whatever I'm working on, then I'll put it aside and take a break or work on something else. Then I go back to it, and I do the hour a day thing until I've gotten all the way through it again. Rest, repeat. Only rarely can I write for more than an hour without it turning into crap.

Do you fall back on any beverages for artistic stimulation?

I don't really stimulate myself with any beverages, but when I write in the evenings I reward myself with a glass of wine or a beer after. Or two. And copious amounts of television.

66 I write an hour a day when I have an idea. . . . Only rarely can I write for more than an hour without it turning into crap. 99

What are you working on now?

I'm working on a bunch of linked short stories, mostly about people in their twenties, set in New York City.

What is your social situation? Are you married? Do you have any pets?

I have a husband named Bruno and a dog named Franklin. ❧

A Life in Books

**Writing and Book Favorites from
Amy Bryant**

Best short story you've ever read?

"What We Talk About When We Talk About
Love" by Raymond Carver.

Best "film of a book" you've seen?

Short Cuts.

Favorite novel that nobody has ever heard of?

Who Will Run the Frog Hospital?
by Lorrie Moore.

Favorite bookshop?

Three Lives & Company, New York.

Author you'd most like to meet?

David Sedaris.

Favorite author?

Ann Beattie.

Favorite "guilty pleasure" as a reader?

US Weekly.

Best writing advice you ever received?

Revise until you're just adding and subtracting
commas.

First book you fell in love with?

The Catcher in the Rye.

Favorite children's book?

I love the Madeline books.

Book you'd most like President Bush to read?

Doctors of Conscience: The Struggle to Provide Abortion Before and After Roe v. Wade by Carole Joffe.

Book you've always wanted to read but haven't gotten around to?

One Hundred Years of Solitude by Gabriel García Márquez.

Favorite literary character?

Enid, from Daniel Clowes's graphic novel *Ghost World*.

Favorite book about D.C.?

Banned in DC: Photos and Anecdotes from the DC Punk Underground.

Book you wish you'd written?

The Burning House by Ann Beattie.

About a Girl

WHEN I STARTED to write *Polly,* I knew I wanted to write about the 1980s, and I knew I wanted to write about a girl who has a series of different boyfriends. But I had no frame of reference without music. How could I write about junior high without writing about "Gloria" or "Centerfold"? Each chapter of *Polly* is about the music as much as the boys, because Polly loves them both. Even Polly is named after a Nirvana song.

My father, Donnie Bryant, still talks about the first time he went to see bluegrass icon Mac Wiseman play and heard the banjo. He was seventeen years old, and he knew what he was supposed to do from that moment on. Hardcore music was like that for me. Like a force of nature. I wanted Polly to feel that way in the book.

My parents met in Arlington, Virginia, in the 1950s. My mother was fifteen and my father was nineteen, and he was already playing the banjo professionally. Three years later, my father was invited to play an extended engagement at the Grand Ole Opry. My mother went with him, and they got married as soon as they got to Nashville. He toured with Mac Wiseman and bluegrass legend Lester Flatt, but finally gave it all up to settle down with my mother back in Virginia and have children.

I was born in 1970, and some of my earliest memories are of waking up to the ear-splitting sound of my father's banjo traveling up two flights of stairs to my bedroom. (I'm the only person I know who has asked a parent to turn that racket down.) My older brother started

> 66 Each chapter of *Polly* is about the music as much as the boys, because Polly loves them both. Even Polly is named after a Nirvana song. 99

8

playing classical guitar when he was twelve, the year I was born, so when I wasn't listening to "Foggy Mountain Breakdown" I was hearing Bach through his bedroom door across the hall. My older sister played the piano, and, needing to copy her every move, I took lessons for years, though I never enjoyed it the way she did. My mother didn't love bluegrass but she did love the Beatles, Bob Dylan, and Simon and Garfunkel, so that was in the house, too.

For me, it started with "A Hard Day's Night" by the Beatles, then "Fifty Ways to Leave Your Lover" by Paul Simon. I danced to them in the living room, entertaining my family. In elementary school the music teacher examined all the girls' mouths and told us whether we would be better suited for clarinet or flute. I didn't want to play either, because by then my sister had wallpapered her room with posters of Bruce Springsteen and the Doors, and I knew flutes and clarinets weren't cool. My brother, weird enough to listen only to classical music in high school, suddenly became obsessed with the Rolling Stones in college. No one merely liked music in my family. It was worship.

As I grew older, I danced with my friends in the basement. I loved the song "Pop Music," by M, and then "Heart of Glass" by Blondie. And I listened to the *Grease* soundtrack over and over and over. I got a toy drum set and a plastic electric guitar for Christmas. My friends and I set the drum set on the coffee table, used a round hairbrush for a microphone, and played Band. We put on my mother's old dresses and wore makeup; we were like tiny drag queens getting together at a bar to lip-synch torch songs. It was my favorite game. ▶

“ In elementary school the music teacher examined all the girls' mouths and told us whether we would be better suited for clarinet or flute. I didn't want to play either. ”

About a Girl *(continued)*

I was in the sixth grade when the Go-Go's came along. I wasn't just a fan—I wanted to be a Go-Go. My friends and I dressed up in mini skirts and performed "We Got the Beat" for the talent show. I was Gina Schock, and my drums were boxes turned upside down on music stands. My best friend, Eileen, was the bass player, Kathy Valentine, and during the guitar solo she leapt into the front row of ecstatic, cheering kindergartners and ran among them as they screamed with delight.

The Go-Go's obsession lasted through junior high. Then the summer after eighth grade I saw *Rock 'n' Roll High School* on cable and fell in love with the Ramones, especially Joey Ramone. I didn't want to be a Go-Go anymore, I wanted to be Riff Randell. Riff Randell was like a cooler, more independent, more modern Sandy from *Grease.* I bought a pair of parachute pants and wore black eyeliner in earnest.

Then I was in high school, and I discovered speed metal. When I heard speed metal I heard my father's fast bluegrass picking, but without that whiny singing and without those cheesy, heartfelt lyrics. Speed metal was rightfully mine, and those guitar players went as fast up the fret board as my dad. Fast was important when I was an adolescent, so I soon replaced metal with hardcore, which was even faster, but also political and more relatable. With hardcore I had found *it.* There were lots of hardcore shows, and I needed to go to all of them. My family understood, even though none of them could stand what I was listening to. I had a midnight curfew, unless I was going to see a band.

> ❝ When I heard speed metal I heard my father's fast bluegrass picking, but without that whiny singing and without those cheesy, heartfelt lyrics. ❞

When Polly goes to her first hardcore show, she hears music she loves and, more important, lyrics she cares about, as opposed to the masculine satanic themes that metal bands sing about. All of the anger and rejection she's feeling from her family and all of her dissatisfaction with the world around her is suddenly being expressed right in front of her, with all the emotion she can't reveal in her own life. My adolescent angst wasn't exactly like Polly's, but I remember what it was like to finally make a connection with something bigger than me or my friends, and it was important for me to get that sentiment into *Polly*. The first time art feels personal is a profound moment in a person's life, whether it happens with a book, a band, a painting, a movie, whatever. As an adult you learn to seek it out, but when you're young you usually just stumble upon it, and it's almost a religious experience.

Music was how we found each other in high school. A band T-shirt would tell you who you wanted to be friends with. The Duran Duran girls wore glittery makeup and rat-tails. The early U2 and REM fans were vegetarians and wore cloth shoes and New-Wave haircuts. There were the metalheads and punk rockers and Deadheads and classic rock kids, and the mods and the goths. On the weekends we got in our groups and listened to our music, and it was the most important thing in our lives. Being in the D.C. area, we were part of a larger movement in music history. Driving D.C. hardcore force Ian MacKaye fronted Minor Threat and Fugazi, and founded Dischord Records. Dave Grohl was from the Virginia suburbs ▶

66 A band T-shirt would tell you who you wanted to be friends with. The Duran Duran girls wore glittery makeup and rat-tails. The early U2 and REM fans were vegetarians and wore cloth shoes and New-Wave haircuts. 99

About a Girl *(continued)*

and played drums in local hardcore band Scream—he later moved on to Nirvana and the Foo Fighters. This is the backdrop of *Polly,* and the backdrop of my own teenage years as well.

Like Polly, I had a boyfriend in high school who played guitar in a band. My mother once reminded me that she had met my father in high school, and that he had been in a band, too. "I know how it is to like those boys," she said. I was completely grossed out. The boys I liked were nothing like Dad. Still, she wasn't afraid of the boys I liked the way other mothers were, and she encouraged the hardcore band that played in our next door neighbor's basement to rehearse as much as they liked.

After my parents divorced, my mother married someone who loved the same bands she did, and my father, who had become a policeman after his music career ended, married a woman who sang in the police band. If I had wanted to be a teenage rebel, I would have had to have stopped listening to music, to cease all album buying and concert attending. Then I would have been truly weird in my family's eyes. But Polly's family is different. Getting into hardcore is a part of her rebellion. Polly's family feels threatened not only by her sexuality, but by her immersion in a music world that's completely foreign to them.

Polly finally finds solace in art and in her college friends—friends who like the same music she does. Once she's out of her parents' house, she's free to explore her interests outside the context of rebellion. The same is true for her relationships. Her parents are no longer there to provide boundaries or offer opinions, so it's up to her to decide what she really wants. Of course, Polly still wants music and boys, and she still finds one a lot less complicated than the other. ⌒

Author Picks
Books and Records

Top Ten Coming-of-Age Books

To Kill a Mockingbird by Harper Lee

Even though this is one of those books everyone reads in high school, for some reason I didn't read it until a few years out of college. I went around raving about it to all my friends, who had read it ten years ago and were somewhat less excited to talk about it.

Catcher in the Rye by J. D. Salinger

I read this book for the first time the summer after ninth grade, and I was sorry I hadn't read it in school because I wanted to talk about it with other people who had read it. This was the first time that happened to me with a book.

Who Will Run the Frog Hospital? by Lorrie Moore

Lorrie Moore is one of my favorite writers. This book is about how best friends grow up and apart in an unpromising small town, and how weird it is to look back on old friendships as an adult.

The Basketball Diaries by Jim Carroll

This book is sexy and scary and all about a New York City that doesn't exist anymore. I read this before I moved to New York, and it made me want to live there even more than I already did.

> ❝ [*Who Will Run the Frog Hospital?*] is about how best friends grow up and apart in an unpromising small town, and how weird it is to look back on old friendships as an adult. ❞

The Bluest Eye by Toni Morrison

This made me cry, and I didn't want it to end. It's about how poverty and racism feed self-loathing.

This Side of Paradise by F. Scott Fitzgerald

This is Fitzgerald's first novel, and I liked trying to figure out which parts might be autobiographical. Fitzgerald makes you want to read his work out loud. The way he uses language in his descriptions is ornate but subtle.

A Good School by Richard Yates

Richard Yates is one of those writers who makes other writers feel as if they have no business even trying to write. This book is set in the 1940s and it's about prep school boys, but somehow I cared. It's about the timeless issue of status.

The Book of Ruth by Jane Hamilton

The main character's naïve point of view guides this story toward inevitable doom, but the ending is still a shock. When I finished this I wanted to go back to the beginning and read it again.

Middlesex by Jeffrey Eugenides

This is about what it's like to grow up and discover you're someone different than you thought you were. It's about family and gender and relationships—all the important stuff.

This Boy's Life: A Memoir by Tobias Wolff

Tobias Wolff's prose has a real rhythm to it. I love how the angry protagonist turns into the famous author.

> 66 [*A Good School*] is set in the 1940s and it's about prep school boys, but somehow I cared. 99

Punk/Hardcore Records

I was lucky enough to come of age in the D.C. area, where a punk rock music scene flourished from the onset of Minor Threat in the early 1980s through the 1990s. I was too young to see Minor Threat, but I did see a lot of shows in the late 1980s. I didn't know this was history in the making: I assumed there were incredible local bands playing in every city. In *Polly* I focused on the Bad Brains and Dag Nasty, but there were so many more, from D.C. and elsewhere. Here are a few of my favorite punk rock/hardcore records from that time:

Walk Together, Rock Together by 7 Seconds
Brats in Battalions by Adolescents
Victim in Pain by Agnostic Front
Rock for Light/I Against I by the Bad Brains
Animosity by Corrosion of Conformity
Can I Say by Dag Nasty
Dirty Rotten LP by Dirty Rotten Imbeciles
City Baby's Revenge by GBH
Joyride/Fun Just Never Ends
    by Government Issue
Food for Thought by Gray Matter
Kingface by Kingface
Double Image by Marginal Man
Music for the Deaf by MFD
Complete Discography by Minor Threat
Energy by Operation Ivy
Rocket to Russia by the Ramones
Three Songs by Soulside
Still Screaming/This Side Up by Scream
Rock 'n' Roll Nightmare by RKL
Learn by Verbal Assault
Sink with Kalifornija by Youth Brigade

66 I didn't know this was history in the making: I assumed there were incredible local bands playing in every city. 99

Don't miss the next book by your favorite author. Sign up now for AuthorTracker by visiting www.AuthorTracker.com.